# Fabulous Nobodies

# Fabulous Nobodies

## Lee Tulloch

AVON
TRADE

*An Imprint of HarperCollinsPublishers*

Grateful acknowledgment is made for permission to reprint lyrics from "Volare."
Lyric by Mitchell Parish and Music by Domenico Modugno. Parmit Music Co.

Hardcover and trade paperback editions of this title were published by William
Morrow and Perennial in 1989 and 1990, respectively.

HarperCollins books may be purchased for educational, business, or sales pro-
motional use. For information please write: Special Markets Department,
HarperCollins Publishers Inc., 10 East 53rd Street, New York, NY 10022.

First Avon Trade edition published 2006.

ISBN-13: 978-0-06-079716-4 (pbk.)
ISBN-10: 0-06-079716-9

*Designed by Kris Tobiassen*

The Library of Congress has cataloged the hardcover edition as follows:

Tulloch, Lee.
    Fabulous nobodies / Lee Tulloch—1st ed.
        p.   cm.
1.  Young women—New York (State)—New York—Fiction.    2.  East
Village (New York, N.Y.)—Fiction.    I.  Title.

PR9619.3.T795 F34 1989
813'.54 19            88029136

06   07   08   09   10   RRDH   10   9   8   7   6   5   4   3   2   1

for Lolita and all the
frocks she is going to wear

# Fabulous Nobodies

# 1.

I'm standing on the door of the Less Is More club, thinking about my fingernails. I'm up here, above the throng, a fashion leader, with the crowd below almost swooning at my feet, and I'm dressed impeccably from head to toe except for three chipped nails on my right hand. Three chipped nails! This has never happened before. I always check my nails before I leave home. I know how tricky nails can be. Not a night goes by without my making sure the nail polish starts at the cuticles and ends at the tips, a perfect unsmudged slash of color. I'm not the kind of girl just to slop it on.

I'm sensitive to little details like chipped nail polish—including the wrong color combinations, or sandals worn with woolen skirts, or pale blue eye shadow—but especially chipped nail polish. Chipped nail polish is almost the most upsetting thing in the universe, after people who wear leg warmers. The fact that I am standing up here with chipped nail polish, even though everyone else is too far away to see it, is a crisis. I know that my nails are chipped, and as far as I'm concerned, I'm the only one who counts.

The nail polish is flaking off almost to the cuticles. It's bubbling and blistering in the heat like leg wax on the boil. Maybe I shouldn't have mixed any of that battleship gray house paint with Revlon Firma Nail. It seemed like a good idea at the time, especially as I didn't have the exact shade of gray at home to go with my silver Courrèges mini, which I had my heart set on wearing tonight. It's a Courrèges kind of night, all steamy and noisy, like a walk down Carnaby Street in the summer of 1965. What a walk down Carnaby Street would have been like in the summer of 1965 if I'd been born then.

I could stick to plain old Max Factor like everyone else. But that's so *predictable.* You can't be fabulous and predictable at the same time; this is one of the facts of life. The reason I am fabulous is that I am *never* predictable. Even I can't predict what I'm going to do next.

I have to act. I just can't stand here like this. Sooner or later somebody fabulous is going to come up these stairs and home in on my nails like an eagle. Fabulous people know about nails. They look for them. Sooner or later somebody fabulous is going to want to shake my hand or kiss it. Which means that sooner or later I'm going to have to take it out of my purse. A girl can't pretend to be looking for her compact all night. I wish I'd worn gloves. Gloves make serious fashion statements, and come in handy, too.

I decide. I dig around in the purse some more—it's got a plastic mother-of-pearl handle that slips neatly over my wrist—and find my emery board. I hold my hand up in front of my face, splay the fingers out, for everyone to see, and start to scratch away at the old polish. The bits of gray paint flake off all over the Astroturf like confetti at a wedding. If you're going to do something unpleasant, you might as well do it with style.

The crowd below is getting restless. They're pushing and shoving and standing on tiptoes to see what I'm doing. I can feel a tremor of irritation as they watch me unscrew a bottle and apply strokes of base coat. They're wondering how I can stand here doing my nails when it's a matter of life and death for them that they get into the club.

As far as I'm concerned, anyone who wonders why a girl would stop everything to repair her nails shouldn't be in a club like this anyway.

# 2.

My name is Reality Nirvana Tuttle, and I was born in 1968. Nineteen sixty-eight was one of the great years in modern history. It was the year Yves Saint Laurent shocked the fashion world with his first see-through blouse. That's why I feel a real *connection* to YSL. His star and mine are linked together. I always get goose bumps whenever I see a YSL across a crowded room.

Constance—she's my mother—is a New Age kind of person. Except she was New Age before the New Age; kind of *old* New Age is the way to explain it. She called me Reality Nirvana during a Marxist Feminist Environmentalist brain wave. It's the only IN thing she ever did. Since then she's been either way IN or way OUT but never right on mark. It's very irresponsible of her. Unfortunately Reality Nirvana as a name was only IN for a millisecond of time, and then it went out again. It was IN briefly again last year. Now it's OUT. Which is darn irritating.

My name has never fit me like a glove. It doesn't sound like the sort of name a fashion goddess should have. Now Ines de la Fressange, *that's* a fashion goddess name, or Victoire de Castellaine, or Lisa Fonssagrives Penn. But I got lumped with Reality. Fortunately most of my acquaintances call me Really, which just blends into the conversation. It's phenomenal how many times they say, "Oh, really?"

At first I used to jump out of my skin when I heard this. But now I don't even blink.

Where I was born—about fifteen miles down the road from Woodstock—is in the middle of nowhere, stylistically speaking. In Phoenicia there's not a single shop that sells Jean-Paul Gaultier. It's *that* behind the times. All the children there have names like Galaxy and Lake and Tribe and Peregrina Nettlespurge. Reality is almost *ordinary*. But here in New York, the fashion capital of the world, it's very distinctive, even though it has two syllables too many to be *seriously* chic.

Why don't I call myself something else? After all, my best friend, Phoebe Johnson, changed her name from Vespa Faske. (I'm sworn to secrecy about that.) The truth is, I've tried. I've called myself Josephine, Diana, Iris, Celeste, Anouk, Anita, Coco, and Dovima, but only for five minutes at a time. Putting on a name is not as easy as putting on a hat. You can't take it off again. Some days I feel very Coco, and other days I feel, well, a bit more Anouk. There's not a single name I can think of that covers all the possibilities. A name that reflects my glamorous life-style and my seventy-two different fashion personalities.

# 3.

I finish doing my nails and put the bottle of blue-gray polish back in my purse. It's not exactly the right color, but it will do in a pinch. I take out my personal flashlight, the one with the shocking pink beam that I like to run over the upturned faces of the crowd. The second I spot an interesting sleeve or a case of clever accessorizing, I let the flashlight linger. This way the person in the spotlight knows she's got the seal of approval. Without my having to yell, which is very unladylike. The person in the spotlight is then up those stairs as fast as you can say Jacques Fath. It's an *honor* to be flashed at by me.

The crowd looks up to me. They literally look up to me because I'm standing twelve steps above them, at the top of a flight of concrete stairs and Astroturf carpet. The Astroturf carpet stops right at my feet, which tonight are clad in my favorite five-inch cork platforms, the ones with the little silver stars stuck all over them. Consequently I loom over the crowd like a monument. Which is *exactly* how I see myself. I'm the monument on the door of the most Happening club in New York.

I'm the one you've got to get past if you want to get inside. I'm the one you've got to please. I'm the one who says Oh Yes Do Come In You Look Fabulous and Oh No You've Got to Get Out of Here You Look Like *Trash*. Sometimes I use Never Darken My Doorstep

Again but only to people who wear red Lycra disco pants. A girl's got to have her standards.

The only way you can get into Less Is More is by looking fabulous. There's no other way. I'm incorruptible on this subject. You can't bribe me; you can't impress me with your bank balance. Why, Mother Teresa couldn't get in here unless she did something about her hair.

Most of the crowd milling in the gutter tonight have about as much chance of getting to the top of these stairs as a size sixteen has of getting into a size four frock. Some people have no idea what fabulous is. Some people think fabulous is a sequined frock with plunging neckline they've seen on a deodorant commercial on television. They think fabulous is a maroon leather jacket with shoulder pads that go all the way to Ohio and a pair of baggy jeans with pockets down the legs. They think fabulous is a three-piece pinstripe suit from Brooks Brothers with matching red suspenders, tie, and pocket handkerchief. They think fabulous is a patchwork jacket with lambskin trim or a silk blouse with a pussy bow at the neck or a sweater with appliquéd sailing boats all over it. Some people think sneakers with socks scrunched down over them are fabulous. Some people go for jackets with the sleeves pushed up past the elbow or lavender sweat shirts cut off at the midriff. It's deeply disturbing that people can get to be like this. They're *sick*.

It doesn't take many *brains* to work out what being fabulous is. If you're fabulous, you have impeccable good taste and impeccable bad taste, too. You can be fabulous in the latest Thierry Mugler and you can be fabulous in an old Pucci print. You cannot be fabulous in peach chiffon, no matter how recent the frock is, or in an old Indian skirt with bells hanging off the hem. You can never be fabulous in anything angora, acrylic, or lapin, unless it's Japanese. There are dozens of rules. If you're fabulous, you know them instinctively. If you're not, you don't.

It's simple.

For instance, there's a girl down there in the middle of the line, which has almost stretched as far as the next corner and has made a detour, like a bride's train, around the sweet old homeless men relaxing on the sidewalk and a chapter of the Third Street Hell's Angels having a board meeting on their Harley-Davidsons in the gutter.

My flashlight freezes on this girl's mouth. You could see her blue lipstick and dark lipline from the *moon*, even though it's gone a bit purple in the pink light. She's one of the ones who think wearing blue lipstick will get them in anywhere. Well, it won't get her in here. You've got to know what you're doing when you wear blue lipstick. You've got to wear it with the right Attitude. This is crucial. You can't just slash a tube of blue across your lips and think that will make up for the fact that you're wearing a rip-and-tear tunic that's at least five years out of date. In my experience, girls who turn up to the club in blue lipstick always wear rip-and-tear things that are at least five years out of date. Don't they read *magazines?*

The girl in the blue lipstick probably has a mother who has told her, just tonight, before she took the train in from the suburbs, "Reconsider your blue lipstick, dear, you look like a corpse, and do you have a token for the subway home?" I know mothers of daughters like that. They're responsible for the whole mess. If this mother had said, "You look divine, dear, the blue lipstick is so chic," the daughter would have been back in the bathroom in a flash, scrubbing at her lips with toilet tissue and reapplying something pink, and we all would have felt a lot better about it.

That girl has no hope of making it into a club like this, unless someone—namely, me—takes pity on her. But it's a vicious circle. If I let her in tonight, she's going to think it was the blue lipstick that got her up the stairs and she's going to turn up forever after at every club in town in blue lipstick, thinking it's her birthright to sashay through the door unchallenged. Worse still, she's going to tell her friends about it, and before we know, we'll be swatting away blue lips like flies.

I wish those other clubs were more choosy about whom they let in. I just bet Ricci down the street at Ready to Wear started the whole blue lipstick thing. She would have been standing around out there, in those appalling leg warmers she insists on wearing even though she's never danced a step in her life, adjusting her headband in a hand mirror or pulling down her sequined bustier to flash more cleavage, and that blue-lipsticked disaster would have walked straight on in her old tunic and Ricci would have not been a jot the wiser. I bet she even gives the nod to *body shirts* and doesn't care. There's no excuse for lowering her standards so disgracefully. We're all in this together if we don't want the world to be overrun by jacquard tuxedos and lollipop pink crushed satin shirts.

The girl with the blue lipstick has rings of black kohl around her eyes and spiky black hair with blond tips and is staring pleadingly up at me like a lovesick panda bear. I give her the pink light. The go-ahead. This white linen suit with a thin leather tie—ugh—thinks I'm flashing at him, and his eyebrows shoot up like boomerangs. I jerk my pocket flashlight again so it's clear who I want. The girl with the lipstick can't believe her eyes, which she is shading from my beam with her hand. I notice she is wearing black lace gloves with the fingers cut out. She starts up the stairs nervously, cowering all the way as if I were going to hit her or something.

"Hi," she says when she reaches the top. I'm towering over her on account of the fact that I'm five-nine in my five-inch platforms and she's only about five-three. "Does this mean I don't have to pay?" She's got her hand firmly clasped over the strap of her shoulder bag, which has insets of acrylic *faux* zebra. Acrylic is not tolerated here. Unless it's worn with fabulous abandon.

"Look," I tell her, "there's no way I can let you in looking like *that*." I say this as kindly as I can.

"Why not?" she whines, her face crumpling up in disappointment.

"That *frock*," I say.

"What's wrong with it?" She makes a big blue pout. I can see that the lipline, which is actually black and crookedly applied, ends just inside her mouth. "It's new." She starts fiddling with a flap of hand-painted fabric that's wrapped around her middle like a mummy's shroud.

"It might be new," I tell her, "but it's still *old hat*."

Her eyes fill up with tears. She's in danger of smudging the black circles around her eyes, which probably took her hours to apply. All of a sudden I feel sorry for her. You have to marvel at people who are so unaware of the fashion world around them. So unaware that blue lipstick and kohl rimmed eyes went out with buffalo girls.

"The point is you're twenty years out of date," I say gently.

"How come?" She sniffs.

"Because the look is 1962 now," I explain patiently. "You're dressed like it's 1982. The way things are going, you'll have to wait at least five years before it's OK to be 1982 again."

"Five years!" She takes in a deep breath. "That's forever!"

"*Exactly,*" I say.

I stand aside to let through the ropes a boy in a peacock green Nehru jacket and a girl in a velvet tent dress, size ten, with a pearl collar. I know the size of this frock on account of the fact I tried it on at Aurora's White Trash, my favorite place in the world, a couple of weeks ago. It was too big by miles. The girl really hasn't got the shoulders for a halter neck, but I say anyway, as she glides past, "*Fab frock.*"

The blue lipstick girl is looking at the couple longingly.

"I wish I looked like *that,*" she says wistfully. "How did she get her hair to go that way?"

"What's your name?" I ask.

"Brooke," she says.

"Look, Brooke, you've got to listen to me. Come over here." I shift her into a pool of green light coming from inside the club. Underneath two slashes of beetroot-colored blusher, there are a pair of cheekbones with *possibilities*.

"If I were you," I say thoughtfully.

"What?"

"I'd do *Maria Callas*."

"What's that?" she asks. "Foot cream?"

I control my temper. It's just like a girl like this not to know about Maria Callas. What do they do at school all day—mathematics? I tell her Maria Callas might just be the very next thing. I tell her I am giving her a hot tip. I tell her she can be the first on her block to do it. I tell her all her girlfriends are going to shrivel up with jealousy. This is what finally makes her smile, a big blue and red smile like a Fourth of July streamer unraveling. She's got the picture.

I spend the next five minutes suggesting she find a black wig, a caftan, and some heavy gold jewelry. I explain how to apply thick black eyeliner. I give her some basic skin care pointers.

"Gee, thanks," she says when I'm finished. "I think my mom's got one of those snake bracelets."

"Now you go home and *practice*, Brooke," I say. "And come back when you've managed to get the eyeliner straight."

"You bet!" She beams and starts to shuffle away, in leather sandals someone has told her are hip.

"You make a fashion statement now," I call after her.

I watch Brooke amble down the street and nearly collide with a pimp in a white three-piece suit with a red satin dog-eared collar shirt. Now, *he* can come in any old time. Pimps have such style. He gives Brooke the once-over and just shrugs. Pimps know a disaster when they see one.

In some ways Brooke is a lost cause, I think. By the time she's learned to master Maria Callas, Maria Callas will be OUT. Anita

Ekberg is going to be the thing. Everyone is going to be splashing around in fountains in strapless evening gowns with blond hair down to their waists. Maria Callas is going to be *passé*. But that's the way it goes, and that's what I mean. Life is cruel to people who aren't fabulous. They're always going to be staggering behind the fashion leaders, tripping over the jagged hems of their unraveling rip-and-tear outfits and madly scrambling to catch up.

# 4.

"Has Faye been here?" demands a voice behind my right shoulder. I whirl around, surprised that someone could have sneaked up behind me. I'm shocked to see it's Hugo Falk, the gossip columnist. I almost faint. Thank heavens I've done my nails, is the first thing that crosses my mind.

"Faye *who*?" I ask, trying to catch my breath.

"Oh, for goodness' sake!" Hugo says impatiently, tapping one chiseled cheekbone with a long finger. "*Faye.*"

"Oh, *Faye*," I repeat, stalling for time. And then I realize which Faye he's talking about. "*That* Faye." I nod knowingly. "You know, I was just thinking about her. Do you know that the Bonnie and Clyde Look is coming back? Not to mention the maxiskirt—"

"I haven't got all night," he interrupts. "Just tell me if you've seen Faye or not."

"Not exactly." I hesitate.

"Thank you," he says crossly, and turns away.

"Hey!" I call after him. "Aren't you coming inside?"

"I don't have time," he says over his shoulder. Then he turns back to me, pauses, takes off his square black-framed glasses, shakes them irritably, puts them back on, and states very grandly, "I've got to meet Paloma."

"Which Paloma?" I ask automatically.

A smirk passes over his face. "Are you some kind of imbecile? There's only one Paloma."

"*That* Paloma." I nod quickly, trying to cover up my gaffe. Of course, I know who Paloma is. I was temporarily distracted, that's all. "Oh, she's here. She's inside. She's wearing a pair of those squiggly earrings. The ones shaped like an X." Hugo examines me suspiciously. "She's with her dad," I add to sound convincing.

"Do I know you?" he asks, looking down his nose at me.

"Of course you do. I'm—"

"I didn't think so," he says dismissively, cutting me off. "I only know famous people."

"I'd be famous if you wrote about me," I say hopefully.

"You girls are all the same!" he snarls, and stomps off into the crowd.

I watch Hugo slip down the stairs. He's tall and slim and almost disappears if you look at him sideways. He's got white skin and black hair cut very short at the neck and long on top so that even though Hugo glides, his hair sort of *bobs*. From the back it looks like a duck's bottom, all gleaming and sleek, with a little kick of a tail at the very end. It's the latest kind of hairdo because, let's face it, Hugo Falk is the latest kind of person. He favors clothes that are the very latest kind of clothes, too, clothes that are so late, in fact, they cause people to stare at him. He favors primary colors and narrow Edwardian jackets that button right up to the throat and trousers that are slender to his ankles, finishing exactly where they should, just above the heel, revealing socks that always contrast with the rest of his outfit and shoes with thick rubber soles.

I once saw him throw a tantrum in a restaurant over the food and then storm out of the place, stuffing his pockets full of peppermint

candies and matchboxes and slipping part of the flower arrangement into his lapel as he left. The pockets he was busily stuffing on
his way to the door happened to be a magenta color. The lapel was
edged in blue. The shirt he was wearing was emerald green. His tie
was hot pink. His socks were canary yellow. And this was in the era
of *pastels.* I think Hugo Falk is an exhibitionist. But then, I don't really know this for a fact. It's impossible to know what sort of person
Hugo Falk is inside because you're so distracted by what sort of person he is *outside.*

I feel depressed as I watch him edge down the stairs. Hugo Falk
always puts me off-balance, and it has nothing to do with my five-
inch heels. That's what he is: *unbalancing.* It's mostly to do with
how important he is. He is *very* influential. He has the power of
putting your name in print. *That* sort of power. It makes me go
all goose-bumpy to think of what this means. My name in
Hugo's column would catapult my career into another dimension.
It would lead to a million things for me. I don't know *what* things,
but I'm sure it would lead to them anyway. That's why I'm trying
to cultivate him. I'm going to have to try harder if tonight is any
clue.

The column is called *"Hugo-a-go-go."* Which is so *cute,* as I tell
him whenever I get the chance. It appears in *Frenzee* magazine every
week. *Frenzee* is distributed free to everyone who lives between Avenue A and Second Avenue, from First Street to Fourteenth Street.
It's not a *huge* circulation, but it's the sort of magazine that gets attention. You get noticed if you appear in *Frenzee* magazine. By people who live between Avenue A and Second Avenue, from First Street
to Fourteenth Street, that is.

It's funny, but some people down here don't trust Hugo Falk.
His column reveals people's intimate secrets. It dishes all the dirt.
But I don't think the fact that Hugo's column dishes all the dirt has

anything to do with Hugo anyway. You have to give him the benefit of the doubt. He doesn't actually dish it. Everyone else does. He just reports it. So it's not really his fault when someone throws himself out a window because of something Hugo's written. Only unstable sort of people do that. They would have thrown themselves out of a window anyway, Hugo's column or not. You can bet on it.

Of course, I don't expect Hugo to write a *whole* column on me straight away. Just a mention would do. My name wouldn't even have to be in big print. Hugo saves that for the truly famous. The all-time great somebodies. Like Peggy Lee. Her name was in big print. In capital letters, too. And in boldface. I'd like to be in boldface. It stands out. Hugo Falk's column about Peggy Lee a few months ago was a huge hit and was single-handedly responsible for the revival of the beauty spot as we know it today.

Hugo is greeted on his way down the stairs by several people. I can see him holding up his hand to brush them aside. When he reaches the sidewalk, he is instantly surrounded by a group of boys with short white hair. He always has several boys with him. They're always different boys. But they always have white hair. Which emphasizes the way Hugo's shiny jet black hair falls in his eyes all the time. These boys are not boys; they're *accessories.* I know what Hugo Falk is up to. I'd be up to it myself if I could find any white-haired boys who are straight.

I let five more people into the club, while I watch Hugo disappear down Third Street. I realize too late that one of them was wearing a sweater appliquéd with a crouching tiger. I hate appliquéd crouching tigers. I must wrench my mind away from Hugo and back to the job or I'll humiliate myself before the night is out.

But for the rest of the evening my mind keeps drifting back to *Frenzee* magazine. If I were in Hugo's column, I'd feel more—real.

That's the word. I'd feel I *achieved* something if someone wrote about me.

The problem is, I'm a stitch away from twenty-one. I try not to think about it, it's that serious. I've got to get my name in print by the time I'm twenty-one, or it will be too late. I'll be over before I've even begun.

# 5.

"Night Cherry. Night Sally. Night Pixie. Night Christie. Night Bambi. Night Millie."

"Night Really."

I'm on my way home early from Less Is More, swinging my pocketbook. I'm walking along Third Street, past all the fashion bars and clubs, bars and clubs with names like PVC and Ultrasuede and Eton Crop and Pink Gingham and The Gauntlet and my current favorite, Café Orlon.

All the hottest clubs and bars have sprung up in this one block. No one exactly knows why. Maybe there is safety in numbers. All the fashionable places ganging up together against all the unfashionable places. Perhaps it's because Third Street always was a very fashionable street. Especially if you're a Hell's Angel. They have their headquarters down the road a bit. Having Hell's Angels on Third Street has always given it a kind of *distinction*.

There is a girl standing in almost every doorway along this stretch of Third Street. Tonight they look exactly like hookers touting for business. Which is confusing, because Third Street is also full of real hookers touting for business. No wonder they call the girls at the fashion clubs *doorwhores*. I don't like this term. It's unladylike. It certainly doesn't apply to me.

"Fab frock," I say to Merry as I glide past Madame Grès. I don't really mean it. It's just the way we have down here of saying hello. It's sort of like "How are you?" in the world at large. Of course, sometimes you come across a frock that is truly fabulous, in which case you say, "*Fab* frock," or, "That frock is *faboo*," or any number of variations. For instance, when I say, "Fab frock," to Merry, she smiles and looks me up and down and says, "Fabulous outfit," warmly. Another way of saying this is "I love your dress." You hear this all the time down here, whether people mean it or not.

I'm really only "Fab frock" friendly to the girls at the other clubs. I'm not *intimate* with them. I don't lend them my jewelry or swap shoes with them. Occasionally one of them has slept in my beanbag, but only in real emergencies when she's lost her keys and the landlord is in Florida. She usually loses my keys the next day, too. That's why I don't offer my beanbag to every Cherry in town. Not these days anyway. I'm too smart for that. You get up in the morning, and not only are your keys gone for good, but your flamingo pink extralash mascara has disappeared from your makeup kit as well. Three months later someone's old boyfriend opens the lock with those same keys at five in the morning dead drunk, and the next thing you know, you're washing his socks and finding him something to wear to the opening of a new bar.

It's late, and the girls are looking bored. To tell you the truth, things aren't so great in some of the clubs these days. The clubs where the management doesn't move with the times. The thing is, the times are moving so darn fast no one can keep up with them. Club 60 just changed its name to Club 61, spent all this money on a new flame red neon to hang over the window bars and on Club 61 matchboxes—in three fashion colors—and already, five days later, they're thinking about moving the name along a year or so to Club 62. No one wants to come to a club called Club 61 anymore. That's how it is. The slightest whiff of a club being out of date, and it's as dead as the dolman sleeve in five minutes.

Maybe they should call the club Club 66 just to be safe. That should keep them in business for at least six months. The problem is, there's always a risk in being *too* ahead of your time. People don't understand you. They don't understand that you're *ahead*. They think you're *way* behind. It's a delicate balance, being a trendsetter.

Sometimes I think things are recycling so fast we're going to whirl right off the planet, just the way frothy little bubbles of bath creme whirl down the drain after my morning soak.

# 6.

I unlock the door to my apartment at 6:00 A.M.

I flop on the bed, exhausted. My platforms come off first. Carefully. I don't fling my shoes around the room the way other girls do. I've seen the way some of my friends treat their things. I've seen where they put their shoes. In the bookshelf. Under a pillow. In the kitty litter. You can't do that to a shoe. You can't separate a shoe from its partner and expect it to be happy. It's like severing Siamese twins in twain. They get *lonely*.

My best girlfriend, Phoebe Johnson, doesn't understand this, even though I've told her a thousand times. She sits on the edge of her bed and kicks her shoes off. Just like that. Up in the air and down again. Hard. Mostly they thud against the wall because, let's face it, her room isn't that big. I've told her flinging and thudding hurt a shoe. I've *told* her to put herself in the mind of a shoe and think what it might be like at the end of a tiring day to be tossed in the air like a Caesar salad. Her shoes must quake in their boots every morning at the thought of it. But Phoebe, who sometimes can be a real bitch, just shrugs her shoulders and pitches her Maud Frizons at the heap at the bottom of her closet. You would expect more from someone who is junior shoe editor at *Perfect Woman* magazine.

My platforms get tucked into a pair of the shoe bags I made especially for them. All my shoes have shoe bags. They're fake fur-lined, like sleeping bags, really, which keep my footwear as snug as a bug in a rug. I like to think that I have the happiest shoes in all of Manhattan.

I unpeel my Mary Quant panty hose, and my feet feel just great flat against the linoleum. I pad around like this for a while just to stretch my toes again. I suppose I should slip into my satin slippers; you've got to be careful of the floors in my apartment. There's a gorgeous pattern on the linoleum—all bouquets of spring flowers and baskets of kittens and swirling gold ribbons—and I don't want to cover it up; but there are great worn patches everywhere and bits of tin tacked down to cover the broken bits of timber. A nail once went right through Phoebe's gold Mugler sandal, and she couldn't go to work for *weeks*. Just hung around in my apartment, reading magazines and drinking Tab. It was exactly like that old film we saw at Theatre 80. What was it? Oh, *yes*—*The Man Who Came to Dinner*.

I go into the kitchen, which is really just an old gas oven that was disconnected when the last tenant used it to commit suicide, a metal filing cabinet where I store all my knives and forks, an electric kettle, and a refrigerator. Actually, the refrigerator is really a Styrofoam icebox, and it hasn't had any ice in it for a week, owing to the fact I have been too busy to go around to Kim's Korean Market and buy a bag of cubes. I have higher priorities than carting ice all the way along Fourth Street. It takes me all afternoon to work out what to wear at night. The shopping never gets done. On account of there being no ice, there's nothing in the refrigerator except the pair of silver hoop earrings I've been looking for for *days*. I wish the kitchen tap hadn't stopped up; it's just too hard having to hold a glass under the shower every time you want a drink. Of course, the fact that the shower is in the kitchen does help a bit. Well, I'm going to have to wash my sleeping pills down with what's left in the thermos flask I always carry with me.

In the bedroom I crank up the blind and tie its cord to the radiator. I push up the window and put my head outside. The morning is coming up and it's summer and the man across the way has gone away from his window. Maybe he's got a girl there tonight. Or a boy. Or something. I haven't seen him around for a week. Perhaps he has died.

All the apartment buildings face into a dark well, and at the bottom of the well is a god-awful piece of junk that some sculptor assembled when this part of the world was bohemian and not half full of suits like it is now. It looks like the Empire State Building after the Bomb has dropped. What's worse, it's a postmodern piece of junk, and everyone knows that postmodern is OUT.

As usual, at six in the morning, all the other windows except his and mine are dark. This is just as well because during the day it looks like the set from *Rear Window*. Much less exciting, though. No murders or little dogs digging up the vegetable patch. Sometimes the laundry flapping in the wind is interesting. It's mostly all frayed flannel shirts and graying tank tops and pink track pants, but a few mornings ago I saw the sun come up on a lovely thirties nightgown, which was far too fine and fragile to be left out in the weather. She was dreamy. I couldn't work out a way of leaping from my rooftop to her rooftop, or I would have gone right on over and rescued her. I haven't seen her since.

I sigh and move away from the window. I wonder if the man across the way thinks of me as the Grace Kelly of my apartment building. Which I am.

I disappear to the bathroom to clean my teeth and then go to the bed and unzip Ralph, my fuzzy black poodle pajama case. I take out Carroll, my pretty little set of pink baby doll pajamas, and lay her carefully on the bed. Then I sit down in front of the window, at my vanity table, pull out my hair bow, and unpin my fall. When I've brushed the fall until all the knots are gone and I've draped it over the hatstand, I open my makeup kit, which really is a Masters of the Universe lunch box with ankhs stuck all over it, peel off my Glamour Lashes, and lay them back on their little plastic tray. Then I take off my charm bracelet, the one with the tiny glass Cinderella slipper on it. My good-luck charm.

My frock Françoise is dying to come off by now. She's so impatient. She's always the first to want to go out and party and the first to want to come home. Her attention span is so short.

There I am, at 1:00 A.M., just settling into a long run of turning away leopard-print spandex unitards and pastel sweat shirts, when Françoise says, "Let's split, I'm bored." Well, a girl just can't up and leave her door like that, even if she wanted to. So Françoise sulks for the rest of the evening.

It's a battle of wills. This is on account of her couture status and the fact that she is French, although I sometimes doubt her background. That Courrèges label just might be stuck on. People sometimes do that. I can't imagine why. A person with true taste can always tell a real Courrèges by the way she fits. That's why I'm suspicious of Françoise; she wriggles around a lot. I admit she has straightened herself out in the past few months, especially since I brought Petula home. Petula is as good as gold. A real sweetheart. Françoise says she's mealymouthed, a British *cochon,* but it's just sour grapes. Petula has been brought up nicely, that's all. I found her at a church bazaar, which ought to say something about her background.

Françoise can't wait to be unzipped. She's on the floor at my feet in an instant. I pick her up and put her carefully on a hanger specially made with little slots so that she can't slip off. Then she goes on her rack, as meek as a lamb because she's all limp and tired. The stand-up collar has collapsed without a neck to cling to. There won't be much gossip in the closet tonight. Françoise is never one to indulge in idle chat with the other girls anyway. She's ready for *sleep.*

I pull on Carroll's little nylon panties and then wriggle into her sheer top. It's a bit tight around the armholes, but I can bear it. I don't understand people who sleep without clothes. It's so *primitive*. I fluff up the pillows on the bed and move all my dolls to the side I don't sleep on. I think of Phoebe for a minute and what she told me last week: Audrey Hepburn hates dolls. What a crazy. Phoebe, I mean. To remember that sort of stuff.

And then the blind goes down, and I'm in between the sheets, with my pajama-poodle next to me. The bedside light goes off, my black satin eye mask goes on, and I'm ready for sleep. I hope the man across the way was watching me. I'm not an exhibitionist. I don't like people seeing me without my clothes on. But it's no fun getting undressed alone. Which is something a girl has to get used to these days. There are so few boys to get undressed for. Or to get *dressed* for. It's the only sad fact in my fabulous life.

The sleeping pills start to work.

# 7.

I'm dreaming that I'm Ursula Andress in *Dr. No,* and I'm wearing this divine little bikini with a wide belt around the hips and I'm lying deep in the warm sand with Sean Connery because someone is shooting at us, when I'm dragged out of my sleep by a banging noise. I say *dragged* out of my sleep because when you're sweating it out with Sean Connery in a sand dune in Jamaica in 1962, there's no way you suddenly want to find yourself in bed with a poodle pajama case in a one-and-a-half-room apartment in the slums of Manhattan more than twenty-five years later.

"Reality!" a voice is calling out, urgently. I have been trying to make it with Sean Connery for *years,* and I'm not going to let him go now, not for any old urgent voice. He rolls over to protect me from the ricocheting bullets, and his hairy chest is tickling my nose. He's got one big strong arm wrapped around my head and the other one across my thighs. The banging sound and the sound of bullets stop, but he's still lying on me, like a dead weight. He's breathing, though: throaty, whiskeyed Scottish breaths. The suspense is killing me. All I can think is, If I had thighs like Ursula Andress, I'd be lying on me, too.

"Reality!" The banging starts again, and Bond is getting lighter and lighter. He's turning to air. What's worse, I can physically feel my

Ursula Andress cheekbones collapsing under my skin. In my crazy half-asleep state I think, If I wake up now, maybe I can keep the thighs.

"Realit-eeeee!" I'm totally awake, and I'm holding on to Ralph as tight as can be. His black acrylic poodle fur is tickling my nose. I push my eye mask up onto my forehead. It's bright daylight outside; this I can tell by the fact the sun is sneaking through the bamboo blind and making little batik shadow patterns on the wall, exactly like the fabric Armani used several seasons ago. I'm thinking how amazing this is when the banging stops and the voice stops screeching and I can hear, in a sharp whisper, "Really. It's *Freddie.*"

The first thing that crosses my mind is that I've promised to go somewhere with my neighbor Freddie Barnstable and I've slept in. The second thing that crosses my mind is that someone has died. The third thing that crosses my mind is that it is Phoebe who has died and she's left me her Cardin pantsuit. I leap out of bed at the thought and throw Gloria, my silk crepe de chine negligee, the one with the heavenly tufts of lilac marabou feather on the sleeves and around the neck, over the baby doll and stagger to the door that joins my room to Freddie's.

There's an old chain belt that serves as a lock wrapped around the door handle, and as I unravel it, I whisper to Freddie through the hole where there used to be a doorknob, "What's happened?"

"This is an *emergency,*" he hisses. "Can't you hurry up?"

"I am!" I tell him, as I try to pull the nail file out of the bolt without breaking my polishless nails. "Is it Phoebe?" I ask breathlessly as I tug at the door, which always sticks. "Push on the door, will you?" I call out to Freddie.

"What?" he asks, and pushes the little wet nose of Cristobal, his Chihuahua, through the doorknob hole. At this moment I give the door an especially big tug and it opens.

Freddie is standing there in a Hawaiian shirt with gold chains like leis around his neck. He's wearing a black Romeo Gigli skirt and lace-up Roman sandals tied in neat bows below his knees. He's got Cristobal under one arm. There's a Jack Lord badge on his chest.

"You locked our door!" he says accusingly as he comes in, and throws Cristobal into the room ahead of him. Cristobal, who is also wearing gold chains, scampers to the bed immediately and grabs Ralph by the throat. "You know you shouldn't do that. You're so *exasperating*."

Freddie lives in the apartment next door. The door that joins his room to mine is there because the building once was an old hotel. I suppose our rooms were once a suite. I usually keep this door open. But sometimes I lock it, with the chain belt, when I don't want to be disturbed. Freddie takes this as an insult. He likes to waltz through the door whenever he needs to borrow a hat or a charm bracelet, even if I'm not home. Especially if I'm not home. He has even been known to take a frock while I'm sleeping. It always happens to be the exact same frock that I feel like wearing when I get up, too, which is uncanny. Freddie and I have this spiritual thing going, like roommates who get their period at the same time. Cristobal is growling fiercely and tossing Ralph around with quick flicks of his little head. His gold chains are rattling, and his skinny body is shaking like one of those vibrating beds you often see in TV shows about Las Vegas. I snatch Ralph out of his nasty little jaws before he can do any serious damage.

"Look," I say to Freddie crossly, "Chihuahua slime." I wipe off Ralph on the edge of the bed and get back in.

"You can't go back to bed," says Freddie frantically, picking up Cristobal and kissing him on the ear. "It's *important*."

"What time is it?" I ask him. "That's important."

"Never mind," says Freddie, which means it's before four o'clock, my usual waking-up time. The other problem with having Freddie an adjoining door away is he is on a different time clock from me. He needs only two hours' sleep a day, which means he's in bed at nine in the morning and up again at eleven. He has perfect skin and therefore no respect for a girl's beauty sleep.

Cristobal starts scratching. He has teenage eczema. "Look, Reality," Freddie is saying. "You've got to lend me some money!"

"Oooooooh," I groan. "I've just paid the rent. You know I don't have any money, since they raised the rent to three-fifty."

He sits down at the foot of the bed and looks at me with those foxy yellow eyes. Cristobal has turned his foxy yellow eyes on me, too, and whimpers for effect. They're a matching set. "Yes, you have," he says quietly.

My head and Freddie's head and Cristobal's evil little Chihuahua head all turn in unison and focus on a drawer in the table next to the bed. "No, you don't!" I clutch at the pillow. "That's my Chanel suit!"

"Reality," Freddie says sternly, and I can see the color of excitement high on his pale cheeks. "Who lent you his very favorite, very precious Charles James evening stole the last time you had nothing to wear?"

"Hmmm," I mumble, and screw up my mouth. The truth of it is that Freddie is as generous as they come when it comes to lending me his frocks. When it comes to lending *anyone* his frocks. In fact, he often insists his girlfriends wear his frocks, so he can exert some sort of quality control on his dates. "But not my Chanel money!" is all I can think to add.

He who hesitates is robbed. Freddie has the Chanel shoe box out of the drawer and the contents all over the bed before I can say Karl Lagerfeld. He's scrambling through the coins like a mad thing, and Cristobal's jumping about, barking, as if it were a new game. I look on helplessly.

"Pennies and five-cent pieces!" he says with disgust after a minute or so. "Don't you have anything *else*?"

"Well, I've got a long way to go," I say dismally. I don't need Freddie to point out my sad economic state.

"A long way!" Freddie exclaims. "Oh, Reality, a Chanel suit costs at least two thousand dollars. You don't even have two hundred cents!"

"Well, there was this gorgeous little red cashmere cardigan with the sweetest jet beading down at Aurora's. Do you want to see it?" I admit it's my Chanel suit fund that I turn to whenever other frock emergencies occur.

"The point is"—sighs Freddie—"I've left this street vendor with my last five dollars in all the world, and if I don't come up with another fifteen in a few minutes, God knows who he's going to sell it to!"

"Sell what?" I wriggle my feet around the heap of coins on the bed. Cristobal has slumped into an ugly little pile of skin on Freddie's lap.

"The blouse! The *Rudi Gernreich* see-through blouse!"

"Rudi Gernreich!" I almost jump out of my skin. "A *real* Rudi Gernreich?"

"Well, the label's cut out and some of the buttons are off, and I think it's been used as some kind of dishcloth, but yes, yes, I'm sure it's genuine." He takes up a corner of my sheet and mops his brow with it. "Oh, you should *see* it. It's *super*. You'd die for it."

He looks like he's about to burst into tears at the thought of it. Freddie has no stamina. It's on account of the fact that he's English and they don't make them properly these days. I mean, he's not *resilient*. Even though he is a policeman's son. I'm sworn to secrecy about this. He's offended by the slightest thing. It was bad enough his family banishing him to New York and the Fashion Institute of Technology because of some drama over his father's not wanting him to wear frocks, but what's worse, he says, is having to put up with all the bad taste.

Just last Friday he takes me to tea at the Mayfair Regent, which is a divine thing to do—all those little pots of strawberry jam and fluted-edged scones with currants in them and china teacups that

clink and sandwiches with the crusts cut off—and as we are about to
settle down to a nice gossip about all our friends, Freddie suddenly
doubles up and looks like he's going to be sick. Well, what can I do?
"Freddie," I say, "have you been poisoned?" and he groans for, oh,
three or four minutes before he straightens up again.

"Reality," he says faintly, and I could swear he is about to suffo-
cate, and I start to look around for one of those posters that instruct
you how to save the lives of choking victims when he points to an
old dame who is taking off her coat behind me. "Really," he splutters,
and shakes his finger, "ask her to get rid of that *ghastly* hat!"

I'm feeling sorry for Freddie now, even though he's thrown my
Chanel savings all over the bedroom, even though he's woken me up
this early in the day. I'm even feeling sorry for Cristobal, who, I suppose, at least shows some savoir faire for a dog. I'm remembering
Phoebe's Yorkshire terrier, Famous, who lasted only a week because
he had the bad taste to chew up one of her Manolo Blahnik jeweled
evening slippers.

"Look, Freddie," I say, "you only need fifteen dollars."

"If the blouse is still there." He looks miserable.

I start counting out the coins on the bed. "You think we've got
two dollars here?"

"Perhaps."

"And I'm sure I've got some change somewhere." I slip out of bed,
go to the closet, which is really only an old curtain draped over an al-
cove that contains a long frock rack, and dig around in the pockets of
Annie, a western-style jacket with black and red roulé cactus and
cowgirls with lassos across the shoulders. I find a bunch of notes and
count them out. "*Nine* dollars!" How could I have overlooked it? I last
wore Annie—when? It was something to do with frozen margaritas.
I vaguely remember some salt around the edge of a glass.

"Gosh," says Freddie, brightening up. "Thanks."

"Eleven dollars," I say. "Can you bargain the guy down?"

"'Fraid not," Freddie tells me. "I screamed when I saw the blouse. He knew I wanted it. I've already bargained him down from thirty."

"Thirty is an awful lot for a Rudi Gernreich blouse that has been used as a dishcloth."

"Blasphemy!" Freddie looks at me as if I'd spit in Christian Lacroix's face. Cristobal growls.

"Four more dollars," I say quickly. "Phoebe might have it."

"I *can't* go all the way over there. I tell you the blouse will be gone! It's probably gone already!" Freddie's knuckles have turned white, and he starts stomping around the room, or as close to stomping as a 110-pound weakling in a Hawaiian shirt and gold chains can get.

"I'll lend you my Lurex bubble skirt," I'm about to say when I have a brain wave. "Tom!" is what I say out loud.

"What Tom?" asks Freddie, a bit irritably, I think.

"Tom *downstairs*," I tell him. Freddie looks at me as if I'm mad, but it's dawning on him. "Let's go!" I say, and run to the front door. Freddie sets off down the stairs after me with Cristobal squawking at his feet.

When we get to the doorway of the apartment building, Tom is fast asleep, like a baby with five days' growth, under his cardboard shelter. He's wrapped up in about ten pieces of rotting blanket, even though it's so hot one of the heels of my pair of slip-on mules goes right through the melting sidewalk. His head is resting on a shopping bag full of empty soda cans that he's scavenged from the street. Empty bottles of Thunderbird are scattered like cigarette butts around his doorway. Someone has written a rude word across his corrugated cardboard roof, and it looks like he's spent the day trying to cover it up with wet bits of newspaper. He's so house-proud.

Tom is sleeping on his side, with his arm hooked around an oversize beer can. I slip it out carefully, so as not to wake him, and crouch down on the sidewalk with my back to the street so no one can see what I'm doing. Tom is always good for a loan, but I'd hate for some stranger to come along and rip him off.

I count the notes. "Fifty-three."

"Fifty-three!" Freddie exclaims. "He's richer than both of us together. That's rather a surprise."

"He makes *heaps* on all those old cans he collects," I explain. "Five cents a can adds up." I count out four dollars.

"Can you make it seven?" Freddie asks. "I need to buy *Vanity Fair*."

I give him eight. "You'll have to return it by the end of the week," I say. "And buy Tom a bottle of scotch as thanks."

"Certainly," Freddie says, and puts the eight dollars in the pocket of his shirt. "Now, I must trot off before the wretched blouse is gone." He looks down at Tom as I slip the beer can back under his arm. "Where do you think he got those carpet slippers? They're *super!*"

Freddie picks up Cristobal, who has just marked out his territory around Tom's house, and plants a big kiss on my cheek.

"Really, you're fabulous."

I clunk back upstairs in my mules and marabou feathers and attempt to tune back in to *Dr. No.* I get *Hawaii Five-O* instead.

# 8.

When I wake up again, it's six in the afternoon. Which is annoying because I've slept through *Thunderbirds*.

I fling off my eye mask and sit up. I flop out of bed and pull up the blinds a bit to see if it's still sunny. The sky is pink and mottled with gray like a chiffon frock I once owned and gave to Freddie. He's more the chiffon type. Anyway, it's steamy hot, which is fine by me. There're so many more fashion possibilities in summer when you don't have to worry about your knees getting cold or a draft blowing up your miniskirt. Not that I ever do. I'd wear a miniskirt in a snowstorm if I felt like it.

I turn on the shower and wait until the peanut butter jar fills up with warm water. If you start the day with warm water, maybe with a squeeze of lime in it, it dissolves all the fat particles in your stomach, washes them right out like a dose of Drano. I read this in one of the beauty books above Phoebe's desk at *Perfect Woman*. I read other interesting things in those beauty books, too, like slices of raw potato over your eyes reduce puffiness and walking on egg yolks is a wonderful way to soften the heels of your feet. The potato trick is a particularly good standby when you've been crawling around the neighborhood at all hours of the morning looking for a bar that doesn't play the Doors. I mean, I *love* the Doors, but some nights a girl just longs for something a bit more lyrical, like the Troggs.

I go back in the boudoir and stop in front of the closet, waiting for inspiration. I hear the familiar sounds of my frocks straining against the curtain, quivering with anticipation, wondering what mood I'm in, where I'm going, who will be chosen tonight.

You can't imagine what pleasure it gives me, this poising on the brink. I'm Reality Nirvana, I'm five-four, I'm one hundred pounds, I've got a twenty-three-inch waist, and I'm twenty years old—almost twenty-one—but I don't look it. I wear a 34B cup bra and a size six frock, and my big toe is shorter than my second one. I've got blond hair with little platinum wisps around my face and the remnants of some henna in it, a few freckles across my nose, and a curve in the middle of my top lip like a little twin-peaked mountain. I've got green eyes like swamp water and white ends on my lashes which need mascara and the beginning of some cellulite on my thighs if I go over them with a magnifying glass. This is me, standing here. One hundred percent natural, except for the silver frosting in my hair and—I admit it— a prominent palate that was fixed with braces when I was nine.

But don't you see what's so fabulous about my life? I can stand here, five-four Reality who's sort of pretty with a sort of good body although it could do with some improvement and kind of scraggly hair that can't make up its mind if it's short or long or platinum or blond, and in half an hour I can be going out that door five-nine Reality in a beautiful Ann-Margret wig curling around my shoulders and sweeping black Elizabeth Taylor lashes that make my swamp-colored eyes look like almond-cut emeralds (with the additional help of a pair of Secret of the Superstars colored contact lenses) and the sexiest Kim Novak low-cut frock that pushes up my bosoms into two white grapefruit and nips me right in at the waist and curves out over my derriere and falls to a little kick pleat to show off the backs of my knees.

Or in half an hour I could go out that door five-five Reality in the dearest pair of white go-go boots with lime green fishnet panty hose and an Op Art minifrock in psychedelic swirls of purple and orange and a white plastic space bonnet with a Lucite visor. I could go out that door in a black leather biker's jacket with a 3-D illustration of Saint Francis of Assisi sewn into the back and lined with an old British flag and a stretch miniskirt that barely covers my behind and striped ankle socks over torn tights and a shaggy white wig that I've recently hacked about with an old razor blade and studded leather wrist straps and a transfer of a bleeding heart stuck on my right cheekbone. Or I could step out in the neatest brown tweed New Look suit with a cream silk blouse and Peter Pan collar and matching cream suede gauntlet gloves—the ones with the pizza grease on them, but you don't really notice as the grease trickled down the seams—and a patent leather pocketbook slung over my wrist and a brown felt turban with a big pearl hatpin stuck into the side and look for all the world like a Sunday school teacher going to a revival meeting.

I can walk out that door a brunette or a pinkette or a Dalmatian if I want to. I can have fuzzy Afro hair or a Louise Brooks bob or soft marcel waves rippling down the side of my face. I can have bloodred lips or innocent pink ones. Slashes of black eyeliner or kinky clumps of blue mascara. A face as pale as a ghost or dusted all over with gold. A polka dot ribbon in my hair or a ring through my nose.

I can be vamp, tramp, flapper, sleaze, mod, postmod, Pop Art, disco, retro, rococo, go-go, gypsy, new wave, new romantic, New Look, Carnaby Street, Cossack, Bonnie and Clyde, directoire, debutante, existentialist, belle époque, buffalo girl, baby doll, Barbarella, punk, postpunk, Pre-Raphaelite, even *preppy* if I want to, which is almost never.

I can be any one of these things, and I never know which one I'm going to be when I wake up in the morning. It's *exciting*. I can lie in bed for ages, snug and warm and full of peace, considering all the possibilities spread out before me, the infinite variety of looks I can create and moods I can be in for the day. Some days I just lie there and try to go all limp and let the muse descend upon me. My dear little muse who whispers in my ear things like, It's a Doris Day kind of day and wouldn't the daisy yellow wool bouclé suit with the three-quarter sleeves and the rolled collar look sensational with your beige and white two-tone sling-back flatties and the white panty hose with tulips embroidered up the sides and the blond flip wig and perhaps the silk faille pillbox hat with the cabbage rose on the front? Other days I need to get up and wander around a bit and have some coffee if there's any and then go to the closet and have a little chat with my frocks, that sort of thing, and just ease into one of them, which is exactly what I am about to do now.

Because I am in a classical mood lately, I select a traditional red-on-white polka dot dress with shoestring straps and a built-in padded bra and waist cinched tightly with a big red elastic belt. The frock's name is Gina—after Gina Lollobrigida, naturally—and she's so tight little wrinkles of fabric form on my hips when I walk. But she's got a *great* sense of humor, a wonderful Italian outlook on life. When you walk in Gina—in six-inch red high heels, of course—you get this urge to hum "Volare" and swing your handbag like mad. I love her *so* much.

I've been favoring Gina a lot lately. This means that some of the other frocks in my closet are seething with jealousy. The ones with Latin blood. Dolores and Carmen and Carmelita are frothing at the hem. They're not pleased with me at all. I'm their most unfavorite person at the moment. (The fact that I'm their *only* person at the moment doesn't make them behave any better.)

I've explained to them, delicately so as not to hurt their feelings, that I've gone off froufrou for the time being, that the last thing I want to wear in the street right now are layers of tulle or big satin bustles or hoop skirts that make it impossible to get through doorways without wearing your frock around your neck. But the girls don't under-stand. They like to rhumba; they like to samba; they like to take a tango or two around the dance floor. They like to shimmy in the spotlight. They're good-time girls.

I can hear Dolores grouching as I close the apartment door be-hind me. They'll go on like this for weeks if I don't give one of them a whirl around the neighborhood soon. Now that it's summer, they can hear the salsa rhythms from the apartment building across the way floating through the bedroom window. It's in their veins, this Latin music. There's no room to cha-cha in the closet. They want *out*.

But I forget them as soon as I step out onto the street. Life is won-derful! There are so many parties to go to and great frocks to wear.

# 9.

Gina takes me for an evening stroll down Third Street. She's vibrating with pent-up energy. She's wiggling like Jell-O as we walk. I'm singing.

> Let's fly 'way up to the clouds,
> Away from the maddening crowds,
> Let us leave the confusion
> And all this illusion behind.
> Volare. Oh. Oh. . . .

It's a *smoldering* evening. The leaves on the trees are bronze against a cinnamon sky, just like Estée Lauder's summer colors. I always look up when I walk. A lady doesn't inspect the gutter. Occasionally she might inspect the trash cans for old Italian *Vogues* which are too expensive to buy and discarded shoes and bits of mirror. But the *gutter* is beneath her. All that the gutters around here contain are used plastic syringes and soggy cigarette papers and condoms with *lipstick* on them. Can you imagine? Who'd want to do that sort of thing? The last condom I looked down at had Lancôme flambée gloss all over it. I'd recognize that color anywhere. It's one of my favorites.

There are dozens of people in the street tonight, and they're all turning around to stare at me. A lot of them say hello. I'm well known in this part of town. I'm well known all the way from Fourteenth Street to First Street and from Avenue D to Second Avenue. Which is the only part of Manhattan that counts. Except for Seventh Avenue and the corner of Fifty-Seventh and Fifth. This is the *universe* as far as I'm concerned.

There are girls sliding by in black leather miniskirts and T-shirts with skulls and crossbones on them and boys in paint-splattered jeans with the knees ripped out. They're looking at me with *respect*. They're thinking, I Wish I Thought of That. I can see it in their eyes. They're thinking, If She's Wearing Six-Inch High Heels, It Must Be OK. They're going to rush right out and buy a pair. People copy me all the time.

"Hey, *gorgeous!*" says a black man with a big smile who is clicking his fingers as he comes toward me. I grin at him. He's on my wavelength.

"Love your suit," I tell him as he goes past in a flash of lilac crimplene.

A boy on a bicycle rings his bell, and a big gray limo eases along the road beside me and then speeds off. Three guys are exchanging money on the corner of Avenue B, and they stop what they're doing and whistle. I tell you, I'm feeling like *something*. I wish there were a construction site nearby. Gina loves to ooze by a construction site. She's a real romantic.

First thing, I go to the Magazine Rack and fight my way through the fashion crowd to get my hands on the latest issue of *Harpers & Queen*. There's a hat on the cover which is to die. It consists of dozens of silk leaves making the shape of a cabbage with a tiny little rubber snail crawling up one side. The silk leaves are tinged with brown, as if the cabbage were dying. Leaves are very IN in hats this year. Especially dead leaves, like overblown roses. Fashion always reflects the times you live in.

I stand there for a while looking at the pictures. Then I put the magazine back on the pile and head out onto Avenue C.

As usual, I stop by at Café Orlon, for the day's gossip.

Faille, the waitress, comes straight over to me. She's wearing a beige Orlon pantsuit with a short-sleeved zip-up top. She's as tall as a beanpole, so the bottom of her trousers barely reach to her ankles. It's a new interpretation of an old look. I tell her I like the outfit.

"Fab dress," she says, admiring Gina, as I squeeze into a chair by the wall.

"Fab hairdo." I compliment her in turn.

"Gee, *thanks,*" she says, patting her bright orange head. "I thought I'd switch to fall colors. For the new season."

"It looks *great.*"

"You, too. Fab nail color."

Café Orlon is packed. It's always packed. Even at four on a Monday afternoon or ten on a Tuesday morning. I mean, I've never actually *been* there at ten on a Tuesday morning, but people tell me this. Going to Café Orlon is what you do while you're waiting for the clubs to open. Most of the people sitting around on wrought-iron chairs with their legs crossed and white faces are fashion stylists. There are a couple of makeup artists showing their portfolios to each other. There are some new frocks being paraded. Stella, the local Psy-chic, is doing a reading in one dimly lit corner. She has a sign in the front window. I CAN READ YOUR FUTURE LIKE THERES NO TO-MORROW, is what it says.

Faille tucks her order book into a pocket in her jacket and puts her pencil behind her ear. "There's, like, big news," she tells me above the din, and leans closer to whisper in my ear. "Ricci's been fired."

"Ricci?" I ask. "Not *Ricky*?" I pronounce her name Ricky, not *Rich-ee,* which is what she calls herself. She spells her name *Ricci,* af-ter Nina Ricci, which I think is pretentious. We all got over L'Air du

Temps when we were fifteen. Which shows how behind the times Ricci is.

"The very one." Faille grins.

"You're kidding!"

Faille nods. "God's truth."

"I knew it! You don't last long around here with *that* much bad taste. Anyone who wears glitter boob tubes has got a *major* credibility problem."

"Oh, it wasn't anything to do with what she *wears*," says Faille.

"Oh? How could it be anything else?"

"She wouldn't let Tina Chow into the club. She didn't recognize her. Can you believe it?" Faille says this very slowly, as if the words were creamy bits of Milky Way bar.

"Holy cow!" I scream, and start giggling. A few people turn around and look at me. When I catch my breath, I say, "Imagine not recognizing Tina Chow! It's a *sin*."


It is *vital* to recognize somebodies like Tina Chow when you're on the door of a club. It's *essential* to make the somebodies feel like somebodies by letting them glide through these ropes like Jesus over water. Important to smooth their way. To make them feel superior to the nobodies who are standing below wishing they were somebodies who could glide through those ropes like Jesus over water, too. The somebodies wouldn't come to the clubs if it wasn't for the nobodies standing around wishing they were somebodies. A somebody just can't sit at home in her sweat pants and say to herself, "Oh, I'm a somebody, so I can sit here all night and be content." A somebody has got to know she's a somebody. Be told lots of times. Be pushed around by adoring fans. Roughed up a bit by autograph seekers. Hear her name running like a ripple through the crowd.

That's why we need nobodies, to make the somebodies feel superior. The somebodies wouldn't come if they couldn't be sure they'd
have nobodies to trample all over. And the nobodies wouldn't come
if they didn't have somebodies to stare at. The club makes money off
the nobodies—somebodies never pay for anything—by charging
them exorbitant admission prices. The nobodies gladly pay. Especially as I hardly ever let them in. The nobodies wouldn't pay to
stand around in a room full of other nobodies. That doesn't make
sense. Especially when that room is just a dusty old ex-bingo hall
with trestle tables and vinyl chairs and dead gladiolus in the alcoves.
Which is exactly what Less Is More is. An ex-bingo hall run by the
Girls for God, a Catholic women's auxiliary. I thought up the name
myself.

But if the nobodies can spot Cher's latest hairdo across a crowded
room or know that it's Jessica Lange who is in that bathroom stall adjusting her slip, they'd sell their mothers for the privilege.

The subtlety of all this—something that obviously escaped Ricci's
attention—is that somebodies sometimes don't look like somebodies. They look like nobodies. Tina Chow is one of these.

She looks like a nobody. A *fabulous* nobody, but a nobody nevertheless. When you're on the door of a nightclub, you've got to know
the difference between a somebody who looks like a nobody and a
nobody who looks like a nobody.

It's elementary.


"So," says Faille, patting her hairdo, "do you think I should apply for
the job? Ricci's job? Before anyone else does?"

"There's probably a line a mile long outside the club already," I
warn her.

"You think so?" Faille sounds dejected.

"Faille, it's a vacant door," I point out. "Everyone in the world wants to work on the door of a club. Even at a club as tacky as Ready to Wear."

"I hate to admit this, but I envy you." Faille sighs, taking her notebook out of her pocket again and her pencil from behind her ear. "Standing up there in a spotlight turning people away. It's *important*, isn't it? Deciding who's somebody and who's nobody? It's like having the power of life and death. Like a brain surgeon. Or the President of the United States. It's a real *responsibility*. I don't know how you sleep at night."

"I try not to think about it," I tell her. "I'd be a nervous wreck if I did."

# 10.

Aurora's White Trash is near the corner of Sixth Street and Avenue C. It's next door to a store that sells fresh chickens and disembowels them in the backyard. The stench is sickening, especially on Sundays, when the whole family is out the back hacking off heads and plucking feathers. But this doesn't deter me one bit. Aurora's shop is *Mecca* as far as I'm concerned. It's my daily pilgrimage. Where else could I find an Emilio Pucci original for twenty-nine dollars?

As soon as you walk into the shop, you forget the chicken gizzards. The smell disappears like magic. Your senses move up into a higher plane of awareness. Your whole body becomes focused on the task at hand. Your whole *being* becomes focused on the task of sifting through the racks of frocks and jackets and antique overcoats, racks dripping with sequins and bugle beads and floating lengths of chiffon, with strands of mink and swaths of silk and swirls of Op Art polyester print. The task of finding the perfect frock for you before somebody else spots it.

Aurora sits behind a display cabinet in the corner with her paper cup of cold cappuchino. The cabinet is crammed with old silver cutlery and broken clip-on earrings and neatly folded linen and the arms and legs—and sometimes balding heads—of ancient china dolls. There are bits of torn filigree lace and yellowing babies' clothes and face powder from the thirties with violets painted on the packages. Sometimes there are beaded evening purses in the cabinet and leather gloves like butter, but these get snapped up in the time it takes to buckle a belt. I've never seen Aurora move from her cabinet. Not once. She's always in exactly the same spot, sitting in a teak chair with orange and green floral upholstery, in a puddle of flesh. Aurora was a hat model at B. Altman's in the late 1940's and early 1950's, and she once met Lisa Fonssagrives. She says she modeled the hats that went with the New Look in 1947.

Aurora has let herself go. Her hair is now like clumps of sofa stuffing, all prickly and pale yellow. In the old days, when she was modeling, she had her hair marcel waved. It curled down the side of her pink cheeks in golden ripples. She used to sleep with a hairnet. She still wears that hairnet, in the daytime. It ought to break her heart to dwell on memories of how perfect she was back then. Compared with what a blimp she is now. It ought to drive her to distraction being a size twenty-two and having to sit all day in a room full of exquisite size six and eight cocktail frocks. It would kill me.

The funny thing is, Aurora doesn't seem to care. She's almost the most contented person I know, sitting behind that counter and relating tales of Elsa Schiaparelli's shoe-shaped hats to us all, in her hibiscus-print muumuu and toweling slippers. Maybe it's something to do with being old. Maybe you stop caring after thirty. I'm going to stop caring when I'm *dead,* and even then there's a chance I'll get to be an angel and chose the color of my robe. A clotted-cream-colored Fortuny gown, all rippling pleats and twists of gold silk cord, would be heavenly.

Aurora shifts herself in her chair when I come in and grunts. She rarely smiles. In fact, she seems quite grouchy most of the time. To strangers, that is. But she's like a mother to me. More of a mother than the one I've got. But I'm not going to go into that *now*. I really enjoy our chats, and I think she does, too. It's like there's a special language of frocks, and we both know how to talk it.

"I've been saving something for you," she says before I can say hello. She pulls out a package from underneath her chair. It's an old newspaper. She unfolds it slowly in front of me. Lying in the center of a headline that reads HERMAPHRODITE IMPREGNATES HIM/HERSELF is a pair of plastic earrings in the shape of a dear little basket filled with vegetables. There are miniature carrots and onions and a tiny bunch of spinach. Aurora knows my taste down to a T.

"How divine!" I say, and try them on.

"Aren't they just *adorable*?" Aurora says, in a thick voice that makes her throat sound as if it's coated in coarse linen. She coughs every third word like she's got a button caught in her windpipe. Aurora says she was born outside Barcelona—which is the fashionable place to be born at the moment—but only last week she referred to her childhood in Vienna. Maybe Vienna is outside Barcelona. "I bought those earrings in Budapest in 1952. I found them again last night. They're so *cute*." She croaks proudly in an accent that is now pure American tourist, like she'd grown up listening to Americans in art galleries. I've seen enough of these tourists in the East Village, fingering the motorcycle jackets and trying on the RAISE YOUR HEM AND LOWER YOUR IQ T-shirts. "Oh, *honey*," the women say. "Aren't these switchblades just *adorable*?" This is how Aurora talks.

"I didn't know you were in China," I say.

"No, honey. I never went there."

"But they have great hats."

"Do they now?"

"Has anything new come in this morning?" I ask. "Anything interesting? I've simply *got* to have a new frock. It's been two whole weeks since I've had one. I'm in agony!"

"Sure thing, sweetheart. There's a little something in blue velvet. Over on that rack." The bangles on her arm rattle as she points to a row of dark frocks, hanging there silently like a whole lot of commuters on the subway.

"Is this the one you mean?" I ask, pulling out a velvet coat with smocked sleeves. "But she's beautiful!" I hold her up against my face. "Who could give something like this away?"

"Lots of people do," says Aurora in her gravelly voice. "There are folks who care about clothes and folks who don't. I wouldn't be in business otherwise."

"Well, I care about frocks," I say, putting my arms through the sleeves and feeling the cool satin lining against my skin. "I think I care about frocks more than I care about people."

Aurora nods.

"I couldn't imagine throwing out any of my frocks. They're my best friends."

Aurora is looking at me with shrewd, old lashless eyes.

"A lot of folks outgrow their clothes," she says.

"But I wouldn't just toss them in the trash!" I protest. "I'd preserve them. For posterity. They're like heirlooms. Even my Zandra Rhodes silk chiffon print is. I didn't throw her out when she went out of fashion. I kept her. Not that I'm going to be able to wear her for another three or four years. But when I do, it's going to be like old home week. What do you think?"

I twirl around in front of Aurora. She puts her fingers to her throat and casts her eyes to the ceiling. "My oh my," she says approvingly. She bats her missing eyelashes. She has applied some eyeliner half an inch thick, and it ends in a painted beauty spot near her right eyebrow. She has an orchid tucked behind her ear which she strokes from time to time. It's brown around the edges.

"How much?" I ask nervously. "I really do love it."

"Fifteen dollars," Aurora says. "But you can have it for twelve."

"It's a deal!" I say. "Can you hold it for me?"

Aurora grunts.

I go down to the old painted closet at the back of the shop where Aurora keeps her layaways. I slip the coat back on its hanger and hook it up in the part of the closet that belongs to me. I've got six things put aside already. Some of them have been there for months. The only trouble with being on a door is that you earn a pittance. Most of that pittance goes on rent, when I remember to pay it. A fashion leader like me has to rely on the kindness of thrift shop proprietors. And what she can find in Dumpsters. It's a miracle that I look as fabulous as I do.

I finger the hem of a full-circle black velvet skirt with the scenes of Mexico hand-painted all over it. It's heaven. I add it to the six other things and sigh. Sometimes I worry that I'm aiming too high in life. With things like my Chanel suit. But if dumb, rich, ugly women can own five-thousand-dollar frocks, why can't I?

## 11.

Phoebe is waiting for me inside Theatre 80. It's pitch-black except for some flickering light from the screen. Phoebe always takes the front-row center-aisle seat. It's as if she's trying to gobble up the film. She says you can see the eye makeup better from there.

She scoops her black purse off the seat beside her so I can sit down.

"Where have you been?" she snarls. "I've had a hard time trying to keep this seat for you."

"Shut up," whispers some person behind us.

"I've been to Aurora's. Do you like my earrings?"

"I can't see them," says Phoebe, who is looking straight up at the screen, not at me.

"I'll get my flashlight out," I offer. I scramble around in my purse. "Where is that thing?" I've got my mirror and several eye pencils on my lap. "There!" I say as I make out the flashlight and flood my face with the pink beam.

Phoebe doesn't even turn a hair. "Sweet," is what she says.

"Turn that thing off!" says the person behind me, and pushes me on the shoulder.

"Yeah!" says someone else up in the back.

I was going to turn it off anyway. I don't know why they're getting so upset. I start putting everything back in my purse. Something drops on the floor, and I feel for it with my feet.

"You've missed all the best bits," scolds Phoebe.

"I haven't missed the pink and silver party frock with the pink tiara," I say smugly, retrieving my mascara. "Or the coral coat with the mink hat."

"But you've missed the black frock with the pearl and jet necklace and the hat with the ostrich feathers and white pompon and the evening gown with the yoke neckline and the four strands of pearls."

"But this is the bus station scene," I say, looking at the screen. "I'm sure the pompon hat comes next."

"You fool," Phoebe snarls. "I've already seen this *twice* today. The pompon hat comes after Patricial Neal in the red turban and black cape but *before* the putty-colored trench coat with the head scarf."

"*Shut up!*" The person behind me pokes me right in the middle of the back with something sharp. I turn around. I can't see who it is in the dark.

"Do you mind?" I say crossly. "I can't concentrate on the film!"

I turn back to the screen, and Audrey Hepburn's celestial face fills me with wonder.


The velvet curtain lurches across the screen, and the lights come up. People wait in their seats for the second half of the double bill, the 9:55 screening of *Roman Holiday*.

Phoebe disappears while I'm kneeling on the floor, searching for a pot of eye shadow that has rolled under my seat. I find her later, in the bathroom, applying soft beige lipstick in big creamy curves.

"You'll miss *Roman Holiday*," I warn her. "It's just starting."

"A girl can't watch that sort of film without her lipstick," she says, totally unconcerned.

I groan. It gets very boring being girlfriends with a clone of Audrey Hepburn. Audrey Hepburn circa 1961 to 1967, to be exact. According to Phoebe, Audrey Hepburn after *Wait Until Dark* is not Audrey Hepburn at all.

Phoebe is always telling me that I should find the look for me and stick to it. This is her major criticism of me. She points out that she discovered Audrey Hepburn six months ago, and she's stuck with her through thick and thin, even through the recent revival of Brigitte Bardot. She swears she will stick with her through Maria Callas and Anita Ekberg, too. We will wait and see. Maria Callas is a very *powerful* image.

I admire Phoebe's devotion to Audrey Hepburn, though. If I were going to be devoted to a look, I suppose Audrey Hepburn is the look to be devoted to. Audrey Hepburn *or* Jackie O. Or Honor Blackman. But you see? There I go again. I can't be loyal to any of them. *All* of them are the look for me. It's impossible to choose just one.

Being Audrey Hepburn for Phoebe has meant putting silver streaks in her black hair and wearing long gloves, even when she is having a bath. It has meant mostly wearing Givenchy, or good copies of Givenchy, and heaping on the pearls and jet beads and then topping it all off with the biggest hats you've ever seen, hats like flying saucers or upside-down pudding bowls with colored scarves trailing. It has meant always wearing a little square handbag over the wrist, *never* the shoulder. It has meant going on shoplifting expeditions for yard-long cigarette holders and little tasseled earplugs to wear with her eye mask at night.

It has meant dating men who look like George Peppard or Humphrey Bogart or Fred Astaire or Albert Finney or Cary Grant or a combination of all five. It has meant being as polite and refined as can be and saying "perfectly darling" all the time and "dear little man" to everybody, even girls. It has meant, most of all, being thinner than thin and doing weird exercises to make her neck "as long as a giraffe."

Phoebe takes a very hard line on Audrey Hepburn. There is a boy who has been pursuing her for months. I wish he would pursue me. He's very attractive. But he made a major mistake with Phoebe last week. He told her that he thinks Audrey Hepburn is "scrawny, like a chicken." That was the end of that relationship. "Imagine not having the sensitivity to understand that it's Audrey Hepburn's thinness that makes Audrey Hepburn so beautiful," Phoebe complained a couple of days ago. "Clothes just hang off those bones of hers like running water. Audrey Hepburn is my heroine because she looks wonderful in everything. That takes real talent. I dropped that boy *flat.*"

Wherever Phoebe goes there is always this *frisson.* (Her word.) I have to hand it to her, she does look exactly like Audrey Hepburn. She wears half-inch heels so that she can be exactly Audrey Hepburn's height (five feet seven and a half) and keeps her weight down to exactly Audrey Hepburn's weight (a hundred pounds) and pads the toes of her shoes so that she can wear exactly Audrey Hepburn's size (10AA).

Phoebe eats two boiled eggs and a piece of brown toast and drinks three cups of coffee for breakfast. She has cottage cheese and fruit salad for lunch and thin slices of meat with two vegetables for dinner. She has been doing this ever since Audrey Hepburn's diet was published in *Perfect Woman.* She never deviates, even for Swedish pancakes, which are my downfall.

Tonight she is wearing a little sleeveless black sheath with tie belt and pleated hemline that looks exactly like the one Audrey Hepburn has just worn in the scene in *Breakfast at Tiffany's* where she's getting dressed to go visit Sally Tomato at Riker's Island. Phoebe has bare legs and black alligator shoes and a giant black sun hat with a scarf and long black gloves and dark sunglasses, and she is spraying her neck with L'Interdit from a crystal bottle with a long black pump. She is not wearing her diamantés because she says diamantés are "tacky" before 10:00 P.M.

"Well," she says, blotting her lips on toilet tissue, "I'm absolute *finito*."

"A maaarvelous mouth," I comment.

"Thank you," she answers crisply. "Are you coming?"

"I'm late for the club," I say quickly. Otherwise Phoebe will insist I join her in the auditorium, which will make the number of times I've seen *Roman Holiday* sixty-three.

Phoebe just flaps her wrist. She couldn't care less. I can tell by the way she's tilting her chin that's she's already half merged into the character of Princess Anne. She floats out of the bathroom and lets the door close in my face.

I back-comb the top of my red wig before I follow her out into the foyer. I find her standing outside the theater doors signing an autograph on the back of a Theatre 80 program. She finishes her signature with a flourish of ball-point pen and hands it to a short girl in a copy of an Azzedine (with a bit of cotton hanging off the hem). As the piece of paper flutters between them, I notice Phoebe has signed her name *Audrey Hepburn*.

# 12.

I am wearing my black ciré jersey jumpsuit and my thigh-high boots. I've got on a shoulder-length brown wig with the bangs pulled back off my face. I am, of course, Emma Peel. I've decided that the theme at the club tonight is the Woman Whose Lipstick I'd Most Like to Borrow. I'd love to borrow Emma Peel's lipstick. I have real respect for a woman who can karate-chop half a dozen men without getting her lip gloss all over the furniture.

There's a theme night at Less Is More every Thursday. The reason why the club has theme nights is that dressing up is the only thing anyone can be bothered doing anymore. *Vogue* calls it the New Languidity, and as soon as *Vogue* made it official, well, everyone started practicing it like mad. This is one of the reasons Less Is More is booming and some of the other clubs are going bankrupt. The clubs that are way behind the times, like Club 61. All they've got to offer is dancing, which went out with stonewashed denim. Less Is More offers lots of great frocks to look at and enough light to see all the details. All the other clubs are gloomy. Less Is More has kept all the original fluorescent fixtures from the original bingo hall that stood in its place, so everything is illuminated brightly. A bit too brightly if your skin's broken out. But it's a positive thing, generally. Everyone agrees that great frocks well illuminated are the best entertainment there is.

Judging by the crowd tonight, the Woman Whose Lipstick I'd Most Like to Borrow is going to be more popular than Stepford Wives, which was formerly my greatest hit. On Stepford Wives night people had to come dressed as if they were off to a PTA meeting, in floor-length print frocks and frilly aprons, pushing shopping carts of cornflakes or some famous brand-name product. Well, the Red Apple wasn't too pleased when all its carts started disappearing in the afternoon, but everyone had a whale of a time playing Dodg'em cars with them the next morning before the police came.

Stepford Wives really cemented Less Is More's popularity. Since then everyone who lives five blocks either way of here waits breathlessly for my announcement of what the following night's theme is going to be. Well, maybe *announce* is the wrong word. I just tell a few very close friends, and they tell a few of their very close friends, and those close friends tell some others, and before you know it, the theme has spread like hot pants through the coffee shops and vintage clothing emporiums of the Lower East Side.

Some people try to wheedle the theme out of me ahead of time by offering to lend me frocks and shoes and things, but the truth of the matter is, I don't plan these things at all. I'm not too good at thinking ahead. My life just unravels like a hem coming down.

Besides, the theme is a matter of inspiration, and you can't plan for an inspiration. I'll spread the word that it's Patsy Cline night, for instance—"I Fall to Pieces" is almost my theme song—but when I get up in the afternoon, I just don't feel in the mood for a bandanna and gingham skirt with two hundred petticoats. You've got to be in a very special mood for bandannas and gingham skirts, and these moods strike only about once a decade.

On afternoons like these I'll decide, for instance, that I'm feeling very *vinyl*, not gingham, and I'm feeling very *seven-inch heels*, not cowboy boots, and I put these elements together and come up with Chelsea Brown as a theme. While everyone else is slipping into hootenanny skirts and fringed shirts with embroidered sombreros on the shoulders, I'm quietly pulling on a red vinyl miniskirt that measures twelve inches from waist to hem and a Day-Glo bikini top. While they're all trying to squeeze into cowboy boots with stacked Cuban heels, I'm fastening a tiny gold chain belt around my waist, sliding into acid yellow fluorescent tights, and digging around in the closet for my red plastic sandals with the seven-inch stiletto heels. While they're trying to tease their hair fifteen inches high, I'm unpacking my Dynel Afro wig and looking under the bed for that pair of gigantic hoop earrings like dinner plates I know I tossed there a month or so ago. While they're rounding the corner into Third Street in ten-gallon hats, chomping on hay and whooping like cowboys, I'm standing at the top of the steps frugging to the Jackson Five. Once they get a load of me, they turn on their Cuban heels and run! They're beside themselves. They can't believe I would have done this to them. But quick as a flash, they're on their way home to change. Twenty minutes later they're back in flared trousers with two-inch cuffs and white mink coats over three-piece polyester suits in pale green with red satin shirts and gold rings with initials like LSD made out in cubic zircons half an inch high. They're back in black Leatherette microminiskirts and white high-heeled sandals over coffee-colored panty hose. They've dug out lime green and lavender nylon caftans with frog fastenings and patchwork suede vests with lambskin trim. They're fabulous now. Naturally, I let them all in.

And all the while the unfabulous ones who don't live five blocks either way of here and don't hang around in coffee shops all day are gawking at my Dynel Afro and are gaping at the invasion of polyester and Leatherette and are thinking, Well, tonight we look better than *that*, until they start to notice that it's the polyester and Leatherette and vinyl and Dynel that are swaggering up those steps and through that wooden door and it's the pinstripe suits and silk pussy bows and Ralph Lauren print frocks that are the ones who are stuck like sink sludge to the bottom of the stairs.

Theme nights sort out the fabulous from the unknowing in a second. It's natural selection.


So far I've counted seven Maria Callases but only one Anita Ekberg. I was right about this the other night. Maria Callas is already on the decline. The minute that there's more than two of somebody, she's *finished.*

I've let in an Estée Lauder, a Josephine Baker with bananas strung around her hips, a Penelope Tree, a Jean Shrimpton, a Jean Seberg, and a Jeanne Moreau, a Veruschka covered in graffiti and blending into the building behind her, a Sharon Tate from the suicide scene in *Valley of the Dolls,* a Suzy Parker, a Dovima, and a Lisa Fonssagrives, who all arrive together, a girl naked from the waist up who tells me she's supposed to be Vanessa Redgrave in *Blow-Up,* a fabulous Honor Blackman with straw in her hair, one Ines de la Fressange, a Loulou de la Falaise, an Anouk Aimée with eyeliner as wide as the Hudson, an Anita Pallenberg, a Nina Van Pallandt, a Marianne Faithfull, a Bianca Jagger and two Jerry Halls, and a Wallis Simpson with a jewel box under her arm.

I've turned away Shirley Bassey, Cher, two Barbra Streisands, one Barbara Cartland, Zsa Zsa Gabor, a 1975 version of Elizabeth Taylor, a Diana Vreeland who was dressed in green silk (imagine that— Diana Vreeland in anything but red and black! Are they kidding?), a Princess Diana in a sailor collar, Diana Ross, Diane von Furstenberg, Dolly Parton, and an Elsa Schiaparelli who was wearing a copy of a Chanel suit. How stupid. Elsa Schiaparelli would have *died* rather than put on one of Coco Chanel's suits. Everyone knows they hated

each other. It's just plain foolish to try and get away with Elsa Schiaparelli while you're standing there, for all the world to see, in a truck-
load of gold chains and a wool suit with gold braid.

Less Is More has its standards. Freddie arrives after midnight. He
pushes his way through a group of Stevie Nickses, who are definitely
*not* coming in, and bounces up beside me. He is wearing the Rudi
Gernreich blouse, miniskirt, and coordinating knee-high socks with
platform shoes. He says he is Peggy Moffit, Rudi Gernreich's favorite
model. He has outlined his eyelids with big black circles and is wearing at least three pairs of my false eyelashes. Cristobal is wearing a
body stocking made from an old pair of ribbed panty hose. He looks
a bit annoyed at the simplicity of his outfit, especially as he is eyeing
the diamanté collar on Jacqueline Susann's black poodle. He's growling deep down in his throat. Freddie is accompanied by a boy in a
smart little two-piece suit. "This is Jackie O," he says proudly. "Isn't
she *fab*?"

I shake Jackie O's big bony hand. He really is something. He's
*impeccably* Jackie O from the tip of his pale yellow pillbox to the toes
of his two-tone white-and-beige pumps.

"It's a *real* Oleg Cassini," says Freddie. "I've been saving it up."
Freddie would have spent all afternoon working on Jackie O, setting
her neat brown wig and searching through his makeup for the exact
shade of pink lipstick. He would have chosen this boy—whoever he
is—for Jackie O on account of his ultraskinny frame and great knees.
I don't understand why boys have the best legs while girls are the ones
who wear most of the miniskirts. This proves to my mind that God
must be a man. Combined with the fact that he created cellulite, of
course.

"Hello," says the Jackie O plaintively from under his wig, a bit
tired, it seems, of being talked about. "I'm Cameron."

"Oh, hi, Cameron," I say. "Love your handbag." It's white leather
with a pearl clasp.

"Cameron is the only person I know with a size thirty-two A chest," confides Freddie as he slips through the ropes.

I'm so distracted by Cameron's Jackie O outfit that I don't even notice a couple in matching red leather trousers and *faux* alligator blouson jackets sneak up the stairs. It doesn't even register until it's too late that they're both wearing imitation Givenchy sunglasses with pink lenses that you can pick up for a song from the street vendors on Broadway. It doesn't even register whether they're men or women or both. (This is typical of nobodies. They still think androgyny is in when in fact, girls have looked like girls for at least five years now.) All I notice is a gold chain on a red purse as it flashes past. I look guiltily around to see if Philip, my bouncer, has seen them. He's over in the corner, giving me the look of *death*.

And then I spot her. It's the blue lipstick. She's standing down in the crowd, staring up at me with an open mouth. It's definitely the same girl. Even though she seems to have a black wig on. The blue lipstick is the giveaway. We make eye contact, and she raises her eyebrows hopefully. I shake my head. She looks at her feet, devastated. Then she disappears into a throng of Julie Newmars with painted-on eyelashes and is gone.

# 13.

There's a boy laid out asleep beside me now, with his T-shirt halfway up his chest and the top button of his jeans undone.

I bend over him and poke him in the stomach. The black hairs that are curling around his navel are just like the astrakhan collar on my red melton forties coat, the one with the swinging pleat in the back and the big covered buttons down the front. He rolls over on his side and grunts. I tickle him under the arm by slipping my fingers up his T-shirt sleeve. He shrugs me off. I grab one of his long underarm hairs and pull hard. I know how to wake boys up.

"Huh?" he says, and sits up like a thunderbolt. His name is Quark. His father works for NASA. I let him into the club a few hours ago, even though he wasn't dressed as the Woman Whose Lipstick He'd Most Like to Borrow, and now he's let me into his bedroom.

I'm excited about Quark. He's the sort of boy for me. He appears in a deodorant advertisement on television. The one where he's cutting wheat in a cornfield and sweating like a pig. The one where he's got his shirt tied around his waist and his bare chest is gleaming like gold sequins.

Quark does magazine advertisements, too. He makes two thousand dollars a day minimum. It seems his freckled lips are the big attraction. *GQ* went *wild* about them.

His apartment building is on the East River, with a doorman, too. There's nothing inside his room to tell you anything about him—I looked—except the labels on all his shirts, which are names like Jean-Paul Gaultier and Giorgio Armani. I've never been able to resist a boy who wears Jean-Paul Gaultier. It's a sure sign that the boy won't mind stopping to look in Barney's windows on the way out to eat. I like boys like that. It's almost my number one criterion for a boyfriend. Tolerance of window-shopping.

Quark has a *GQ* on the chrome coffee table, too, which is a good sign. Even though the *GQ* is on the coffee table because he's photographed inside.

We've spent most of the night looking through his portfolio, and then he fell asleep. The portfolio is still on the floor near the bed, open at a photograph of Quark on a tractor wearing Ralph Lauren.

"You've been sleeping." I smile as he focuses his fawn eyes on me and runs his hand through his blond hair, which is trailing like a waterfall down one side of his face.

"When?" he asks dreamily.

"Almost right away," I say.

"Shit," he says. "What's the time?"

"Let's turn on the television and see." I've been dying for an excuse to turn it on. He's got a forty-five-inch screen. I've never watched one before, except perhaps at a video fashion show at one of the clubs. I've been sitting here for about three hours, I think, looking at the blank screen. I didn't want to wake Quark up. I thought it only fair.

I reach for the remote control, which is exactly where it should be, on the bedside table. This room could be a set for a commercial. It's perfect. Even the sheets are gray with fine black grids all over them. There are drawings of women's torsos framed in black on two walls. It's so masculine.

I zap around for a while until I find *The Flintstones.* "It's eight," I tell him. "Don't you just adore Pebbles and Bamm Bamm?" I sit there giggling. Cartoons always make me laugh at eight in the morning. Quark jumps to his feet and goes into the bathroom.

He is *still* in the bathroom when *The Flintstones* finish. The door is open. I can see him standing over the washbasin. He's staring in the mirror, trying to get his hair to fall a different way.

I dangle my legs over the edge of the bed and call out to him, "What are you doing?"

"The studio at nine," is all I can hear of what he calls back over running water.

He steps into the doorway of the bedroom, trying to squeeze the contents of a tube of hair gel into an open palm. The tube makes little gasping sounds. "You don't happen to have any of this stuff on you, do you?" he asks, tossing the tube in a gray plastic bin.

"Sorry," I say. "I'm over gel."

He stands there, blinking at me. His jeans now have three buttons undone. They're wrinkling and pouching in all the right places.

I'm starting to have real problems with Emma. These femmes fatales get so hot under the collar. I can feel the steam coming out of the bottom of my sleeves and around my neck. I bend over to pull my thigh-high boots back on, and Emma takes this for a sign that I'm ready to unpeel her. Before I know it, she's popped her zip and the whole of my front is exposed. She's wriggling around now, like a can of worms, struggling to slip off my shoulders. I'm valiantly trying to hold her together.

"Sorry," I say to Quark, clutching at Emma's sleeve and pulling it back over my shoulder. "I've split my jumpsuit."

"Oh," he says, shrugging his shoulders. "I've got a nine A.M. call. I've got to run."

"Oh, it's OK," I say pleasantly.

He runs his hand through his hair again, and I can see he's hesitating. Then, in an instant, he's over on the bed, pushing me firmly against the pillows.

While he's rubbing his fly against my leg, I'm thinking what a fabulous film this would make: me on the bed with my wig spread out on the pillow and my long nails clawing and my lip gloss gleaming in the moonlight. It would be just like one of those great B-grade Italian things with Monica Vitti in it. The director would naturally shoot it from way above, probably from over there above the built-in closet. I toss my head around and try to imagine myself from a different angle. I think I would be very good at steamy scenes in a B-grade movie. I've got a long throat. You always see more throat than anything.

I open my eyes and look at Quark. He's staring over my head. He's pushing me around now as if he's annoyed with me. And then in a flash he jumps off me and wriggles on the bed like a chicken after its head's been cut off or like someone holding a live wire. I get up on my elbow and look. He has unbuttoned his jeans all the way, and his hand is plunged down them. It's sweet of him to practice safe sex, but I really wasn't that worried.

When he's finished, he expels a little puff of air and lies still for a while. Then he pulls his jeans up with one hand but doesn't try to button them. He clasps his other fist around something, slides off the bed, and goes back into the bathroom. I can see him quite clearly through the door, standing at the mirror again with his jeans pushed low on his hips. He opens his palm and runs the contents through his hair, pulling and teasing it out until the hair stands up in a stiff cascade.

He catches me looking and smirks. He washes up and comes back into the bedroom and puts his sneakers back on.

"You've got to go," he says. "My cleaning lady's coming in a minute."

"OK," I murmur.

"Just close the door behind you when you're ready. I'm off."

"Thanks," I tell him.

"It was nothing," he says modestly, and picks up a sweater from a chrome and wicker chair. He rattles his keys and turns before he gets to the door. "Thank *you* for the hair gel." He smirks. "I was all out."

I curl back up on the bed and cuddle into one of my ciré boots. That was nice, I'm thinking, and go immediately back to sleep with the boot in my arms.

The housekeeper wakes me up awhile later, and I quickly gather up my things and bundle myself into the corridor to avoid her critical looks. I shuffle to a bus stop, all the while trying to keep Emma's broken zipper together with one of my hands.

I wonder what Quark thinks of me. It's hard to tell. He's the strong, silent, deodorant-commercial type. I wonder if he sees me as the sort of woman who is shot from above in B-grade Italian movies.

Or does he just see me as a *hairdo*?

# 14.

"I think Quark is so handsome," I say to Phoebe in one of the third-floor dressing rooms of Bergdorf Goodman, one with a view across Fifth Avenue. I can't see much of the view right now as I have the waist of a pink wool Chanel skirt caught on my nose and one arm twisted the wrong way through a sleeve of the jacket. This is the Chanel suit I've been saving up for. Or a variation on the theme. Phoebe and I come into Bergdorf's whenever we're bored and range all around the couture department, trying on everything in sight. The saleswomen hate us, of course, but they can't freeze us out with their icy stares. When you've got the fashion passion, you could melt Alaska.

"I'm sure he likes me. He's very considerate. And he's working with Bruce Weber today. Imagine that."

"He's OK." Phoebe is leaning against the door with her arms folded across a frothy tulle ballerina-length petticoat she has just said she'd die for. She's standing against the door so that the saleswoman who is hovering in earshot won't come barging in to see what we're up to. "If you like that sort of thing."

"What sort of thing?" I ask, trying to untangle my arm.

"*Men.*" Phoebe sniffs. She screws up her nose.

I manage to pull the skirt down over my nose with my free arm and twist the bodice of the jacket to the front.

"What's wrong with men?" I ask.

"Sex is."

"What's wrong with sex?"

"I don't know what all the fuss is about, that's all," she says, shrugging one shoulder. "It takes so long to get dressed afterwards, and you ruin your hair, and you end up with mascara right down your cheeks and *worse* between your legs."

"How would you know?" I look at her in surprise.

"I've *asked*," she says stubbornly.

I slip both my arms through the sleeves of the jacket and tug at the skirt so that it squeezes over my bosoms and slithers down to my hips. The first few hooks at the back won't do up, even though I've pulled in my stomach, and no matter how deeply I inhale I can't get the jacket to button up at the front.

Phoebe looks at me critically. "You spend too much time thinking about men anyway."

"Well, I wouldn't if I had one of my own," I say defensively. "If I had one of my own, I'd hardly give him a second thought."

"Hold your stomach in."

"I am!"

Phoebe has a serious expression on her face. She's looking me up and down.

"Face the music, dear one," she says. "You're too fat."

"I'm sure the label says size six," I say.

She tucks the tulle petticoat under her arm, comes over to me, and starts to tug at the bodice. "There's at least two inches too much of you. You need a bigger size."

"But it's the only one."

"Too bad. Maybe it will fit me."

"Forget it!" I yell, and turn sharply around to push her away. "I saw it first!"

"OK. OK." She shrugs and backs off.

"Maybe I could take it home anyway and hang it over the fridge and eat sushi for a month," I suggest brightly. "Just on the off-chance it will fit later."

"Don't be *ridiculous,*" says Phoebe. "Anyway, I'm not going to jail for a suit that doesn't even fit."

It's my experience of life that the very frock you'd die for will never do up around the waist. For this Chanel suit, I would gladly throw myself under the Broadway local, provided I came out of it with no disfiguring marks on my face. The trouble is, I can't see how it would look on me. It *is* too small. I can fantasize about it, though. No one can stop me from doing *that.*

"Well, do you want it?" asks Phoebe impatiently, stuffing the tulle petticoat into her alligator purse and trying to close the clasp.

"It's three thousand dollars." I sigh.

"That's not what I mean!" she says through narrowed eyes. Phoebe has been dying to lift something from Bergdorf's couture department, but so far we've only managed a single Tokio Kumagai boot from the shoe department, a few pieces of lingerie, and a careless Anne Klein sweater left over a chrome chair in a fifth-floor fitting room. The tulle petticoat has come from lingerie, and Phoebe has been carrying it around blatantly for an hour.

The trouble with the couture department is that all the frocks and suits are drawn together by plastic ropes that let off an awful siren if you so much as look at them. The saleswomen unlock them with a key before taking you into the fitting rooms. I think it's disgraceful to chain frocks up. It's unconstitutional. Don't they know about Abraham Lincoln? I'm thinking of writing a letter of complaint to Bergdorf's, but I might give myself away. For future heists, I mean.

I take off the jacket and skirt and sigh. "One day," I tell Phoebe, "I'll be able to come in here and order a sackful of them. I'll be invited to all the showings. I'll be invited to lunch with Karl Lager-feld."

"Don't hold your breath."

I slip the jacket back onto its satin hanger and loop the skirt underneath. The sales assistant is rattling at the door.

"Would you ladies like any *help*?" she calls out, with an edge of frustration on the last word.

Phoebe jams her crocodile purse under her arm to conceal its bulge and puts her hand on the doorknob, but not before she says to me, "Will you ever learn? You've got to leave your things on the floor for other people to pick up. Dump that suit!" I put it on the chair carefully, and Phoebe gives me a withering look.

"Well, I don't think it's fair," I explain.

"How much money do you earn?"

"Not much," I groan. "I owe Tom sixty-seven dollars, too."

"Well, that saleswoman's making a bundle," Phoebe is telling me as she opens the door abruptly. "Let her pick it up."

Phoebe walks calmly to the escalator with her purse tightly wedged under her arm. I keep a good three paces behind her in case she gets caught. I am sure she will get caught. There're *yards* of tulle sticking out the back like a ballerina's bottom.

Phoebe is standing serenely on the escalator and is gliding down to the first floor, a wry little smile on her face. To me she looks as guilty as hell, but to everyone else she probably looks like a well-heeled Park Avenue brat who has just run riot with a credit card. Phoebe is actually a well-heeled Long Island brat with a Bergdorf's credit card, but she doesn't want anyone to know. I'm sworn to secrecy on this. She thinks it's ideologically unsound to have a father who owns a factory that makes rip-offs of Reeboks. She's certainly right.

When we get to the first floor, a lot of people turn to stare. Phoebe just sails on by, in the direction of the revolving doors.

"Good for you," says Phoebe when we're out on Fifth Avenue.

"Everyone's so busy staring at your ridiculous getup that they don't even notice me."

Phoebe and I don't shoplift to *shoplift*. Only boring people do that. It's so *common*. Phoebe and I shoplift to liberate frocks. We have a *moral* responsibility to go lifting. That's why we do it. It's nothing to do with the slips and gloves and tortoiseshell combs we manage to take. We're not materialistic. We're on a *mission*. We've come all this way uptown—which might as well be Siberia—because we have made a pact that *somebody* with taste should. All those poor frocks and jewels and four-hundred-dollar shoes, why, they need women of style and sensibility to stroke them and try them on and slip them into their pocketbooks.

When you've got no money but lots of taste, you build up a sort of *reverence* for frocks, which those old dames with platinum American Express cards will never understand. They just go on into Bergdorf's like shredding machines and gobble up everything in sight. They don't know the difference between a really heavenly frock and a bit of old garbage some local manufacturer has whipped up and slapped a big price tag on. They don't know, and they don't care. They are buying the price tag, not the frock. Which means that a whole lot of awfully nice frocks go to the wrong families.

It's like adoption, really. The richest and the most powerful people get the first pick of the babies, but they might not make the best parents. All those closets full of frocks that have only been worn once or twice, why, it's *criminal*.

In the ladies' room at the Plaza Phoebe takes the petticoat out of her purse and tries it on again.

"I used to 'ave one of them when I was a little girl," says the attendant, who has her palm out for change. "Ten layers of tulle it 'ad. Ten of them."

"I'm sorry I don't have a quarter," says Phoebe as she finishes drying her hands. "Perhaps this will do." She hangs the petticoat over the startled old woman's wrist.

"Why did you do that?" I ask in the lobby.

"I don't believe in tulle anymore," is what she says. "It's *tasteless*."

# 15.

Phoebe has told me she doesn't believe in tulle. I believe people need to believe in something. I think all my friends who say there's nothing to believe in anymore except the miniskirt are wrong. There are lots of things. Dignity, for one. That's important. Girls should always be impeccably groomed, have their nails French-polished if possible. And modesty. If someone says you look fabulous, you should always say, "Oh, thank you." There's charity, too. I regularly go through the racks at the Salvation Army to see if there are any frocks that fit me. And honesty. I believe in telling people who turn up at the club in truly horrible things, "Go home, you look like *trash*." They appreciate it in the end. It gives them something to aspire to, especially in a world where there's nothing to do because everyone's done everything before you anyway.

And there's fashion. If we didn't believe in fashion, where would we be? We'd be sitting at the racetrack in powder blue nylon stretch pants without a scrap of makeup on our faces. There's no dignity in that. Without fashion, there'd be no waiting at the Magazine Rack at three in the morning for the latest edition of *Vogue* to be dropped in the gutter, there'd be no scrambling through it for the newest things in the shops, there'd be no ripping out of pages to stick to our walls and frantic raiding of our piggybanks to see if we can afford any of it. There'd be no mooning over Thierry Muglers in Barney's windows and no fun in spending a whole afternoon in the changing room trying on heavenly things we could never afford but that make us look a million and a half dollars for a minute anyway. There'd be no thrill whatsoever in discovering an old Mary Quant mini at the back of some thrift shop in a suburb where they don't know the value of these things and buying it for a song and taking it home and sliding into it slowly, the zipper going up and up, and watching the jealousy grow on our friends' faces when they see us in it for the first time. No, without fashion, we might as well all be dead. As far as I'm concerned, fashion is like *oxygen*. You can't breathe without it.

# 16.

I'm having a dream that I'm a bag lady roaming the streets of New York with all my favorite frocks bundled up in shopping bags under my arms when the phone rings and wakes me up.

"Yes!" I pounce on it and almost knock my blackamoor jewelry stand off the bedside table.

There's silence, and then a voice says in a very concerned way, "You're *home*. What's *wrong?*"

It's my mother.

"Oh, it's you," I say, disappointed.

"I was sure you wouldn't be home."

"Well, I am," I tell her defensively. Constance always has the habit of saying the wrong thing. She's probably drawing attention to my being home deliberately. "What do you want?"

"Oh, I'm calling to see how you are," she says cheerfully.

"You are not."

I can hear her sigh deeply. "I thought we could have a civilized conversation—"

"You're not coming to New York, are you?" I ask suspiciously. "You're not coming to spy on me?"

"Whatever makes you think that?"

"The *last* time you came to New York, that's what."

"I only tried to talk some sense into you."

"You and about a dozen members of the animal liberation movement. For your information, I'm still wearing fur, and I don't care what you think."

"But, Reality, if you only knew what they did to those poor little animals—"

"If you're going to lecture me, I'll hang up."

"You're my daughter," she says. "I'm just concerned about your state of mind."

"I am *not* your daughter," I point out. "I'm your *mission*."

It's true. I'm Constance's mission. I'm her crusade. Or her part-time crusade. She's so busy turning everything in sight into wall hangings, she hasn't got much time to devote to me. But every now and again she tries. When she's been to one of those meetings with her women's collective. Her *whales* is what I call them. They're all fat and blubbery, just like whales, and they sit around for hours, spouting tired old nonsense about ozone layers and affirmative actions and other things that are totally out of date.

It turns my stomach to see women like this. You've got to move with the times. It doesn't matter if you go backwards or forwards, but you just can't stand still. You can't have a 1969 attitude in 1979 or 1989. You can't have a 1969 attitude on January 1, 1970. Constance and the whales have slept through all the great events of the last twenty years: the Maxiskirt, Le Smoking, Punk, Buffalo Girls, Oversize, Japanese, the Big Shoulder, and the Crinoline. What I want to know is this: Did they sleep through all the great events of the fifties and sixties as well? Did they go to school and college and have babies without being aware that everything was changing around them? Did they suddenly wake up one day and think: Wow! I love this moment in history! and stay stuck in it forever?

Actually, I feel sorry for Constance. It's only twisted, perverse, and deeply troubled people who feel, for instance, that any woman who puts on a fur coat—even the most gorgeous ankle-length stranded sable you've ever seen—is a murderer of animals. Can you imagine? As if the woman actually traipsed up to the woods of Canada in snowshoes and strangled the little critters to death with her own hands. It's just too ridiculous to bear thinking about. You hear of other old hippies—I know Constance has got mixed up with this lot—roaming the streets in gangs of one or two, stalking and attacking innocent women who have dared to step outside in anything as harmless as a squirrel cape. The thing is, these women are jealous. It's not my fault they've come of age in a socially conscious world and found themselves marooned in a material one.

It's envy, pure and simple. Envy of my fabulous lifestyle. If Constance had her way, I'd be still back in Phoenicia working in the Rainbow Thrift Shop and coming home at night to that horrible pottery-filled house with the squeaking veranda door.

I'm a total misfit out there. Like those hand-me-downs Constance kept forcing on me until I was twelve. People in Phoenicia don't understand anything about fashion. You just have to look at them to know that, the way they clomp around in smelly old wooden sandals and sew little bells to the crinkled hems of their Indian cotton skirts. They never read magazines, or at least not magazines that count, just dreary old rags about baking bread when everyone knows that whole wheat flour went out in 1975. If they did read the right magazines, they'd know that it's absolutely insane to make patchwork quilts out of any frock made before 1966. It's inhuman, too. Let a silly old hippie loose in your closet, and the first thing you know, she's shredded all your vintage Puccis and crocheted them into dolls to scare the crows off the marijuana plants.

Constance wants me back in Phoenicia to reform me. Not because she really cares about me at all. It's an eternal source of humiliation for her to have a daughter with a sense of style. Well, it's humiliating for me to have a mother who is a hippie. Why doesn't she ever think of *that*? I've certainly never told anyone about her. Except Phoebe, who has skeletons in her own closet.

I'm sick of being told my head is filled with nonsense. Constance says that she and her friends have worked for twenty years trying to free women like me from frocks and makeup and inferior roles in society. Whoever heard of such a thing? I'm on the door of the hippest nightclub in New York. Being on the door is not an inferior position. I'm just a couple of steps down from fashion icon and moving up fast. All I need is a few press clippings. I don't want to be liberated from frocks and makeup.

It's ridiculous. Without frocks and makeup you just can't call yourself a woman. Constance must be mad. I don't know what she's talking about.

If Constance did something about her eyebrows—she's *never* plucked them—and let me take her shopping, she might look almost decent. She even looks a bit like me, except her hips are twice as wide. She's only forty-two after all. It's not really as ancient as it sounds. Lots of women are older than forty-two and don't let themselves go the way Constance has. Look at Raquel Welch. There's a lesson in Raquel Welch for Constance, but she won't learn it. You can understand why I usually hang up on her when she calls.

There's silence on the line.

"Constance? Are you still there?"

All I can hear is the clicking of a loom. She's probably hard at work, making one of her hideous sperm whale hearth rugs, the ones people snap up at $350 a pop.

"Constance?" I repeat. "I'm going to hang up."

"Don't do that, Reality," she says. "I was thinking."

"Well, there's no time for thinking. Don't you realize what time it is? It's nine in the morning! I've got to get my beauty sleep."

"Are you still working at that—discotheque?"

"It's not a *discotheque,* Mother." I groan. "It's a nightclub."

"I'm only trying to catch up on your news."

"Well, if you really want to know what's happening to me, I'll tell you. I'm having a fabulous time. Life couldn't be better. I think I might have a new boyfriend. He's a model. Even you might have seen him on television. I'm saving up for a Chanel suit. A pink silk one. I tried it on the other day. You should have seen it. It's heavenly. Except that it costs three thousand dollars and—"

"You wouldn't waste three thousand dollars on a *dress?*"

Constance sounds shocked. I knew I shouldn't have raised the subject of frocks. That's the trouble with being woken up in the middle of the morning. You forget whom you're talking to.

"Why not?" I ask.

"That's disgraceful."

I think I can see what she's getting at. "I don't think they're cruel to silkworms. Are they?"

"I'm not talking about silkworms. Aren't there other things you'd like to spend three thousand dollars on?"

"Oh, yes, there'd be lots of other things."

"Like what?"

You know, I just can't think of anything in particular. So I tell her, "Shoes and great hats and maybe a new bag. Oh, and I saw some fab earrings last week—" I stop because there's a frosty silence on the line. "Well, isn't that what you wanted me to say?"

"No, it isn't," she says crisply. "Haven't you ever thought of spending your money on those more unfortunate than yourself?"

"I paid twenty-five dollars for a ticket to Fashion Aid," I tell her. "And I had only twenty-seven dollars in the bank at the time."

"That's not what I mean."

"Well, I don't know what you do mean then. Frocks need as much support as Ethiopians."

"You're being flippant."

"That's not *true*. You've only got to see the terrible things people do to their frocks! They pinch them in with tight belts and put cigarette holes in the fabric and throw them out at the end of each season without the *slightest* bit of compassion. Or they cut them up into little pieces and use them for rags. Even for rag *place mats*." I put this in to annoy her. She loves making rag place mats. Her house is full of rag place mats and handmade flower mobiles and pottery bread crocks. "You can't even believe the way the stores look after their frocks! It's like the Belsen horror camps or something. Why, they jam them all together on racks where they can't breathe, and they don't protect them at all from people pulling at them and rubbing their sticky fingers all over them and scrunching them up on the fitting-room floors when they've finished trying them on. It's torture!"

"Reality, don't make tasteless jokes."

"Jokes! If you only *knew* how they suffer!"

"I'm trying to help you."

"Help how?" I say. "If you really wanted to help, you wouldn't be snooping around after me and writing all those pamphlets about women being oppressed by frocks. A frock never oppressed anybody. It's the other way around—"

"Why do you always get our conversations out of proportion?"

"But I'm the one who has everything *in* proportion! I'm good at proportion. Ask Freddie. Frocks need our help, and all you women have been doing is putting them down since the sixties. Everything was just *fine* before you came along. It was just dandy. Women cared about their frocks. They cared about gloves and hats and dressing up for cocktail parties. They spent *hours* working out what they were going to wear to dinner. They loved their frocks, they really did. And you come along in your Indian cottons and crocheted ponchos and tell them it's superficial to care about what you wear. You don't realize how much damage you did!"

"Calm down," says Constance. "You've got to understand my point of view. We haven't spent twenty years fighting the good fight just to raise a generation of daughters who are obsessed by Laura Ashley!"

"Mother, you don't understand *anything*," I say. "I am not obsessed by Laura Ashley! Her clothes are OUT."

I slam down the receiver and slip under the bedspread. With a bit of luck, Constance will forget about me for another year. I'm probably just a reminder note on her Greenpeace calendar. She's probably putting a line through my name right now.

# 17.

Where does my good taste come from?

Freddie says he inherited his taste from his mother, who wore Norman Hartnell right through her pregnancy. He says that from inside her belly he could read the labels on all her frocks.

Phoebe says the very first thing she saw in her whole life, after she had come out feetfirst—typically perverse—from the womb, was a divine pair of blush pink sling-back flatties one of the mid-wives was wearing. She says the shoes were the first thing she re-members ever wanting to die for. And, she points out, she was only just *born*.

But it's just too difficult to believe that a girl like me, with im-peccable taste, could be the offspring of a woman who makes ceiling mobiles. It makes me wonder if I'm really Constance's daughter. I mean, they slept around a lot in the sixties, unlike now. Constance would have slept around before she decided she didn't like men. I'm sure of it.

As for my father—that *creep*, running off and leaving me with a house full of feminists—I guess he just woke up one day, took a good look at that disgusting pair of green overalls Constance still wears when making breakfast—bran muffins, of course—and couldn't take it anymore. I think my father must have taste, but I have never found out where he lives to see if it's true. Maybe I got my fashion sense from him. I certainly didn't get it from a woman whose idea of dressing up is to put on an embroidered peasant blouse and a tiered skirt with tiny mirrors around the hem.

I once sent Constance a fab canary yellow wool Balmain coat I found on Avenue A—the *smartest* thing you've ever seen—and do you know what she did with it? She turned it into a soft sculpture.

No, I *couldn't* have inherited my taste from her.

# 18.

Someone is throwing a cocktail party for Hugo Falk's new book, *Falked Tongue*, at Houndstooth, a new restaurant way over on Eighth Street. The senior junior shoe editor at *Perfect Woman* has been sent an invitation, and Phoebe has scooped it out of the wastepaper basket on her way home. I've almost had to strangle her to take me along. In the end I promised she could borrow my mulberry suede gloves for the occasion. So here we are standing by a column in the middle of the room, trying to catch the attention of a waiter. And anyone else who comes along.

I'm wearing a candy pink Jean Shrimpton frock with a high bodice and dainty cornflower blue satin piping around the neck and cuffs. It's perfect. All the floors and walls and banquettes and tables and china and napkins at Houndstooth are covered in little black-and-white checks. All the guests are wearing black or white or both. It's like staring at a polka dot skirt and going cross-eyed. I'm the only person wearing candy pink, which gives me a distinct advantage, photographically speaking, over Phoebe, who is wearing black (and mulberry-colored gloves).

"Have you read the book?" I ask Phoebe as we stand around with a group of people in black, collarless jackets, which is the latest thing.

"Don't be ridiculous," she says, slipping her dark glasses to the end of her nose so that she can see better.

"What will we say if he asks us if we like it then?" I ask.

"What will we say *when* he asks us if we like it?" Phoebe comments, pulling one long glove off by the fingertips. "He's just spotted us and waved." Phoebe nods her head in the direction of the bar. I can see Hugo from here because he's so tall. And because he's wearing a candy pink flannel suit, almost identical in color to my frock. I can see that he's patting his jacket pocket as if he's looking for a pen. I can see that a woman with gray hair in a black lace Bettina blouse is handing him one.

"I don't think he's waving at us," I say. "I think he's waving at someone behind us."

"Anyhow," says Phoebe, not to be contradicted, "he's moving in this direction."

"Quick, let's ask somebody about the book," I suggest. At this particular moment we're both squashed against the black-and-white column as a stream of people push past us. "I don't see anyone I know. Anyone I know who *reads.*"

"Hey, watch out!"

"Sorry." I turn around to see whose foot I've just trodden on. It's Biba, the girl who does my streaks for free on Mondays.

"Oh, Reality, it's you. I didn't recognize you in that wig."

"Hi, Biba. Fab frock. Have you read Hugo's book?"

"No, I haven't. It doesn't look very big. There are copies over there."

"I've got one!" says Phoebe, who has smiled sweetly at the man next to her and turned back to us with his copy of the book.

I don't know whether he gave it to her or she just took it. She flips quickly to the end. "It's only fifty pages long."

"Well, what's it about?" I ask anxiously. "Hugo's gaining ground."

"Seems like it's about Hugo Falk to *me*," Phoebe says, peering closely at the page.

"Nice pictures, though," says Biba, looking over Phoebe's shoulder. "There's one of Hugo at PVC. Is that Faye Dunaway in the background?"

"Let me look," I say. "Oh, yes."

"And here's a neat one of him with a cocktail. Who's that sitting next to him? He's adorable."

"It's Thierry Mugler!" I say.

Biba just shrugs as if she doesn't care about Thierry Mugler. Hairdressers are so *insular*. "Well, all I can say is I wish he had asked me to do his hair. It's all over the place, and I'm desperate for a credit. Are there any magazine people here?"

"There's me," says Phoebe, who is always annoyed when she's not included in the conversation.

"Oh, Biba, this is Phoebe. Phoebe works at *Perfect Woman*. Phoebe, this is Biba. Biba does my hair."

"We've met before," Biba reminds Phoebe. "I didn't know where you worked, though. I like thought you didn't do anything. I've seen you out the salon window lots of times. Do you think you could introduce me to the beauty editor?"

"If you touch up this blond streak," says Phoebe, pulling at her hair, "I could put your portfolio on her desk."

"Thanks," says Biba. "It's a deal. When do you want to come in?"

"How about Thursday afternoon?"

"Sure thing."

They shake on it.

We all help each other out downtown. It's quid pro quo. I let Biba into the club for free. She does my hair. She does Phoebe's hair. Phoebe puts Biba's portfolio on the beauty editor's desk. The beauty editor gives Biba a job. Biba does the beauty editor's hair. Biba does

Macy's hair. Macy does Biba's nails. Macy does my nails. I let Macy into the club for free. It's a whole ecosystem down here.

I have enough time to read all of Hugo's book before he reaches us. I'm a speed reader on account of all the times I've had to read whole fashion magazines over people's shoulders in the subway.

"So nice of you to come," Hugo says. He shakes all our hands formally, in the same way he has just shaken all the hands of the people standing in a half circle in front of us. Before he's even got a response from us, he's looking over my head to the door.

"Hell-o, Cary. So glad you could come. What do you think of my book?" He asks this question of someone behind me. I can't hear the answer. "It is, isn't it?" is what he responds.

Hugo tries to push past me, but I'm jammed between the pillar and Phoebe and Biba. He looks down. "Oh, it's you again," he says with a hint of bad temper. "You haven't seen Darwin, have you?"

He's referring to Darwin Black, the book critic. Darwin specializes in neovulgarity, which is the current mode. Hugo is supposed to be a neovulgarist, although I don't know what that means in books. In frocks it means skirts made out of brushed Day-Glo acrylic and anything vinyl. "I haven't seen Darwin," I tell Hugo. "Maybe he's not coming."

"That's impossible," says Hugo. He takes off his glasses and tries to polish them with a lime green handkerchief. "Without his spectacles he looks like—who? Oh, yes, I know, Prince Planet.

"Of course, Darwin will be here," Hugo says coolly, and stuffs his handkerchief back in his pocket. "I specifically didn't invite him."

"Well, if you didn't invite him, it's OK then." I shrug. "He won't come."

Hugo looks at me the way I look at girls who wear tan-colored panty hose: total disgust. "But he's *supposed* to come. He's supposed to gate-crash, so I can have him thrown out."

"That's not very nice," I say, meaning it as a joke.

"It's my party, and I'll do what I want to," is what Hugo snarls back at me.

I am about to ask Hugo if he wants to ask me what I think of his book, but he has already turned away and is asking a white-haired boy in white cycling shorts and a white tank top with LOVE HURTS on the front if he likes it. "It's OK," the boy says tonelessly. I'm annoyed. I could have done better than that.

I wander off from Phoebe to try to find a drink. By some miracle, a waiter hands me a pink daiquiri. It's the wrong kind of pink to go with my frock, but I'm thirsty. I'm about to go over and say hello to Macy to ask her to do my nails on Wednesday afternoon if she's not too busy when an intense hot light suddenly floods my corner.

It's then I notice that Hugo is standing near me, roped off from everyone else behind a red velvet cord. I notice this because the blinding light is over his head. There's a person with a video camera and an assistant with a white reflector board standing outside the rope, filming Hugo reading his own book. He's holding the book close to his face so the cameraman can film the cover. It's got lime green words on a hot pink and purple plaid background. Exactly the colors of the outfit Hugo is wearing tonight. Pink suit, purple shirt, lime green pocket handkerchief and socks.

"Talk to someone, Hugo," suggests the cameraman. "Anyone will do."

I know a cue when I hear one. "Hello, Hugo," I chip in, as if I haven't seen him for weeks.

"Oh, hello, er . . ." Hugo's voice trails off.

The cameraman turns around to kick a cable away and spots me. "This one will do," he says, pointing to me. "She's color-balanced."

"Sure," I say eagerly. I'm pushed behind the rope, and Hugo and I stand there, looking at each other with forced grins on our faces.

"Now talk, both of you," orders the cameraman. "Make it natural."

"They must be kidding," I say. "Have I smudged my mascara?"

There's a silence. "I hate smiling." Hugo grimaces, all the time looking at the camera. There's another silence. "Do you like my jacket?" he asks eventually.

"It goes with your book."

"Yes, doesn't it?" There's a silence.

"Don't stop!" orders the cameraman.

"Hmm," says Hugo thoughtfully, looking directly at the camera all the time and away from me.

"I saw an interesting film last night," I say, just to say something. "*The Day the Fish Came Out*. It's very groovy."

"*The Day the Fish Came Out?*" Hugo says to the camera. "A friend of mine was in that."

"Who?" I ask. "Who was your friend?"

"Candice," he says, drawing out the "ice" to "eeeees."

"Oh, she was great! I loved her outfits! Didn't you think the whole thing was fab?"

"Oh, yes?" he says vaguely. "It was all right."

There's another silence.

"Have we talked enough?" Hugo asks the cameraman impatiently.

"Got it," the cameraman answers, and the lights go cold.

"Well." I giggle. "I guess that's it. It was a pleasure to be photographed with you." I say this in my sweetest voice.

Hugo looks down at me. "You're cleverer than you look, aren't you?" is what he says.

"Thank you," I say. I start to unclip the velvet rope to let him through, out of habit. "See you at the club."

"What club?" he asks distractedly. He's looking around the room again. "I wish Faye had been here by now," he adds. "I would have liked to have been photographed with *her*."

"I'm worried," I admit to Phoebe when I finally find her in the bathroom, cleaning the soles of her shoes. "Hugo Falk doesn't seem to know me. I've let him into the club at least a dozen times. I always admire his outfits. I tell him all the latest gossip. Of course, Hugo Falk knows me. Doesn't he?"

Phoebe says nothing for a minute, then lowers her wraparound ski glasses to the point of her nose and gives me a long appraisal from the toes of my Mary Janes to the top of my club-cut brunette wig. "I think," she says slowly, "that it's *this* you he doesn't know."

# 19.

The *Perfect Woman* offices are just down on Lafayette, in a big old iron building that's green and sooty with age. Inside, though, the lobby and rooms are all unblemished beige, the sort of beige that looks good with the black that everyone wears. Even the doorman wears beige, with a strip of black grosgrain around his cap. He looks embarrassed about the grosgrain bows on his epaulets.

Phoebe's office is on the third floor, tucked away in a corner behind a beige partition. I've been here before, after hours. Phoebe often has to stay back and put masking tape on all the soles of the shoes so they won't get scratched during photography. Actually, what she really does is wear them around on the carpet. It's a sensual experience for her. The only sensual experience she has.

There's a receptionist who looks at me as if I'm a piece of lint on her black silk blouse. Above her head on the wall is a poster of the cover of the next issue. LOOK WONDERFUL WHOEVER YOU ARE, it reads. The receptionist calls Phoebe on the intercom and gets my name wrong.

"Memory Tattle is here to see you," she announces. She points me in the direction of Phoebe's desk.

"Thank you. I *know*," I tell her, just to let her know I know. She curls her lip. It's beige, to go with the carpet.

I pass a group of girls sitting around a desk giggling over a magazine. They stop when I go past. They must be admiring my jumpsuit. It's red vinyl. There's a burst of sniggering as I reach Phoebe's partition. She's bent over a hand mirror, tweezing her eyebrows.

"You shouldn't do that," I tell her. "Thin eyebrows are OUT."

"Ssssh!" she warns me. "They think I'm writing captions."

She looks up, one eyebrow raised. "Anyway, for your information, I'm not making my eyebrows thin. I'm making them *arched*. Arched eyebrows are coming back. Most women don't realize that eyebrows are the *focal point* of a woman's face."

"I know that."

"Anyway, what are you wearing? You look like a messenger."

"*Thanks.* You're supposed to be my best friend."

"Well, you could have at least blended in. You know they're paranoid about spies from *Vogue.*"

"A spy from *Vogue* wouldn't be wearing a red vinyl jumpsuit, would she?"

"You never know. They're cunning. Red vinyl is the *last* thing you'd imagine anyone with any fashion sense to wear."

Everyone on the magazine wears black, without exception because, Phoebe tells me, wearing only black means that nobody can tell that you're wearing the same outfit ten days in a row, which is what some editors at *Perfect Woman* usually do. Besides, Phoebe adds, it's the only color in the universe absolutely *guaranteed* to be chic in any circumstance.

When pressed about this, Phoebe admits that no one at *Perfect Woman* has the nerve to wear anything else now. They're so used to black they have no idea how to handle pink or pumpkin or Prussian blue. They don't know where to wear cream. They're paranoid about purple. They're absolutely *terrified* of yellow. When I point out to Phoebe that this hasn't stopped them from going all lyrical about lime in the latest issue, she just looks at me as if I'm stupid.

"Look at *this*." She pulls out a long brown brow hair and holds it in the air like a laboratory specimen. "At least two-thirds of an inch!"

Phoebe's desk is immaculate. It's immaculate because all she is paid to do is to keep her desk immaculate. Oh, and go shopping all day for shoes for the shoe editor to use in photography.

I look at the way her pencils are laid out in a neat line, their points perfectly sharpened. Her black leather notebooks are in a stack by her elbow, the bindings all facing the wall. There's a shelf of perfume bottles near her head, arranged in graduations of size. I head straight for a bottle of Coco and pull out the stopper.

"Don't *do* that!" she snaps at me.

"I just wanted a little splash," I explain. "You've got enough to last you all year."

"That's not what I mean." She sighs. "It's not perfume."

"Oh, I don't mind eau de toilette."

"It's not eau de toilette."

"Well, then, what is it?" I'm getting cross.

"It's dog's urine."

"What?" I hold the bottle up to my nose and then put it down quickly. "Ugh!"

"We've got a thief," Phoebe explains wearily, "someone who's been stealing all the perfume samples. So we've filled half the bottles with dog's pee. Cristobal was darling about it. I just kept giving him champagne, and he, you know, *obliged*." I thought Phoebe had been a bit more charming to Freddie than usual.

"Anyway," she continues, "you can't use it. The thief is supposed to come along and spray herself all over with Coco or Bal à Versailles and come out smelling like Second Street. That's how we're supposed to catch her. It was all my idea. Aren't I brilliant?"

"Which bottle is safe?" I ask. "I'm desperate for a fix."

"You can try the Youth-Dew. No one ever goes near it."

I actually *like* Youth-Dew. It reminds me of women in sweater sets with their hair hair-sprayed into helmets, the ones who always carry a lace handkerchief. Soaked in Youth-Dew.

"Can't you spritz somewhere else?" Phoebe says, crinkling up her nose as I mist the perfume across my cleavage.

I sit on the edge of Phoebe's desk, making her move her chair away. There's a clear Lucite IN tray on the desk next to me and a clear Lucite OUT tray, too. The OUT tray is almost full. The only thing in the IN tray is a single beige straw shoe with ribbon laces.

"What's this?" I ask, picking it up.

"*The* shoe," she says, still struggling with the tweezers. "The *only* shoe for next season."

"The only shoe?"

"The only shoe you're allowed to wear. Isn't it elegant?"

"But I thought you said *the* shoe for spring was going to be a crocodile-skin sandal with stacked heels. I read it in the last issue. I'm sure I did. Your spring preview-preview issue."

"Oh, that. We changed our minds. Look in the OUT tray."

On closer inspection the OUT tray is full of Polaroids and torn pages from other fashion magazines. Phoebe has scrawled OUT in black felt-tipped pen over every picture, including the one of the crocodile-skin sandal with the stacked heel. I pick up a Polaroid of a Romeo Gigli skirt.

"Why is this marked OUT?" I ask. "It's only just arrived in the stores. I saw it at Barney's last week."

"Precisely," says Phoebe, blotting a bleeding hair follicle with a tissue.

"Oh," I say, putting the Polaroid back down. "Are you doing the IN and OUT lists now?"

"I *told* you. Don't you listen? I'm *typing* them up for the fashion department. It's a *chore*. Say," she says, placing the tweezers on the desk, "would you be a darling and type it for me now?"

"I can't type," I say. "You know that. Can I have a look at the closet? I want to see what Montana's doing for spring."

Phoebe looks at me with disgust. "Trust you to go for Montana. You always did like the *show-offs*."

"Just point me at them," I say impatiently.

"Not yet." She makes a pained face. "Bathroom Sophie's locked up in there."

"Oh?" Phoebe's told me about Bathroom Sophie. She's an editor, and she's always locking herself in the bathroom with the galleys or whatever they're called on deadline day, and she never comes out of there until the editor in chief tells her, through the keyhole, how wonderful she is. "Why isn't she in the bathroom?" is what I ask.

"Louise has bolted herself in there, crying her eyes out. Her boyfriend told her she was too old to wear Vivienne Westwood."

"Look, Phoebe, I never get to see the closet. Can't you let me have one peek? A tiny one?"

"No."

"Can I see the next issue, then?" I ask, noticing an advance copy on Phoebe's desk.

"No, you cannot," she says, putting her hand protectively over the cover. "You might be a spy. You can do that typing for me instead."

"But my manicure," I protest.

"I'll turn a blind eye if you want to add anything to the IN list. I do it all the time. No one ever notices."

"You mean it?"

"Here's the paper." She hands me a single sheet of beige. "Do what you like. I don't care."

I move across to the manual typewriter on a bench behind Phoebe. This is too good an opportunity to miss. I could influence *millions*. My nails are so long they get caught underneath the keys, so I use Phoebe's telephone dialer to type one letter at a time. Soon I have an IN list that's thirty items long. I show it to Phoebe.

She looks at it critically. "We said TANGERINE was OUT last month and now you're saying it's IN. Oh, well, it doesn't matter. I don't think they're going to go for HOT PANTS, though. You better white it out."

"Beige it out, you mean," I say, but Phoebe ignores my comment and goes back to her mirror.

"And don't forget to put in ARCHED EYEBROWS," she says over her shoulder.

# 20.

It's Friday night, and there's a line of suits a mile long outside Less Is More. I've always hated Friday nights. The suits go out drinking and lose all sense of reality. They think I'm actually going to let them in.

The one thing I absolutely, definitely, nonnegotiably won't allow in the club is a suit. I'm famous for it.

I don't mean the Yohjis and the Commes des Garçons and the rubberized Gaultiers with their slim little hips and Gary Cooper shoulders. I don't mean the Paul Smith tweeds and the cute check Kenzos and the occasional Perry Ellis if the jacket is done up.

I mean regular suit suits. Single-breasted pinstripes with narrow shoulders. Fitted jackets with two vents at the back. Little slitty pockets on one chest, with a triangle of handkerchief sticking out. Wide lapels. Four buttons on the sleeve. Half an inch of cuff and anchor-shaped gold cuff links. Slim-line trousers with flapping hems held up by Gucci buckles or red suspenders. The smell of stale cigarettes trapped in the weave. Poly/rayon/Scotchgard obscenities. I've never been to Wall Street, and I'm never going to go. All those suit suits packed like sardines: they could give a girl a recurring nightmare for a lifetime.

I'm proud of the fact you won't find a single suit inside Less Is More. It makes the club more fabulous to the ones who know what fabulous is. I've been threatened with bodily harm, and I've still stood my ground. Suits are absolutely forbidden. Especially suits wearing Burberrys, male or female. That's double trouble.

When I arrive tonight, there's this suit standing at the bottom of the stairs, giving us a hard time. Phillip, the chief bouncer, is just ignoring him. As I step up to my pedestal, the suit turns on me. He calls me doorwhore. That might be OK for the other door girls around here, but it make me see red.

The suit thinks he's funny. He's looking around at all the other suits as if he expects them to applaud him. The fashion crowd that is down there with him gives him dirty looks. They're all fanning themselves with takeout menus from the Chinese deli next door. One of them has a little personal fan strapped to her wrist. It's hot. And I'm wearing Goldie, my heliotrope plastic miniculotte suit. And this suit is getting more obnoxious by the second.

He is a suit who thinks because he is an Immigration Attorney worth two hundred dollars an hour—this is what he is telling me— and because he's got a timid little secretary on his arm in a brown crepe suit with a silk cravat at her neck, and because he's come all the way down here, to the end of the world no less, in a stretch limousine with a fully stocked bar in the back that I am going to fall on my back and feel privileged if he tramples all over me.

I tell him to go home and come back as Samantha Eggar in *The Collector* and I might consider him.

He looks at me as if I've just escaped from a straitjacket. "Who the hell's in charge?" is what he calls up to me.

"I am," I say automatically. I say this ten times a night. "I am in charge."

"That's not what I mean," he yells. "Who's in charge of you?"

"Don't give me Attitude," I say. Actually, Eunice, who is executive vice-president of the Girls for God, is in charge of me, but I happen to know that at this very moment she's in the back room, attending to the leaking urn. I nod at Phillip, who steps forward to stand next to me, his arms crossed like a cigar store Indian. Except that Phillip's got tattoos all the way from his cuticles to the base of his six-inch-high Mohawk.

"Look," says the suit, who thinks he can appeal to Phillip man to man, "I've come all the way down here—"

"So?" interrupts Phillip.

"So I wanna *drink*!" the suit almost wails.

"There's a gay bar down the street," says Phillip. "You might get a milk shake there."

"Look, you little smart ass," says the suit, "you're both going to be looking for new jobs tomorrow."

"Oh, yeah?" says Phillip, and he's moving down the steps like a robot on a rampage.

"Yeah!" says the suit, and pushes his chest forward. I have seen these suits before: The chest always goes forward, but the feet take a step back.

"Don't, Kevin," says the secretary, who has taken one look at the bicycle chain twisted around Phillip's right wrist and is squeezing her date's arm like crazy.

"I wanna see the *manager*," insists the suit, who is shrinking into his three-piece navy-blue pinstripe so that the collar is up around his ears.

"I've told you," I say, and start flashing my flashlight around the crowd again, "I am the manager."

The suit gives me a really filthy look as if he's thinking a girl like me couldn't manage her way out of a frock at bedtime.

"So *disappear*," says Phillip.

The suit looks at his secretary, who is scrutinizing her nails closely. The tips of her ears are fire engine red.

"Why don't you get a haircut?" he says snidely to Phillip as he backs away.

"Why don't you get a *life?*" Phillip smiles between broken teeth. Phillip is from Manchester, which is why he has bad teeth, at least according to Freddie, who is from Birmingham and has good ones.

The suit turns on his heels and then turns back and gives me a sly look. "And as for you . . ." He spits, digging into his pocket and rattling some change. He pulls out a quarter, holds it up for the crowd to see, and tosses it right up the stairs, where it lands at my feet. "Buy yourself something *decent* to wear." He disappears into the crowd.


At the same time as the suit is leaving us, a woman in an expensive but boring pair of blue trousers with a navy blue cardigan strides up the stairs as if she's expecting me to unclip the velvet ropes for her there and then. These people really have *nerve.*

"Oh, go away," I bark at her.

There's a distinguished-looking white-haired man with her. He's about to say something, but the woman has turned on her heels and fled like a deer. The man gives me a cross look and follows her. Good riddance, I think.

I flash my light at a very striking Greek girl in a dark wig. She's wearing a great pair of square glasses with black frames. The look is *very* Nana Mouskouri. I let her in.

# 21.

How was I to know that the woman in the navy blue cardigan was Jackie O? The *real* Jackie O? The one I said, "Oh, go away!" to? The one I almost threw down the stairs? But it looks like it was.

Freddie has come into my bedroom this morning with a copy of the *Daily News,* folded to a small picture on Page Six. A picture of Jackie O and a distinguished-looking man getting into a limo on Third Street. "Jackie's night on the town," the caption reads.

It's unfair to expect me to have recognized her. She wasn't wearing a pillbox. That cardigan wasn't an Oleg Cassini. I take a closer look at it in the *Daily News* photograph. It even looks like it might have been bought off the rack. Jackie O buying things off the rack! I think she was trying to trick me.

Anyone would have made the same mistake. If Jackie O wanders around town in a navy blue pantsuit, not looking like Jackie O, what hope have we all got? I mean, Freddie's friend Cameron makes a better Jackie O than Jackie O does. Jackie O has got a responsibility to all of us to look like herself. She's a *goddess* after all. For a goddess to look like a real person, well, I think it's *dishonest.*

I'm very disillusioned.

# 22.

It's the next night and I'm getting ready to go to Less Is More when Freddie comes flying through the door that joins our apartments. With Phoebe, who is cross.

"Don't look at me like that," says Phoebe defensively. "Freddie dragged me out of *Funny Face before* the ballerina-length wedding dress with the short veil. I'm livid." She goes to my bed and flops down on it, with a pillow under her stomach, and jams an Yves Saint Laurent Ritz cigarette into her ebony cigarette holder. "Where's the lighter?"

Freddie, being a gentleman, takes a folder of matches out of his quilted purse and tosses it at her.

"What's wrong *this* time?" I ask, noticing Freddie's red face. "My shoe box is empty."

"No, no," says Freddie breathlessly. "That's not it at *all.*"

"Well, what is it? I've got to get to the club."

Phoebe and Freddie exchange glances.

"Aren't you going to tell her?" says Phoebe to Freddie impatiently.

"Tell her what?" I ask.

"Would you like a cup of tea?" Freddie asks me.

"She better sit down," says Phoebe, taking a deep drag on her cigarette. Little ashes flutter around her face like fireflies.

"I don't want a cup of tea, and I don't want to sit down! Will someone tell me what is going on!" I sit down anyway, in a purple beanbag that has always been too low to the ground. From this angle I see that there's a giant hole in the inner thigh of one of my lime green fishnet stockings.

"*Marvelous* garter belt," says Freddie, looking in the same direction.

"Just tell me, Freddie," I demanded. I'm getting hysterical.

Mostly about the hole in my stockings but also because of the black looks on the faces of my two best friends.

Freddie bites his lip.

"Oh, *really*," says Phoebe, crossing her legs in the air and leaning down harder on her elbows. She looks at me levelly through eyelashes coated in ash. "You've got the sack."

At first this doesn't mean anything. "What sack?" I ask. "And who does it belong to?" Freddie's straw tote bag, the one with the drawstring top, flashes into my mind. "I gave it back to you *months* ago," I say to him.

"She doesn't mean that, I'm afraid," says Freddie, wincing. "You've been superseded."

I look at him blankly.

"*Replaced*," translates Phoebe.

"Recycled," says Freddie, looking down at his bronze Pancaldi pumps.

"*Fired*," Phoebe concludes, almost triumphantly. She crisscrosses her ankles.

"Very funny," I say.

"It's true." Freddie looks up at me again with sad eyes. "Eunice is furious about Jackie O. She found someone else."

"But there isn't anyone else! I'm the only one!"

"Not anymore," says Phoebe.

Freddie scowls at her.

"What do you mean, she's furious about Jackie O? It wasn't my fault Jackie O turned up in that—that—*cardigan.*"

"As far as Eunice is concerned, Jackie O can turn up in whatever she likes. And get in." Phoebe yawns.

"But she has no right coming to a club not looking like herself. It's Jackie's O fault, not mine."

"Blasphemy!' says Freddie.

"How could Eunice fire me when I haven't even gone to the club yet? I've been here repairing Tallulah's hem. How could she fire me when I've just been sitting here all alone repairing a hem? There's no justice in that."

"We don't care what you've been doing or where you were," says Phoebe haughtily. "We only care where you were not."

"The club," says Freddie. "That's where you were not."

"But why didn't Eunice *call* me?"

"I don't know. I only got there thirty minutes ago myself."

"To find a *riot* going on," adds Phoebe smugly.

"It was ghastly," says Freddie. "You wouldn't have wanted to be there."

"She wasn't," Phoebe points out.

"There were people pushing and shoving. There were more pink sweat shirts than you could poke a stick at."

"Oh, God!" I have to giggle. The club without me is a natural disaster.

"And thousands of pairs of Converse high tops with the laces undone."

"No!"

"And *leg warmers!*"

"You're joking!"

"Freddie says it was too tacky for words," pipes in Phoebe, who is now grinding her cigarette out on the windowsill.

"You couldn't breathe for the smell of Obsession!"

"You're *horrible*," I tell Freddie, and try to get up out of the bean-bag. "I'll get dressed, and we'll go sort this mess out."

Freddie and Phoebe just stare at me.

"You don't understand," says Freddie, looking a bit agitated.

"What don't I understand?"

"Everyone was having a *fabulous* time."

"As a matter of fact," says Phoebe, removing Cristobal from the bed with two fingers as if he were a moldy old orange you find under a pile of frocks, "Freddie says there were more people there than ever."

"There were dozens of somebodies."

"Who?" I ask Freddie. "Which somebodies?"

"Oh, just the ones you don't let in."

"That's OK then." I sigh with relief.

"Eunice was *very* pleased," says Phoebe. "They are making *loads* of money."

"Everyone has to pay."

"They're *charging* the somebodies as well?"

"Oh, yes. It's revolutionary. But you don't have to worry," adds Freddie quickly. "It's not the sort of place you'd want to be seen in anyway."

"But, Freddie," I say, "until last night it was the only place I wanted to be seen in."

"I'd forget it," he advises. "It's not your fault people don't have taste. It's not your fault the club is packed and making more money than it ever has and attracting more celebrities than ever."

"Thanks," I say.

"Ricci just had first-night luck."

"Ricci? *Ricky!*" I almost roll off the beanbag.

"Ricky's at Less Is More? I don't believe it! She turned Tina Chow away from Ready to Wear! She turned Tina Chow away before I turned Jackie O away!"

"Jackie O is worse," says Freddie.

"Besides"—Phoebe exhales—"people have short memories."

"But Ricky's got no taste!"

"Precisely," says Freddie.

"That snake in sheep's clothing!" I say. "I should have guessed she'd be up to something."

"She wouldn't be up to *anything* if you did your job properly."

I glare at Phoebe. "Eunice will have me back."

"I don't know about that," she tells me. "Eunice approves of Ricci. She's a *Catholic*."

"Well, I'm a lapsed one."

"Ricci's got a strand of the pope's hair pinned to her denim jacket."

"I've got a three-D portrait of Saint Francis of Assisi on the back of mine."

"Saint Francis of Assisi doesn't rate against the pope."

"I *loved Brother Sun, Sister Moon*," comments Freddie.

"Face it. You were IN yesterday, but now you're OUT." Phoebe gets up off the bed and brushes some lint off her black frock.

"Think of yourself as an item on that list you typed."

"Very funny," I say miserably.

"Anyway, we have to go," she adds.

"*Where?*" I ask. "Where are *you* going?"

"To the club, silly," says Phoebe, spitting on one finger and running it over her (arched) eyebrows.

"Which club?" I ask, in a daze.

"*Less Is More*," says Freddie, looking apologetic. "We promised Ricci."

"But I thought you hated Ricci!"

"Not now that she's on the door," says Phoebe blithely, stuffing one of my Hermès scarves into her purse as she goes. "Bye!" she says, and pauses for a minute with her finger on her chin. "You should do something about your hair."

"Freddie?" I cry.

"Sorry," he says, and shrugs his shoulders. "Really I am." He whistles at Cristobal, who leaps into his arms and then slips into the inside lining of Freddie's eighteenth-century frock coat, the one he salvaged from the Met's costume sale.

"Well, I'm coming, too."

"Don't be silly," says Phoebe, flouncing out the door. "I don't think they'll let you in."

# 23.

It all happens so fast. I'm sitting in my boudoir repairing Tallulah and fuming. The next thing I know I'm marching up the steps to Less Is More. Between the apartment and the club not a thought goes through my mind.

Ricci is standing up on my step—*my* step—in apricot-colored stirrup pants and a raspberry-colored T-shirt with a black satin bra over the top. The nerve of her, wearing stirrup pants when she knows I hate them.

What makes me madder is the way Ricci's fudge-colored hair is falling into her eyes as if she hasn't combed it at all. It doesn't look messy enough to be worked on. She could have at least *tried* to meet my standards, even if she and the whole world know she hasn't got a chance.

What's worse, she appears to be letting in any old person through those ropes, in groups of four and two, as if it were Noah's Ark or something. A pair of Burberrys go in. This is too much to bear. As I push my way through the crowd, I notice that one or two fabulously dressed people are the ones who are waiting in line. There's a pair of ice blue palazzo pajamas I would have let in in a flash.

I stomp right up beside Ricci and grab the hem of her T-shirt.

"Get out of *my* club," is what I say.

"Take your hands off me!" she says, trying to twist away.

"I'll do what I want. It's my door you're standing in."

"Phillip!" she squeals. The coward.

"It's me, Phillip," I tell him when he moves in. "It's Reality." I'm holding the T-shirt in a tight bunch. Unfortunately Ricci is taller than I am—I'm mortified to realize that I'm wearing my fluffy slippers, which I forgot to change—and *much* heavier, so I can't hoist her off the Astroturf.

"Well, now, it is you Reality," Phillip says amiably. "What are you doing, love?"

"I'm getting rid of this—*person*."

"No, you're not!" says Ricci. "Get off me!"

"This is my door," I insist. "And I want it back."

"You goofed. You *can't* have it back. Now give me back my shirt!" Ricci snarls.

"You don't deserve it," I say, loudly, so that the crowd can hear me. "You're letting in *sweat pants*. I've seen you!"

"So what? A lot of very nice people wear sweat pants."

"You're so *stupid*!" I let go of the T-shirt and give her a little push. "It doesn't matter whether they're nice or not. It's the principle of the thing. You're *ruining* this club. The next thing we know, you'll be letting in Earth shoes."

She smiles at me smugly and tilts her chin. "I have already. *Two* pairs!"

The thought of Earth shoes in my club makes me wild. I give her a really hard push. She stumbles and twists her ankle. One of the heels of her black sling-back shoes gets caught in the edge of the Astroturf and snaps off.

"Look what you've done!" she screams, and dangles the shoe in front of me.

"I did you a favor," I tell her calmly. "Those shoes didn't go with your pants."

She glares at me.

"Come to think of it," I continue, "nothing in the universe would go with those pants."

"Phillip!" she screeches. Her face is going banana-colored. Which, against the raspberry of her shirt and the apricot of her pants, makes her look like a fruit salad. A week-old fruit salad.

I can feel Phillip behind me, moving in. Ricci is still waving the heelless shoe in my face. As I reach to snatch it and fling it away, he twists both my arms into a knot at the back.

"Throw her out!" Ricci commands.

Just then Eunice comes out from behind the cashier's window, rubbing her hands on her pinafore.

"Now, now," she scolds. "What's going on?"

"She let in Earth shoes!" I tilt my chin accusingly, at Ricci, who is now hopping around on one foot, trying to squeeze her crooked toes back into her shoe. I shrug my arms to make Phillip let go of them.

Eunice looks at me crossly. "We have a rule you know, Reality, dear, that our guests have to wear shoes. We can't have any bare feet in here. The Blessed Virgin wouldn't approve." I tell her she'd better change her ruling soon. Sandie Shaw is going to be the next thing, after Maria Callas and Anita Ekberg, of course.

"This girl is talking *nonsense,*" says Eunice to anyone who will listen, putting a hand to her gray head and tucking a stray hair into her bun. "Will someone tell me what she means?"

There is silence. Everyone—the whole crowd—is looking at me.

"Eunice, I've got to talk to you," I plead. "This club is going to be *dead* in two weeks. You can't allow her to keep on letting in Earth shoes and Reeboks. They're tasteless."

Everyone then looks at Eunice's feet, which beneath her print frock and dark tan support panty hose are clad in yellowing Reeboks with pink terry-cloth trim. "I don't know about that," she says, sounding hurt.

"Sorry," I say.

"Besides, dear," she goes on, "we've made more money for the collection plate tonight than we made all last month. The Girls are very happy. Ricci's doing a lovely job. Such a sweet girl."

"There!" says Ricci. "You go home. Before I sue you."

A suit on the third step bounds over to Ricci at this point and hands her a business card. "Call me if you need me," he says.

"I'm not going home until I get through to Eunice!" I turn back to Eunice, who is smoothing her apron and readjusting the crochet hook and skein of wool in her pocket. "You've got to listen to me, Eunice. Look at all these people." I point to the crowd that is milling below. The ones out of earshot are pushing and shoving impatiently. "There's hardly a fabulous person there. And if the fabulous people don't come and mill outside, the somebodies will never come!"

"Oh, I don't think a few running shoes will make any difference, do you?" Eunice asks, with a worried look on her face.

"But they will!" I protest. "Not to mention all that spandex. It's an epidemic—"

I'm just warming up to make a speech when Phillip interrupts. "Trot along, love." He puts a firm hand on my shoulder.

"But I've got something to say! Where's Freddie? Where's Phoebe? They'll tell you!" I look around me.

"They're inside." Ricci, who is standing with one foot on a higher step than the other, to balance out the heel-height discrepancy, smirks. "*They* don't seem to mind all the spandex."

"Go strangle yourself on your stirrup pants!" is what I cleverly say to her as I make a very dramatic exit, the crowd on the stairs parting in recognition of my superior sense of style.

* * *

All anyone cares about these days is money. Even the Girls for God. It's heartbreaking. No one cares about the important things in life anymore. They don't care how anyone looks. When people like Ricci rise to the position of doorwhore at a club like Less Is More, you know the world is getting to be a very ugly place.

# 24.

"Cristobal Balenciaga!" Freddie sighs, as we're standing in front of a spotlit coat in the exhibition room at the Fashion Institute. "Have you ever seen anything so *divine*?" he asks, pressing his hands together under his chin as if he were going to get down on his knees and pray.

I must admit I haven't.

We've made up. Freddie has apologized to me for going to Less Is More. He explained that it was so rivetingly awful he couldn't resist. I've told him I've forgiven him. He's told me he's forgiven me for throwing Jackie O down the stairs, even though I have to keep on pointing out I didn't *throw* her. He has taken it upon himself to write Jackie O a note of apology and is expecting a handwritten acknowledgment any day now. This has given his week an unexpected point of reference, he says. I think he realizes he has me to thank for this great opportunity to start up a correspondence with one of his heroines.

Consequently his plan is to keep me busy, because if I weren't so busy, I'd have nothing to do. I read one of the catalog cards out loud to Freddie: "Evening coat. Tulle covered with bright green ostrich feathers by Judith Barbier. Winter 1964. Worn by the Comtesse de Martini."

"Oh, *God,*" groans Freddie, in ecstasy.

"And look at this!" I say, pointing to the display next to it. "Evening coat. White organza with applied flowers made of pink and white parachute silk. Summer 1964. Lent by M. Hubert de Givenchy, Paris."

"Oh, God," moans Freddie again. "It's *beyond!*"

"How do you think I'd look in this?" I ask, contemplating a mannequin swathed in "Bubble dress, violet nylon tulle and organdy appliqué. Winter 1961." "Do you like the color?"

"I *love* the color," he says. "I'm *devoted* to violet," and turns to another mannequin, one that is wearing "Evening gown, black silk crepe with 'chou' cape. Winter 1967." "But this is the *dernier cri.*"

There are about two dozen mannequins on platforms under lights in the room. There are wedding gowns in silk faille and ivory satin shantung zibeline. There are cocktail dresses in white guipure lace with black satin bows and full-length frocks in violet "faveur" lace on silk-covered horsehair ground. There is a jacket in variegated brown coupe de velours in broken stripes on a black silk ground and an ivory satin duchesse evening gown with rhinestone shoulder straps. There's a long trailing frock in black silk velvet with a divine foliate cutwork pattern and a baby doll in heavy black silk with embroidered dots.

"I think heaven looks like this," whispers Freddie.

We stroll among the frocks. There are about five other people in the room, some of them taking notes, the others floating around as if they were mesmerized. It is so quiet you could hear a hem coming down. Until two girls in tacky bleach-splotched jeans come in and start giggling at one of the exhibits, an unbelievably adorable pink shot silk taffeta evening frock with a big bustle at the back.

"Sssssssh!!!!" snaps Freddie. "You wouldn't giggle in church, would you?" The girls make faces at him and move on. I wander into the room next door, and Freddie catches up with me a few minutes later. We are both staring at a purple mohair coat.

"Look at that," he whispers, pointing to the way the sleeve is pleated. "Isn't that one of the most beautiful things you have ever seen? The man was a genius. He takes something from nature like a petal, and what does he do? He *improves* upon it. He's *immortal.*"

He looks at me intently, and little pink heat spots appear on his cheeks. "That's what I have to do, Reality. I've got to be up there with Balenciaga." He takes my elbow and leads me out of the room into the stairwell, where he can raise his voice. "I've got to be remembered. I've got to leave a legacy. I'd just *die* if I died before I did something important."

"Did something important like what?" I have to ask.

"Like making a beautiful sleeve that unfolds like a rose. Or a skirt that billows like a sail. Divine things that make people divinely happy."

"You'll do it, Freddie," I say encouragingly.

"If only there weren't so many parties to go to," he muses, mostly to himself.

# 25.

I'm lying around on my bed, trying to work out what to do today. I reach for my bedroom drawer and take out my scrapbook. It's got a periwinkle blue cover and the airbrushed photograph of Jackie and John F. Kennedy holding hands by a lake with swans gliding by. This makes me feel sad.

I flop the book open and study the photograph of me I've glued to the first inside page. It was taken the night of the opening of Less Is More, and I talked the photographer into giving me a print, in return for getting into the club for free for life. The photograph is on a page all by itself, which I can afford to do right now, owing to the fact that the rest of the scrapbook is blank, like my future.

The photo of me is just black-and-white, nothing really special, a snapshot. Everyone says it's a good likeness, though, even if I do look like a junkie. The thing is, if I had known they were taking it, I would have looked directly at the camera, chin down as I've practiced in front of the mirror, not off into space like a zombie. My big chandelier earrings look more fabulous than I do. It's too annoying to be captured in print, for the whole world to see, when you're looking anything less than sensational. I do think it's true that photographs are little bits of your soul, trapped in paper and chemicals. I'm super-

stitious about that. You are how you look, and if you look terrible—
even in a photograph—that's how you are. It's elementary.

I close my scrapbook and feel more depressed than I did when I
opened it. If that's possible.


"*Quel* horror," Phoebe says at the other end of the phone. "Paige is
sick, and they want *me* to tidy up the fashion closet. It's four-fifteen
already."

"It's not going to take you more than two hours, is it?" I ask
wearily. "I thought we had a date to meet at Orlon. I'm not going to
get up if you're not coming."

"Well, I'm not going to make it at this rate. The closet's a mess.
We've been opening the door and just tossing things in there, thinking that Paige would be back at work today. Now the little cow has
pleurisy. Can you believe it?"

"Can't you find someone to help you?" I ask. "I was looking forward to breakfast."

"You eat too much," says Phoebe. There's a silence. "Maybe," she
says, drawing out the word so it's more like "may-beeee," which
means she wants something.

"What?" I sigh.

"You could volunteer to help me clean up."

"I can't be bothered." I yawn. "It's too far."

"Oh, really! Five blocks is too far?"

"It's *emotionally* too far. You know what I mean."

"Are you sick or something? I have asked you to help me tidy up
the *closet*. The closet you've been dying to get into ever since I've met
you."

"I've lost all interest in life," I tell her.

There's another thirty seconds of silence. All I can hear is someone in the background typing one letter every ten seconds and the clinking of glasses. Phoebe eventually speaks up, in a little-girly voice. "So you're not going to come and help your best friend in her hour of need?"

"I'm busy."

"Don't be ridiculous, Really, you don't *do* anything anymore. How could you be busy?"

"I've just remembered a button I've got to sew on."

"I'm not accepting that excuse. I expect you here within the hour. Don't take too long to get dressed. We've got a lot of work to do." And then she hangs up. Just like that. Just like Phoebe.

I put the receiver down and bury my head under a pile of pillows. I feel like a limp piece of fabric that has been torn down the middle. I want to do something, but there's nothing I want to do. I want to get dressed, but I can't be bothered. I want to have breakfast with Phoebe, but I don't want to help her tidy up the closet. I want to tidy up the closet because I've been desperate to see the samples from the European spring collections, but I don't want to do it because it means walking five blocks. My mind feels like one of those wooden Russian dolls, the ones that open up to find more dolls inside. I keep on opening compartments and finding new reasons not to do anything. The trouble is, I'm soon going to come to the last doll and I know there's going to be nothing inside.

In the end, in a panic about the last doll, I decide to flop out of bed. When I'm standing up, I suddenly see in my mind's eye all those sunny little Ungaros swinging on a rack in the *Perfect Woman* closet. I come to my senses. Phoebe has just presented me with the opportunity of a lifetime. To talk to a rackful of Ungaros! Without sales assistants hovering around! A girl could learn a lot from an uninterrupted hour with an Ungaro.

\* \* \*

The fashion closet is down a narrow passage from Phoebe's partition. It's just a door in the wall. Phoebe puts a key in the lock and turns the handle. The door opens about five inches and jams.

"Oh, bother," she says, and pushes her shoulder against the door. She manages to open it enough to slide through. I don't quite make it.

"I've got more curves than you," I protest.

"Curves are *vulgar*. Push harder."

There's a box blocking my path, so I stay in the doorway while Phoebe turns on the light. The sight that meets my eyes is breathtaking and shocking at the same time.

It's not a closet but a large room. It's overflowing with cardboard boxes and opened suitcases and racks of frocks squeezed together against the walls. It looks as if Phoebe and her colleagues have been tossing things helter-skelter into here all year. To my grave I won't be able to forget the sight of all those poor frocks and shoes and bags and hats all jumbled up in a heap on the floor and shelves as if nobody loves them at all.

Phoebe and I have managed to find about a square foot of clear space in which to stand.

"Oh, Phoebe," I groan. "This is going to take us *decades*."

"Well, we don't need to *really* tidy up," she says with a foreign note of apology in her voice. "We just need to tidy up enough to look as if we've tidied up."

I start moving boxes out of the way. "Look at this!" I say, emptying a green plastic trash bag onto the floor. "A Galanos gown! All scrunched up with a pair of cheap panty hose!"

"Oh, *that*," says Phoebe when I hold it up for her. "It's just a dead dress."

"She's not *dead*," I protest. "Just a bit bruised."

Phoebe looks at me as if I'm crazy or something. She has not an ounce of compassion in her whole body. I fold the Galanos into a neat bundle.

"I'm taking her home to rehabilitate her. It's too insulting for a Galanos gown to be tossed into a trash bag as if she were a gob of old chewing gum. Why, a Galanos gown is so picky she doesn't even like sharing the same rack with anything less than an Yves Saint Laurent, and even then she feels superior! It's going to take her months to get over this."

"Suit yourself." Phoebe, who has a shoe box under her arm, shrugs. "I wouldn't get in a state over an old rag like that. It's last season's."

I start sorting and folding and hanging and ironing.

Somewhere along the way Phoebe gets called out to the phone. She doesn't come back. I don't mind. I feel like that boy in the great harem pants—Aladdin—in a cave full of glittering treasures.

I'm in a sort of rhapsody, fingering silks and rubbing angora against my cheeks and whirling bits of chiffon around my waist. I pull skirts over my hips and slip into silk frocks and try on tweed jackets with half belts at the back.

I move through the racks and shelves rapidly, my neck and wrists strung with costume jewelry, my head piled high with hats, my shoulders weighed down with scarves and belts. I get to know every *inch* of that closet.

This is what I find. The shelves go up to the ceiling on three sides, and out of them spill these things: half-open boxes filled with ropes of pearls; shiny lengths of ribbon unwinding themselves from spools of purple, green, and gold; silver lamé gloves with their fingers dangling; bright silk scarves knotted together like a magician's hat trick; lashings of tulle and stiff white netting; fluffy piles of cashmere wraps in the colors of sugar candy; creamy bundles of antique lace; bunches of gleaming feathers; hats swathed in mists of veiling; falls of synthetic hair and shaggy nylon wigs; fob watches with engraved cases and beads of polished wood; gold-heeled shoes and sequined satin slippers, hand-painted sneakers and alligator-tipped cowboy boots; twists of ankle socks like scoops of sherbet; drifts of pastel panty hose with sheer elongated feet; iridescent pleats of taffeta in mother-of-pearl shimmerings; slippery ivory camisoles with hand-rolled hems; necklaces with translucent strings of sun-bleached seashells; clusters of black Ray-Bans with mirrored glass; loops of plastic bangles in zebra stripes and cheetah spots; big pom-pons of silk flowers with green plastic stems; hanks of dyed wool in sunset colors . . .

And on steel racks beside all the shelves, peeping out, are flounces of bright layered skirts, red and canary yellow piped with gold braid; crisp sleeves in plain linen and checkerboard wool; cheeky stand-up collars with buttoned throats; cuffs in coffee-colored lace over satin wrists; the plush forearm of a white Mongolian lamb jacket, dripping soft, crimped hairs; a glimmer of gold button on a smart epaulet; the sparkle of a diamond on a pocket; the greasy shine of a sleeve of a black leather jacket; the curved thigh of a pair of loden jodhpurs . . .

And on the benches beside the racks beside the shelves I find a dozen coat hangers quilted in baby blue satin with blue forget-me-nots around the neck; a huge rattan snake charmer's basket with its lid off, full of scraps of fabric and needles and giant safety pins; an open suitcase with layers of crumpled pink tissue paper inside; a battered set of heated rollers with a melted lid; a single brown shoe without any laces; three rolls of masking tape; a steam iron with a blackened bottom; a bottle of methylated spirits; a half-eaten pack-age of mint chocolate chip home-style cookies; a map of the Paris metro; an empty card of Valium; a pair of Bloomingdale's hand weights; a herbal teabag; a clothes brush covered in lint; a few loose press-on nails; and underneath it all, a blue satin Halston gown completely ripped in half up the back seam and in terrible pain.

I pick up the poor gown and stroke her. She must be ten years old. Which means she might have been lying here for almost that long.

As I hold her in my arms, I am suddenly filled with a terrible rage at the injustice of it all. These magazine people must be *animals*. Treating frocks like this. Tossing them like old rags on the floor. Ripping them in half and leaving them without so much as a stitch. Smudging makeup all over them and not bothering to clean it off. Mixing Halston gowns with ready-to-wear; Christian Lacroix with Liz Claiborne, Galanoses with old panty hose. It's the worst discovery I've ever made in my life. It's like finding out that your mother once owned an original Fortuny and gave it to the Salvation Army.

If there was one thing in the whole world I believed in, it was that fashion editors cared about frocks. That they loved them as much as I do. But a fashion editor having such *contempt* for a blue satin Halston—it's as if the whole fabric of society has been torn down.

I rush out of the closet with the Halston in my hand and find Phoebe sitting at her desk, giving herself a French manicure.

"Phoebe!" I cry, waving the frock at her. "How could you stand by and let this happen? You've got to respect frocks if you want them to respect you!"

"That old thing's been there for years," she says, taking one set of fingers out of a bowl of soapy water and shaking them. "Nobody wears that kind of blue anymore."

"But she's been suffering," I say. "You should be ashamed of yourself."

"It's nothing to do with *me*. I'm not the fashion assistant. I'm just following her orders."

"Oh, Phoebe," I say, "haven't you seen that movie?"

"What movie?" she asks.

"*Judgment at Nuremberg.*"

"I hate religious films."

"Couldn't you hear the *noise*? All that shrieking?"

Phoebe looks at me blankly. She never did understand how to talk to frocks: "You took your time," is all she says. "It's seven o'clock."

"I don't care what time it is!"

"*Quel* bad temper."

"You wouldn't treat a *person* like this!"

"Wouldn't I?"

I ignore her. "What makes you think that frocks aren't people, too? It's your responsibility to make these frocks comfortable. They're your *guests.* I don't care how your fashion editors feel about Halston these days, it's a crime to treat one of his frocks as if, as if"—I'm searching for the right comparison—"as if she's a Tommy Hilfiger! What sort of woman are you? Do you have ice in your veins? I wish I could wring your neck!"

All of a sudden there's a cough behind me. I fling myself around angrily. If it's one of the fashion editors, I think, I'm going to let her have it. It's not. It's Hugo Falk.

"Oh!" I say, mortified.

"Well, what a performance!" He looks amused. "Do I know you?"

"No." I smile thinly. "I'm *sure* you don't."

"You look familiar."

"I'm not!" I protest. "I'm not familiar at all!" The thought of Hugo Falk seeing me like this, all wrinkled and covered in dust from the closet, not in the most advantageous light, fills me with horror.

Phoebe, for once observant, notices my distress and comes to my rescue. "Don't worry about her, Hugo. She's nobody."

I'm not sure what Hugo says next because by then I've started to back away down the hall. I run for the exit and clatter down the iron stairs, the torn Halston wedged under my arm and flapping in the jet stream behind me.

# 26.

"Hell-o!" I can hear footsteps behind me. I keep on walking down Lafayette. *Fast.* Or as fast as my silver star-studded platforms will take me.

"Hell-o! Stop a minute!" The footsteps are catching up to me.

I speed up a bit. I don't want to talk to anybody. I want to get that Halston home and have a good cry. I feel all unraveled and off-balance. And then to prove this, I twist my ankle on a broken bottle of Heineken. "Ouch!" I cry, and pull up short.

"Don't run away!" the voice says from two feet behind. I bend down and grab my ankle and look up to see Hugo Falk hovering above me. I must go white, because he says in a voice that I suppose is meant to be kind but comes out snappish, "I'm not going to bite!"

"My darn foot," I say to the sidewalk, because I'm too embarrassed to look Hugo Falk in the eye. "I've hurt it."

"Forget about your foot," he says, slipping a hand under my arm and pulling me upright. "I want to talk to you. Come on." He drags me along by the armpit for a few feet.

"Hey. What do you think you're doing?" I say when I've come to my senses. I try to push him away. "That's no way to treat a lady."

"It isn't?" he asks, and seems genuinely surprised.

"Well, you don't grab *Faye* like that, do you?"

"Faye? She's not a lady. She's a *star.*"

"For all you know, I might be one, too."

"If you were, I'd know you," he says.

"Anyway, my foot's twisted," I tell him. "I'm not going anywhere."

"Don't be a crybaby. Come on, I'm taking you to a bar. We can *talk.*" He says this last word importantly.

I don't know why I'm irritated with him. I just am. "What if I don't want to talk?" I say stubbornly.

"Well, it doesn't matter then," he says, sounding offended and dropping his grasp of my armpit. "I'll write about somebody else."

My heart does a roll like a French twist. "You're going to write about me? I mean, I'm not surprised, not at all, it's just that you said you don't know who I am!"

"I don't need to know who you are. I know everything about you by just looking at you. I have a highly developed visual sense. That's why I'm such a brilliant chronicler of New York life. It's never what people say that counts—I always make that up anyway—it's how they look. You look *fabulous.* That's enough for me."

I suppose that's reasonable.

"So are you coming?" He starts striding ahead of me.

"Sure!" I call after him as I scramble to catch up.

There are twelve fashion bars in one block of Third Street. Hugo insists we stop in every one of them.

Hugo tells me he has to meet a girl who is the friend of the best friend of the managing editor of *Esquire* at the Boa Bar. The girl isn't there; but I have a frozen margarita, and Hugo has a Kahlúa and milk anyway. Someone pays for the drinks, but it's not Hugo. At PVC Hugo is supposed to rendezvous with the assistant art director of *Frenzee,* but he's not there either, so we have two glasses of red wine on the house. It's too early to meet anyone at Eugenie, so we go into the Delineator and have four beers while Hugo tries to find the *Times Magazine*'s copy editor at the bar. I have a banana daiquiri and Hugo has a port at Paisley, and someone buys us a bottle of Spanish champagne at Ultrasuede. At Frizon, after a vodka gimlet or two, Hugo catches up with a woman who once worked at *Vanity Fair* but she doesn't have time to talk. Chambre Syndicale is too full and Eton Crop is too empty; but we find a couple of stools at Zazou, and Hugo leaves me to stare into my planter's punch while he goes off in a corner with one of the messengers from *Town & Country*. I forget the rest, except for a great piña colada at Page Boy and a drag queen miming to "My Guy" at Pink Gingham. Oh, and Hugo borrowing lots of quarters from me to make phone calls.

"Why am I here with you? Remind me," Hugo asks hours later in the street. I've managed to get him out of the Twin Set and away from a conversation with a boy who works for a legal firm on the floor below *Interview* magazine. I don't know how I did this. I think my not having enough money to pay for our last drink check—Hugo ordered a round for the whole room—helped a bit.

"Me?" I ask, looking around. I've hardly exchanged a word with Hugo all night, except for drink orders. His curiosity about me seemed to vanish as soon as we walked into the first bar. I know how a pocket handkerchief must feel now. Hugo paid as much attention to me as he did to the triangle of acid yellow cotton sticking out of his top pocket. Less—he took it out once and wrote some white-haired boy's phone number on it.

"Yes, you," he says. "It's funny I've never seen you before. I thought I knew every girl in town."

"You met me at *Perfect Woman*," I tell him.

"I did? When?"

"*Tonight*," I insist.

He peers intently at me. "Oh, yes. I *loved* the way you defended that dress."

"You did?" I feel myself blushing. "So you do remember?"

"I happen to have a photographic memory," he says proudly. "What was your name again?"

"R-E-A-L-I-T-Y," I repeat.

"That's a very seventies name."

"It is not!" I protest.

"Are you sure I don't know you? Your face looks familiar. Although your hair—"

"You do know me," I decide to admit. "From the door at Less Is More."

"But Ricci's on the door of Less Is More."

"Don't remind me!" I exclaim, and fling my arms out so angrily one of the charms on my charm bracelet catches the corner of his glasses and makes a little cracking sound.

His lips twist into a sly smile as he takes off his spectacles and examines them for damage. "You're a bad-tempered little thing, aren't you? I'm bad-tempered, too. It's good for my career. People are in *awe* of me."

We start walking again. Everything in the street, including Hugo's narrow shape, is starting to look like one of those funny mirrors at Coney Island, distorted like the ripples in strawberry sorbet 'n' cream. We pass Cummerbund, an after-hours club. Margie is standing alone outside the door in a skirt and fifties cone-shaped bra with a cardigan over her shoulders, stamping out a cigarette with her foot.

"Hi, guys!" she says brightly, toting for business. "Wanna come in?" Hugo ignores her. Cummerbund hasn't been a success. They let in so many people on their opening night that nobody wanted to come on any of the nights after that. Margie looks so pathetic standing there, I say, "Fabulous cardigan," to let her know I care.

"Hugo?" I screw up enough courage to ask, as we pass by Ready to Wear.

"Yes?" He smiles at me.

"Before—outside the magazine—you said you were going to write a story on me. Is it going to be a *column*?"

"Oh, for goodness' sake, don't be so pushy!" he suddenly snaps at me. He starts stalking ahead.

"Wait a minute!" I call out.

He stops and lets me catch up with him. "Look, I've got a writer's block. I can't talk to you about anything like that now," he says as I struggle to catch up with him. My feet can't quite find the sidewalk, which always happens when I've had a cocktail or two. The sidewalk is two inches lower than I think it is from up here, which means every step hits the concrete like I've got a brick tied to my foot.

"Is it serious?" I ask.

"What's serious?"

"The block? The writer's block? It sounds awful."

"Yes, it is. I knew tonight was going to be a disaster."

"Why?" I ask. "Didn't you connect with the right people?"

He looks at me sharply. "Of course, I did. That woman who used to be at *Vanity Fair* is now at *Redbook*. But she's going to go to *Vogue* next month."

"Oh, I see."

He hesitates for a minute and then decides to explain. "Look, it's just that whenever people demand too much of me, I get a *terrible* writer's block. I can't make any deadlines. I have to sit in bars all day until it comes back to me. Last week I couldn't write a word of my column because some dreadful woman kept pestering me about a story I promised to write on her silly restaurant."

"But that can't be right, Hugo. I just read your last week's column yesterday."

"Oh, *that*," he says, waving his hand in the air as if he's shooing away a fly. "It was just an old one with new names put in. I recycle my columns all the time. No one notices."

"What are you going to do?"

"About what?"

"The writer's block?"

"Will you stop reminding me about it! It will get worse."

"I'm sorry." I touch his elbow to show him I mean it.

He stiffens visibly and shrugs me away. "Well, good night," he says suddenly. "I can't stand talking to you anymore. I'm getting wrung out. You're putting too much pressure on me."

"What kind of pressure?" I ask, amazed.

"You're putting pressure on me to be brilliant. I can only stand people in small doses. They either bore me or put pressure on me. Sometimes I wish I weren't so clever. I depress myself." He starts off down the street at a tremendous pace.

"Hugo!" I shout after him.

"I'll call you!" is what he shouts back at me, over his shoulder, as I watch him round the corner.

# 27.

"You really made a fool of yourself last night," Phoebe says over breakfast at Café Orlon. "Hugo Falk thought you were *bonkers*."

"So bonkers he says he's going to write a story on me," I announce.

Phoebe takes off a polka dot glove and flings it on the table. "You? You're crazy. Hugo Falk tells everyone he's going to write about them. He never does. Why would he write about you? You don't do anything. I, on the other hand"—she flings off her other glove—"am a perfect subject for a story, now that I'm *senior* junior shoe editor at *Perfect Woman*." She waits for my reaction.

"You are?" I ask. "When did this happen?"

"This morning." She makes a dramatic pause, drags on her cigarette, and explains. "Lydia Brooke Cooke is going to *Poise*."

"She is?"

"Yes, and I can tell you it's been a madhouse all day. The top brass is livid."

"What's she going to do there?"

"My dear, she is going to be senior vice-president in charge of beauty questions and answers!"

"No! What does she know about beauty? I thought you said she's been in the Semiprecious Gemstone department for*ever*."

"She has. She's an expert on Elsa Peretti. All that will go to waste now. Well, let me tell you something," says Phoebe, who leans marginally closer. "I'm secretly pleased although it would be sudden death to let on I feel that way in the office. Lydia is going to *Poise* and Paige Brown Bentley is moving up a step to Semiprecious Gemstones and Boo Le Beau Crow is coming across from Big Earrings to take Paige's place and Joan Jennifer Talbot is going to Earrings from Lingerie and Claudia Plumb Somers is moving up to be executive lingerie editor even though I personally don't think she's ready for it and I am going to step into Claudia's shoes and become senior junior shoe editor!"

"That's fab."

"I suppose so. However, it hasn't been announced yet, so I'm trying not to think about it. Do you think I should add a middle name? It's the done thing. What do you think about Carmichael? Does it sound like my family has a country house with dog hairs all over the sofas?"

"Do you actually get to go on *fashion shoots*?" I ask.

"You bet. *Quel* about time I'd say, too. I'm sick to death of spending all day taping the bottoms of shoes and wrapping them in tissue. I'm sick to death of that moldy old fashion closet." She stubs out her cigarette on the table and grinds it into the woodwork. "So, does the Halston fit?" she adds quickly before I can launch into another plea for compassion for the frocks in the closet.

Faille comes over to take our order. "I've always loved that jacket," she says, admiring my egg yolk yellow tufted cotton jacket with the white plastic daisy buttons. She doesn't admire anything of Phoebe's. Faille and Phoebe don't get on. I think there was a fight about backcombing in Phoebe's Patti Page period, which coincided with Faille's Lesley Gore period, but that was too long ago to remember clearly.

"Iced tea," Phoebe says impatiently, tapping her tortoiseshell cigarette case on the table. "With a *long* straw."

"*Lo-ong* straw. A-ha," repeats Faille, going into her waitress act. "Would you like it candy-striped or plain?"

"Plain," answers Phoebe with dead seriousness.

"Swedish pancakes, Faille, and, oh, an extra-large glass of Tab. With a squeeze of lemon," I say.

"Swedish pancakes," repeats Faille, "Uh-huh."

"I've been working all day, and a carrot stick is enough to get *me* by," says Phoebe critically when Faille goes away. "I think you should see a doctor about your metabolism." She jams a cigarette into a long black onyx holder.

"Phoebe, I haven't put on a *pound* since I was sixteen."

"That's all very well and good," she says. "But you're getting older. Your system slows down. You don't want to be the queen of the pig people, do you? You don't want to be the Shelley Winters of the East Village by the time you're twenty-five?"

"Well, I'm allowed one food sin," I argue. "You smoke."

Phoebe looks down her straight, bobbed nose at me. She says the following words very slowly, as if I'm some kind of idiot or something. "If-I-gave-up-smoking-I'd-put-on-*weight*."

"And die of cancer," I say smugly.

"Well, I'd rather have a short, thin life than a long, fat one," she tells me curtly.

She turns her back to me when the pancakes arrive. To tell the truth, they suddenly don't taste so good. I think of all my darling frocks and what might become of them if I ballooned into—horror of horrors—a size *ten*. I couldn't give them to Phoebe because she treats her frocks so *mean*, doesn't even hang them in a closet but piles them on the floor in groups according to occasion, groups called Evening, Cocktail Hour, Thé Dansant, Desperation, that sort of thing. She even keeps her underwear in the *refrigerator* in summer, that's how cruel

and thoughtless she is. I reluctantly agree with her. It would be irresponsible for a girl like me to become a size ten. Even an extra *inch*
here or there would make dozens of frocks homeless. I put down my
fork and push the plate away.

"I'm finished," I tell her. Phoebe turns back toward me and looks
at the plate.

"Aren't you glad I'm your conscience," she says rather than asks.
"Every girl should have one." She takes a small sip of her iced tea.
"I'm full," she says, and bites on the straw. "Let's split."

I'm about to untangle my jacket from the back of my chair when
a reason not to leave enters the room.

"Don't *move*," I tell Phoebe. "Look over there. But don't look like
you're looking."

"What?" says Phoebe, far too loudly. "What am I looking like I'm
not looking at?"

"Shut up," I whisper. "He'll hear."

"Who will hear?"

"It's *Quark*," I tell her,

Quark has come in alone and is slowly taking off a denim jacket.
He's looking all around the room. Maybe he's looking for me. I
smile, but he looks right through me. He could be nearsighted. "I'm
going to say hello," I tell Phoebe.

"If you *insist* on throwing yourself at every man—" she starts to
say, but I'm over at Quark's table before she finishes.

"Hi," I say, smoothing my crumpled linen skirt down over my
hips.

"Hi," he says, squinting into the sun that's streaming through the
big glass window and bouncing around the room off a metallic
bracelet here, a beaten copper earring there.

"I saw you in *Interview*," I say.

"Oh, yeah?" he says. He gives me a big, expectant sort of grin.

"You looked *great*," I say.

He nods his head in agreement and runs his fingers through his hair.

"How's the hair?" I ask.

"Fine." He looks at me curiously as if trying to work out what planet I've come from. He must be still half asleep.

"Just checking," I smile. "Oh, well."

"Fine," he says.

"I'm going to be in a magazine soon, too," I say brightly. "*Frenzee*. Hugo Falk is going to interview me for his column."

"Great," he says.

"Oh, well," I say. Quark doesn't say anything. "OK then," I go on. "I'm in a *big* hurry. I've got to be interviewed. By Hugo Falk. For *Frenzee*. Look out for it. See you around."

"See you around." His freckled lips curl into a half-smile. I can't see his eyes because they are obliterated by shards of sunlight. Like that big robot in *The Day the Earth Stood Still*.

"See you around in *magazines*, then." I wave and wander back to Phoebe, glancing back at Quark over my shoulder. He's running his fingers through his hair.

"You took your time," says Phoebe. "I'm going."

"He's so shy," I tell her. "You can tell he's mad about me. Isn't he?"

"I wouldn't say *that*," Phoebe pushes the table away from her. "I think he's madder about *himself*."

# 28.

Nothing happens for days. I don't hear a peep from Hugo Falk. I don't even see him around, although I arrange myself decoratively in bars and coffee shops all over the neighborhood. He must have flown off to London to one of those nightclub openings he's always writing about. That's one of the advantages of being a somebody. People fly you all around the world on free tickets, and all you have to do in return is stand around and drink their cocktails. I can't wait for this to happen to me.

The trouble is, I told everyone I was going to be in *Frenzee* next week. Well, it's next week now, and my credibility on Third Street is running out. So far the boys behind the bars are still passing me free drinks. But it won't go on forever.

I don't know how I find myself in the men's business suit department at Barney's. But it must be fate. I'm wandering around the store, women's and men's departments, trying to fill up the afternoon by getting acquainted with the new fall shipment of Issey Miyakes and Claude Montanas and Yohji Yamamotos. Some people might think I'm being aimless, but there's nothing aimless in furthering your fashion education. I further my fashion education every day, while I'm waiting for my big break, by going window-shopping and reading magazines. It's important for me to keep up-to-date. Being up-to-date is my profession after all.

I have been stroking all the sweaters laid out on display on the first floor and feeling the weights of all the trouser fabrics on the second. I've been roaming around the European designer section, examining the coat linings and shaking the sleeves of the outstanding jackets and shirts. In the back of my mind I have also been looking out for a salesman I've seen here twice before, who has a dimple in his chin and usually leans by the racks on the second floor, polishing his nails with a checked handkerchief, the best linen naturally, and watching all the other sales attendants fold sweaters.

I've somehow gotten myself into the Zegna department, and I've made a right turn down some stairs. Before I've even realized it, I'm in the thick of the business suits. This department always makes me nervous, all those rows and rows of navy blue and charcoal gray pinstripes sitting smugly on their hangers like a roomful of executives at a shareholders' meeting. They make my flesh crawl.

I start to turn back and retrace my steps, but I keep on running into more and more racks of gray suits. Two people ask me if they can show me something. I wave them away. I've got to concentrate on getting out of here. There's nothing to do but go deeper and deeper into the department and try to find the elevator. I feel like Hansel and Gretel in the forest after the birds have eaten all their breadcrumbs.

I round a corner and stumble on six salesmen standing in a half circle around a person who is apparently trying on clothes. The salesmen are weighed down by jackets and trousers and long coats over their arms. There's a brown leather overstuffed sofa in the corner, and it's laden, too, with tweed jackets and flannel pants and cable sweaters and cotton shirts unbuttoned right down the fronts.

There's a sort of closet near the sofa, a pine one carved with a garland of roses along the top and scrubbed to look like something from an old estate. There are silver-framed pictures grouped on a small table next to it, on a lace cloth, with photographs of models in the frames so they look like family heirlooms. There's a moose head on a plaque on the wall over the table with a plastic nose and an antique pipe in a crystal ashtray in the arms of a plaster black boy in breeches.

The closet is stacked with sweaters, in yellows and eggshell blues and celadon greens, with diamond patterns and plaids and giant snowflakes over some of them. A whole bunch of the sweaters are on the floor, in tumbling piles. Standing in front of the closet, in the closet actually because the mirrored doors are wide open like arms, is the person who is the object of all this attention. One of the salesmen crouches down at this person's feet and starts to measure his inner thigh.

Hugo Falk has his hands by his side, and he's looking irritated. He's wearing a heavy purple tweed jacket with a ticket dangling down from the sleeve over a black turtleneck. He's got on a pair of very baggy pleated chocolate brown pants, which are too long and are folding around his shoes—natty two-toned oxfords—like molasses off a spoon.

The salesman at his feet has taken the tape measure and is measuring from the ground to a hollow about an inch under Hugo's right ankle. Hugo looks impatiently at him.

"They're still too long," I hear him complain.

"But, sir," pleads the salesperson, "you can't be seriously thinking of having them any shorter." The other salesmen grunt in solidarity.

"I intend to have them *much* shorter," says Hugo, and bends right down to tug at the hem. He's at least six feet, so it's a long way to go. "Like *this*," he says smugly, and rolls up the hem until it's just grazing his ankle.

"But, *sir*," says the salesman again, "that's not the done thing."

"Are you questioning my taste?" Hugo asks.

"No, sir," answers the salesman sulkily.

I clear my throat. "Actually," I say from behind them. Part of the word gets caught in my throat. It comes out sounding like "chully." All the salesmen turn to look at me. "Actually," I say more clearly, "it's the thing to stop your cuffs just at the ankle. It's the current mode."

The salesmen look astonished. They've been selling pinstripes to stockbrokers for too long. I go on. "It's better if the legs of the pant taper, of course, but it's perfectly acceptable to a have glimpse of sock, preferably *white,*" I make a point of saying, noticing Hugo's geranium-colored sock, "even with wide trousers."

"You see," says Hugo, hoisting the trouser leg up even further to show off a curvaceous white calf with dark hairs springing up all over it. "We have a fashion expert in our midst."

"Very well." The salesman, who has a shiny bald patch in the back of his head, sighs. He makes a clicking noise with his tongue, and when he stands up, he turns and gives me the look of *death.* "Short trousers are IN, are they?"

I watch while Hugo instructs all the salesmen about his purchases. "I'll have this and this and this and, oh, that sweater, in yellow, not blue, and three of those cotton shirts, all pink, and I don't know about that jacket. What do you think?" he asks me from over the heads of half a dozen salesmen who are running around picking up sweaters and scooping up trousers and smoothing down shirts.

"Me?" I ask, and look around.

"You," he says, and holds up a red jacket. "What do you think? Is it too ordinary?"

"Hmmm." I contemplate the jacket. It's very traditional.

"What's the label?" I ask.

Hugo digs around in the lining. "Young Man."

"American," I say, and fold my arms. "Personally I'd steer away from anything American. French and Italian are the only things. Look"—I go over to the overstuffed sofa and pick up an Armani jacket—"*this* would look great."

"Let's see," he says.

I hold out the jacket for him to slip his arms through. As he's buttoning it up, I brush it down for him.

"Well?" he asks, pulling the cuffs down. "Isn't it a bit dull?"

"It's *perfect.*" I drool. "You look like a matinee idol."

He pulls it off in one swift motion and tosses it at a passing salesman. "Wrap this, too," he says. He turns to me. "It seems as if I'm lucky you came along."

"You're welcome," I say.

"I'm Hugo Falk," he says, holding out his hand.

"I know," I say, not to be put off, taking his hand. "We met the other night. You're writing a story on me."

"Remind me," he says, looking suspicious.

"I was the one who was throwing a tantrum on the third floor of *Perfect Woman* magazine. You said I was funny."

"Oh, *you.*" He sounds relieved. "The girl with a crusade. It's hard to remember all you downtown girls. I know so many people."

"Oh, I understand," I say.

"Do you have a card?" he asks.

"No," I tell him truthfully. "Only suits carry cards."

"It's just as well. I always throw them away at the end of the day anyway."

"You can always find me at Aurora's White Trash. And, you know, I *get around.*"

"I'll look you up next time I'm going shopping," he says, turning back to the mirror and straightening his black turtleneck.

"But what about the article on me?"

"What article?" He doesn't turn around.

"The one you're writing."

"I'm writing lots of articles."

"The article on *me.*" I almost scream in frustration. "You said you'd write about me."

"Oh, I'm always saying that." He shrugs as he brushes a few stray hairs off his shoulders.

I glare at him. He catches my eye in the mirror. "Of course, that doesn't mean I'm *not* going to write about you."

"Well, will you make up your mind!" I lose my temper. "I can't go on not knowing about a thing like this. I mean, I've told everybody that you are, and now you say you might not be. If you don't, you'll ruin my reputation."

I realize this is the wrong thing to say when Hugo turns around and tugs at his sleeve cuffs. "I never write about anybody who *needs* publicity. If you need publicity, you aren't fabulous. And if you aren't fabulous, well, you're just not fabulous enough for me." He slaps his hands together. "I have a million things to do now," he says. "Call me when you do something spectacular. Where *are* those parcels?"

"Maybe we could go and have some coffee," I suggest. "And discuss the whole thing. You've already told me I *look* fabulous. I can look more fabulous than this. I'm just wearing any old thing today." The bones down the sides of Dolores's bustier suddenly pinch my skin. Dolores is letting me know in her own way she's not happy about me calling her "any old thing."

"I'm not drinking coffee this week," Hugo says. "But you can help me carry these parcels out of here." He points to a salesclerk returning with several Barney's shopping bags.

"It's a deal," I say.

It's only later on the street, after I've carried all his parcels and helped him into a cab and called out for him to call me sometime and waved good-bye as he sped away from me down Seventh Avenue, that I realize I've just made a deal but I don't know what the deal was that I just made.

# 29.

Freddie is taking me window-shopping along Fourteenth Street. Fourteenth Street is where Freddie and I get a lot of our inspiration. Fourteenth Street is where we find plastic flowers and old bath towels that can be sewn together to make great muumuus and nylon wigs with silver tinsel through them. Fourteenth Street is the mecca of recycling, and just about everything in our lives is recycled, including our lives, according to the Psy-chic. Fourteenth Street is *poignant.*

"Oh, Freddie." I sigh, as we stop outside an old nightclub, long ago deserted for Third Street. A street vendor is showing us the cutest little battery puppy that spins on its tail and barks. "What am I going to do? I'm counting on Hugo Falk. But I get the feeling I shouldn't count on Hugo Falk. Maybe Phoebe's right. He tells everyone he's going to write about them."

I bend down and pick up the puppy in the palm of my hand. "It was so *horrible* at Madame Grés last night. It's *awful* being high profile and having people come up to you and ask you what you're doing now that you haven't got a door and not having an answer ready. As far as some people are concerned, I'm just a doorgirl without a door, which is close to being *useless.* If I don't do something soon, I'm going to lose all my contacts. All the free haircuts and manicures and samples of makeup. It's going to set me back six months. If I don't have anything to offer, no one's going to give me anything in return. You know how it is."

"Don't worry," he reassures me. "Maybe you could go back on a door until you get a brain wave. You could save some money and go to Paris to see the collections."

"Oh, Freddie, that would take me *months*. None of us have that long. That's *forever*. Besides, I can't go back on a door. All the clubs are owned by sleazebags in white linen suits with the sleeves pushed up. I *liked* Eunice. She was sweet. She always starched her aprons. I don't want to work for some creep who wants me to sit on his lap all the time."

"That's silly. Eunice never asked you to sit on her lap."

"That's what I *mean!*"

"Now, Really," says Freddie seriously as he strokes the head of my puppy, "you've got to pull yourself together."

"Hugo Falk said to call him when I do something *spectacular*."

"That shouldn't be difficult. There must be something you can do."

"Oh, Freddie, I don't think so. I don't know how to do *anything!*"

"That's not true. You know how to dress. You know how to do a great French twist. You should be more *visible*."

I look down at Samantha, my fluorescent pink chiffon A-line minitent frock with the halter neckline and two rows of fringing around the hem. "I'm *trying*," I tell him.

# 30.

The television is flickering when I wake up. I must have had one Sambuca milk shake too many at Zazou. I've been out on the town with Freddie. We've been racking our brains about something spectacular to do for Hugo. We still haven't come up with anything. Anything that is consistent with my fabulous life-style.

I can barely push myself up on my elbows to see what time it is. Everything is complicated by this dead weight that seems to be lying across my legs. When I try to move them, the weight groans.

"Oh, goodness," says Freddie, pushing his hoop skirt down as he sits up. "Did we fall asleep?"

"It's *you*." I frown. "For a minute I thought it was Hugo Falk. I don't know why. I must have been dreaming." I peer at the television set. "What happened to *The Champions*? Did they get that secret formula or did the world blow up?"

"Weren't we watching *The Mod Squad*?"

"It was *The Champions*. I'm *sure* it was. The girl's hair stood up on her head in loops. The girl in *The Mod Squad* has hair that just hangs straight."

"Well, ta-ta. I'm going home." Freddie stretches. He searches under the bed for his slippers. "I've got a class at eleven. Isn't that *cruel*?"

"You don't have to go, Freddie. You could stay here with me and watch television. It's only seven. *The Jetsons* will be on soon. I know how you love them. Please?"

"I *can't*. It's *imperative* that I go to class. If I fail, Mummy will send me to South America."

"What's wrong with going to South America? Carmen Miranda and Yma Sumac came from there. It can't be all bad. You could wear plastic fruit on your head and no one would notice."

"Then I'm *certain* I'd hate it. Have you seen my gloves?"

"I wish you'd stay," I say. "It's awful having friends who are so involved in their careers. I'm bored."

"I told you there was a vacancy for a life model at our fashion drawing class. It pays rather well, I believe."

"But you said I had to take my clothes off."

"I thought you liked doing that."

I pick up a pillow and throw it at him. "Beast! I couldn't let a whole room of strangers see me without my clothes on. What would they think of me? I've never even let a soul see me without *makeup*."

"I've seen you without makeup."

"No, you haven't. You've just seen me with the No-Makeup Look."

"Here they are," says Freddie, picking up his long white satin gloves off the floor. "I've *got* to go," he says apologetically, coming over and kissing me on the cheek. "I've got to work out what to wear today."

I crawl to the end of the bed and turn the dial on the television set. "Freddie, look at this! There's a film just starting. It looks great! Keep me company, won't you? I've spotted a mohair sweater. This film looks very you."

"Oh, well, just for a *minute*," Freddie says reluctantly, and settles down on the floor.

The film is called *The Young Swingers* and turns out to be about a girl who is trying to save a nightclub in Greenwich Village from being torn down by her mean aunt, who is a real estate agent. The girl falls in love with this boy, a nightclub singer, and there's a great song called "Watusi Surfer." The club burns down, and the girl has her twenty-first birthday. It's *so* moving. I instantly dissolve in tears. Freddie, who is still on the floor, gets out his handkerchief.

"That girl's twenty-one"—I sniff—"and she's got a club *and* a boyfriend. It's not fair."

"That was the sixties, Reality," Freddie says, unraveling the handkerchief and offering it to me. "You could have two things at once then."

"Well, it's the eighties, and I haven't got *one* thing at once. You would have thought we would have progressed by now."

"You shouldn't mope about like this," Freddie says, blotting my tears. "You'll get lines around your mouth."

"Who's going to care anyway?"

"I care."

It's sweet having boys as girlfriends.

"That's nice of you, Freddie, but I want a boy to care. You might as well be a girl."

"What's wrong with being a girl?"

"Oh, Freddie, there's *nothing* wrong. It's just no fun around here without a boy to dress up for. Or a club to dress up for. A girl without a boy *or* a club is just a *nobody*."

"Well, I think it's *lovely* being a girl," he says. "It's wonderful wearing bras and garter belts and high heels. It's *gorgeous* hearing your skirts squish and your bracelets tinkle."

"I suppose so," I say reluctantly. "I suppose those things *are* nice. I suppose it *is* really sexy listening to yourself go clop-clop-clop down the street."

"It's so *erotic* to breathe in your own perfume!" He sighs.

"And so *sensual* to lie in a bubble bath and point your toes while you shave your legs. It's *voluptuous* to dust yourself all over with a powder puff."

"And to smooth on night cream."

"Or to unroll a nylon."

"Or pluck out a stray eyebrow hair."

"It is?"

"It makes me go all *shivery.*"

"Every day that I'm a girl I'm so *grateful.*"

"If only there were more boys around to appreciate us."

"We don't need boys."

"Oh, but I do," I say. "If I don't get at least one wolf whistle a day, I get so *depressed.* Who do you think we are doing all this smoothing and unrolling and plucking for? You sound like Phoebe."

"We're doing it for *ourselves.*"

"Oh, I don't think so, Freddie. I don't think you can say *that.* I don't think I'd go to the trouble of brushing my wigs one hundred strokes every night if there wasn't someone out there waiting for me to come out with fabulous hair. I don't think I'd go to the trouble of finding a top in the exact shade of purple to go with my fuchsia flapper skirt if there wasn't someone out there expecting me to be perfectly color-coordinated from head to toe. I don't think I'd crawl around in the bottom of the closet looking for my missing plastic daisy earring if there wasn't someone out there demanding that I make an earring statement. That's why I never show my face outside this door without makeup. There're a dozen people out there waiting for the day I don't wear makeup so that they can say, 'Isn't she plain?' "

"You mean, if there weren't a lot of people waiting in ambush to critique your wardrobe, you'd wear *sweat pants*?"

"I don't mean that at all! Who do you think I am? My mother? I just mean that it's no use being a girl if there isn't someone to look at you."

We sit quietly for a while. I can see straight into Freddie's room from here, as the connecting door is wide open. The room looks like the inside of a robin's egg. The walls are covered in a porcelain blue silk which he found rolled on a bolt at the back of some Seventh Avenue loading dock. Freddie has sewn the silk together in long panels and pleated it so that it falls in shimmering lengths and trails on the carpet, which is cardinal red with a swirling pattern of brown autumn leaves. He has attached big streamers of the fabric to the sides of the ceiling and then scooped them up so that they fasten in the middle around the plastic chandelier he bought for a song at an American Ballet Theatre props and costume sale. Even his bed— which is really a child's cot with railings around the sides—is covered in blue silk. Oh, and so is Cristobal's little *maison*, which is two tiny stories tall and has miniature drapes tied with gold rope in the upstairs parlor. From this angle Freddie's room doesn't look like a room. It's a *cocoon*.

"Your room's so pretty," I say tenderly.

He twists his head and smiles gratefully up at me. "I'm actually thinking about redecorating," he says. "Eggshell blue is so last year. What do you think about disco pink walls with a big mirrored ball in the ceiling?"

"Oh, that sounds fine." I shrug. I'm not really listening to him. I'm thinking about that darn movie about the girl and her nightclub.

"You think so?" he asks. "Well, I really *must* go home now. Cristobal's sleeping pill will be wearing off." He leans on my leg and pushes himself off the floor. "Night-night," he says, kissing the top of my head.

"Night-night." I smile. I start unpinning my wig. I go so far as to take if off and put it on its plastic dummy head. I go so far as to start unzipping Carmen.

Disco pink walls. I *hate* disco pink.

"Freddie!!" I scream.

"What?" He comes rushing out in his panty hose.

"Disco pink!"

"I *knew* you'd think it was an awful idea!"

"That's not what I mean! You *idiot!*" I rush over to his door. "Look!"

"What?" says Freddie. "What am I looking at?"

"Your room!" I tell him. I grab the door handle and close it. "My room!"

"Yes, well, that's all very interesting—"

"Your room." I open the door. "My room." I close the door again. "*Our* room!" I lean against the door and spread out my arms. "Freddie, don't you see? Our room. Our apartment. My nightclub!"

"Your *nightclub*? Really, our two rooms together aren't as big as the girls' powder room at Ultrasuede!"

"So what? It will be exclusive. It will be *truly* exclusive. We can bolt this door open and we can seal off your front door so they don't sneak in that way and we can use my front door as the entrance. We can use the kitchen as the coatroom and your kitchen as the bar and your bathroom as the bathroom—"

"But my loo doesn't have a door."

"We'll put a curtain up. Don't be so shortsighted. Everyone spends all their time at clubs in the bathroom anyway. This will be the first time the bathroom is the club! It will be *sensational!*"

I open the door and wander into his room. "We'll have to get rid of the bed, of course, and move some of this furniture out."

"But where am I going to sleep?"

"I don't know! Stop being a spoilsport. We'll think of something. Now, what about music? I'm not sure we should have any. Do you think music is still fashionable?"

"I don't think any *new* music is fashionable," Freddie says after a while. "We could have something really old. What about Herman's Hermits?"

"Oh, no, I think they're *too* old. We've got to be ahead of our time. Maybe Burt Bacharach. Burt Bacharach is back. He might be groovy.

We'll have to think about it. We're going to have to get a turntable. But we'll worry about that later." I sit on the edge of Freddie's bed and clasp my hands between my knees. "Won't it be fantastic?"

"It's silly." Freddie giggles. "We wouldn't make any money."

"Who cares about money?" I say sharply. "We're in this for the *prestige*. Running a nightclub is about the most glamorous thing a girl can do. Why didn't I think of it before? I'm going to call Hugo Falk right away!"

"Why?"

"He's going to have to write about me now!"

"I suppose we could charge a *bomb* for drinks," Freddie volunteers. "How many people do you think we could fit in?"

"You see, Freddie! You're already sold! You're already thinking of the great credit you could get in Marketing One and Two for this!"

"I could, couldn't I?"

"And you wouldn't even need to go to class. You could sleep in all day."

"When do we open?"

"Oh, Freddie, I love you!" I fling my arms around him. He feels like he's going to snap in two.

"Steady on," he says, straightening his shoulders. "There's rather a lot of things to think about."

"Don't be silly, there's nothing to think about. We'll do it by instinct."

"It would be rather a good excuse to run up a new outfit."

"You silly thing," I say, "who needs an excuse for that?"

# 31.

"I want to know *everything* about your club," Hugo Falk tells me in a corner banquette at Houndstooth. "Although I can't guarantee I'll write about it. There's a club opening every minute."

"Not like this one," I tell him. "My club is going to be more intimate. More intimate than you'd ever believe."

"Well, I admit there's something to be said for smallness. Large things are out of date. Like big paintings and grand gestures. I personally *like* trivial things."

"Oh, me, too!" I say enthusiastically, even though I don't have a clue what he's talking about. I flutter my eyelashes and smile deeply. If I gush all over him now, he'll gush all over me later in print. I'm instinctively good at being interviewed.

"Now what I usually do—may I call you Really?—is get my interviewees something to eat, and then we talk about life, death, the universe, and their favorite restaurants."

"You mean I have to talk with my mouth full?"

"It's more human, don't you think? And I can write things like 'She crossed her cutlery and uncrossed her legs.' It's part of my style. It's called juxtaposition. You said you liked my style, didn't you? Where is that captain? I hate to be kept waiting."

"I'm nervous," I tell him.

"Don't be," he says, and pats my hand. "Everyone likes being interviewed by me. It means they have my seal of approval. *Almost* my seal of approval. There are five stages to go through before a person reaches fabulousness in my estimation. This is only the first. But it's a *big* leap from just being any old nobody that I'd walk past in the street. Those girls over there, for instance." He nods in the direction of a table in the middle of the floor. "You'll notice that they're looking over here constantly. They know who I am, and naturally, because you are with me, they are curious to know who you are. They wouldn't give you a second glance if you were here by yourself."

"These stages of fabulousness. What are they?" I ask.

"Oh, let me see. There's looking fabulous. You've passed that test, although, if I may say so, there's something a bit *seventies* about that dress you've got on." Before I can defend myself—and Germaine, my Betsey Johnson "noise" frock with the grommets hanging off the hem—Hugo keeps chatting away. "Then there's *talking* fabulous—saying things that *sound* fabulous enough to attract people's attention, even if it's only for a few minutes at a time. You can skip the talking bit if you do something fabulous like take your pet boa constrictor with you everywhere you go—"

"Or run a club," I squeeze in hopefully.

"Yes, yes, but that depends on what sort of club."

"Oh, I *agree*," I say wholeheartedly. "What kind of club matters tremendously. You wouldn't be fabulous if you ran a club where the walls were covered in video screens. That was fabulous three years ago."

"I can see you are catching on," he says.

"Hugo, I know what fabulous is," I remind him. "Making decisions about fabulousness is my career. Being fabulous is my *life*."

"You might be right, but that's for me to decide."

"It is?" I bristle at this. "How come?"

"I don't know whether you're at the fourth stage of fabulousness yet."

"Which is?"

"The fact that you have to ask suggests that you're not."

"Well, Hugo, if you tell me what it is, I'll tell you if I'm at it!"

"It's not that easy. It's a certain *je ne sais quoi.* It's impossible to describe, even for a person like me who is so clever with words. I can never quite put my finger on it. It's a state of *being.* A state of being that makes you hold your breath. It's difficult to say more, except that whatever it is, it's *fabulous.*"

"Hugo, if it's that fabulous, how come there's one more step?"

"What one more step?"

"Five steps. You said there were five stages of fabulousness."

"Oh, *that.* Everyone knows what the last stage is. It's obvious. It's being fabulous once and then coming back to be fabulous again."

"You mean like Peggy Lee?"

"Precisely. Where *is* that captain?" He waves in the direction of a waiter in a black-and-white checked jacket and then holds up two fingers. The waiter nods and turns toward the bar. Eventually two dry martinis materialize in front of us.

"Hmm," says Hugo, sipping his complimentary drink. "Delicious. Free things always taste more delicious." He looks at me, suddenly intense. "You know, if you think we're just sitting at a corner table at Houndstooth sipping martinis, you're wrong. We're making martini sips in history."

"We are?" I ask. I pick out the olive carefully and drop it in the ashtray. He takes it out of the ashtray and dusts it off.

"You should keep everything. Even this olive. For posterity. I make a point of it. All my bits of paper, when I don't lose them. One day they're going to write a book about my life, and they'll need all the research material they can get. One day they're going to write

about me, and about you, and about everyone we know. We're going
to be a movement."

"Do you think we're a movement? Already?"

"If you're interesting enough, you're always a movement. Eventually. In hindsight. The trick is just to keep on going to the same
restaurants."

"But the restaurants never stay the same, Hugo. Why, Houndstooth was called Empire Line until a few months ago, when that look
went right out of fashion. And it was called Le Pouf before that.
Don't you remember?"

"Oh, yes. You're right. I do. It's tougher these days to be consistent, isn't it? It's almost as impossible as being original. Look at that
Bloomsbury set. All they ever did was wear paisley and lie around
under rugs on chaise longues. But they were the same chaise longues.
They lay around long enough for someone to stumble over them."

"I *am* keeping a scrapbook."

"You are? You'll have to show me. For the article."

Before I can pin him down about the article—now that he has
mentioned it without prompting from me—we are interrupted by a
smart woman in a red and black Adolfo rip-off of Chanel, who
whispers in Hugo's ear for a minute. He writes something down on
a table napkin. I can't make out what it is, on account of the fact that
every second check on the napkin is black.

"Now," Hugo says when the woman is gone. "What were we talking about before we were so rudely interrupted?"

"We were talking about the article."

"No, we weren't. We were talking about me being a movement.
My favorite subject. It's the last stage of fabulousness, being a movement. You can be a movement only in retrospect. It's the biggest
comeback of all. The problem is that not only will you not be around
to enjoy it, but your critics won't be around to know they've been

wrong about you. But that's how it goes. I believe everybody comes back. Everybody comes back in one shape or another to read their biographies."

"When they write these biographies—about us being a movement—are they going to write about what we are wearing?"

"Of course! That's the whole point. The whole point of *you* anyway. As for *me*, well, they'll certainly write about my suits. I'm *known* for my suits. You know that. Do you like my shirt? It's an original Ken Scott fried egg pattern. It's verging on the seventies, but I can get away with it, unlike you. But there's more to me than just my suits. I've got an extra layer, you know."

"Like a vest or something?"

"If you put it that way, yes. Posterity will recognize my vest. If there *is* any posterity. If the holocaust doesn't come."

"Oh, Hugo," I say sincerely, "there won't be a holocaust. I don't believe it!"

"You don't think so? I don't know what to think. Everybody said there wouldn't be a holocaust in 1936 and look what happened."

"Hugo, there *can't* be. I mean, can you imagine all those beautiful frocks hanging in closets all over the world with no one to wear them? It would be a *tragedy*. It's more of a tragedy when you think of all the beautiful frocks that are going to be made in the next thousand years. All those space age clothes in fabrics we've never heard of before, all those clever shapes we haven't dreamed up yet. Why, by the year 3000 they will have invented a frock with its own panty hose built in, or a gown that helps you lose weight. It's too much to think that we won't be around to enjoy wondrous things like that."

"You're right," Hugo says, smiling at me through gleaming tortoiseshell-framed lenses. "It's bad enough we live in a boring era, without having the chance to look back at it and pretend it was fascinating. You're an odd little thing, aren't you? You make me feel so relieved. I'm *so* glad I discovered you in that pet shop."

"Me, too," I say with feeling, not daring to correct him in case it breaks the mood.

"Don't worry," he says reassuringly, patting my hand. "History will recognize us for what we really are. I'll make sure of that." He lets his hand linger on mine. "I'm glad I can talk to you like this. You know, I almost forget that you're not famous."

Hugo finishes his martini and downs the rest of mine, and much later, when our food arrives, he helps himself to slices of my eggplant parmigiana and spoonfuls of my zuppa inglese and big slurps of my cappuchino alla romana. While he has his mouth full, I've taken the opportunity of chatting away about my frocks and the plans for my club and who is on the invitation list. He seems to be fascinated by everything I say. He keeps absolutely quiet while I talk. To fill in the silences while he's eating, I tell him all about Freddie and all about Phoebe and all about their intimate secrets. About Freddie's father being a policeman. About Phoebe's father's Reebok rip-offs. There's something about Hugo that makes you want to spill the beans. He looks so *trusting*. Which means he must be trustworthy.

"Promise you won't tell anybody what I just said?" I giggle after my third martini.

"Scout's honor," he mumbles as he sneaks the last sliver of my chocolate florentine.

He pushes his drink away and wiggles a finger at the waiter, who is beside us in a flash. "Here's your check. Pay it and let's go," he says to me.

He nods to the waiter to hand me the plastic tray. I turn over the piece of paper. The only thing I can make out is the total. Ninety-eight dollars. I feel like crying.

"Give him a generous tip, will you?" Hugo says as he gets up. "He lets me eat here for free, you know."

# 32.

We've finally decided to call the club The Closet. Freddie says it has a ring to it the fashion crowd won't be able to resist.

The decision has taken us days. We thought about calling it Reality's and then we thought about calling it Freddie's and then we squabbled for a bit. I pointed out to Freddie that I am the identity around here, I am the one who is going to be in Hugo Falk's column, and the club should be named after me. Like Régine. Like Bricktop. I'm the glamour element. Freddie got all hurt and said it was half his and nobody would come to a club called Reality's. It's *too* late sixties. Then I felt insulted and we fought some more and I said I was tired of him thinking of my apartment as an extension of his closet and then we both burst out laughing and that's how the club was named.

Tom is going to lend us his life savings from the refunds on soda pop bottles. Two hundred dollars. He says he doesn't mind being on the breadline for me. He was on the breadline before anyway, even when he was rich. He's used to it.

Freddie is trying to work out a way for us to make some money to pay Tom back in installments. But it's tricky. We're not going to charge anybody for coming into the club, and we're not going to mark up the drinks. It's a matter of principle. Stylish people deserve to be rewarded for being stylish. They don't deserve to be charged fifteen dollars for a margarita. Suits deserve that, but not girls in plastic miniskirts. As I'm letting in only stylish people—that's the house rule, never to be broken—we are not going to earn a *bean*.

Freddie says this doesn't matter. He says that once the club is a hit and I'm written about in all the magazines, we'll earn lots of money from endorsements. He says in no time we'll have our own fashion program on cable television and our own line of menswear and I'll license my name out to panty hose manufacturers and fragrance houses. Reality, he says, is a *fabulous* name for a line of fragrances. It could be the Charlie of the nineties. He's been speaking to Revlon already, in his new capacity as my press agent. Actually he's been *trying* to speak to Revlon. They haven't returned his calls.

# 33.

Freddie has found a sofa down on Avenue B that he thinks will be perfect for the club.

"You'll really love it," he is telling me as we walk quickly along the edge of Tompkins Square Park. "It's red vinyl, very sixties, with these *stupendous* buttons right in the middle of each cushion."

"Will it go with that chintz vanity chair you found yesterday?" I ask.

"No, it won't go at all. That's the point. The club's look is Poverty Deluxe. It's very eclectic. There's one thing I should tell you about the sofa, though." He coughs as we round the corner into Avenue B.

"Oh?" I ask.

"There are two chaps making love on it."

There are. Freddie is not exaggerating. Two old men in scruffy coats with their arms around each other. It's broad daylight and it's Avenue B on a Sunday, which means the avenue is scattered with people going in and out of the various fashion boutiques. The old men couldn't care less. It's sweet. One of them is out cold with a smile on his face, but the other one—all stubble-cheeked and toothless and reeking of Thunderbird—is lying on his side with one tattered trouser wrapped around his friend's leg. Somehow he has managed to undo the other man's trousers and is searching around in the old guy's underpants.

"What passion!" says Freddie, who is standing behind the sofa, looking down on the old men. A few other people stop to look and then walk on quickly. I think they've stopped because Freddie is wearing a bright red mohair sweater over a tweed micromini with multicolored striped leggings underneath and black lace-up combat boots. And a Hawaiian-print beanie. He's such a fashion leader.

"How are we going to get them off?" I ask. "I haven't got all afternoon."

"Yes, you have," says Freddie so smugly I could almost hit him. "You've always got all afternoon. Even when we open the club, you're going to have all afternoon." He goes around to the front of the sofa. "Excuse me," he says to the man who is awake, "would you mind awfully if we moved this couch?"

This has absolutely no effect. "I'll have to pull his legs," Freddie says.

"That's unkind," I tell him.

"Have you got any better ideas?"

"We could ask a cop."

"Look around you, Reality. Do you see any?"

"Not exactly *any*. No, I wouldn't say that."

"Maybe I could poke him with something. Here!" Freddie leaps across to the trash can on the corner and pulls out a broken umbrella. "I'll stick him in the ribs with this."

"Why done ya leave ush alo-one?" growls the old man when Freddie pulls at his collar with the handle of the umbrella. "We're jusht two guysh be-in' friendly." He grunts and tries to snatch the edge of Freddie's skirt.

"This is not working," says Freddie. "I wish I had brought Cristobal. He can bite, you know."

"Well, I'm not hanging around any longer," I say, and start to walk. "Maybe you can appeal to them as a fellow queer. Bye!"

"Reality!" Freddie screams. His voice goes up several octaves, and some ballplayers in the park turn around to look. "We've got to have this sofa! It will single-handedly make the club a hit!"

"Bye!" I repeat. I'm almost at the corner by now.

"Realit-eee!" Freddie's voice sounds high-pitched and pathetic.

"Yeeeoooowww!" I suddenly hear, followed by a crunching noise and a lot of scuffling. I turn around.

"I've done it!" Freddie calls out. "Get back here!"

He has simply gone around to the back of the sofa and pushed hard. Since the sofa has been resting precariously on the corner, one red vinyl foot in the gutter, it has been easy for him to tilt it so that the whole thing tumbles over. Both old men are now in the gutter. The unconscious one is still unconscious, smiling broadly, his active partner still holding him in an embrace. Freddie walks backward with one end of the sofa, and I take the other end, stepping over the former occupants. I can't believe it. The amorous one has got his tongue in his buddy's ear.

"Isn't it *splendid*?" Freddie says from his position at the front of the sofa as we carry it back along the park. "Don't you love recycling?"

Tom looks surprised when we get the sofa back to Fourth Street. "That there's Barney and Burt's bed," he points out.

"I knew we shouldn't have taken it," I tell Freddie later when we've placed it in his room and are testing out the springs. "Barney and Burt don't have anywhere to sleep now."

"There's lots of cardboard around." Freddie sulks. "You'd think they'd be pleased to donate it to a worthy cause. Besides, they don't care what they sleep on. They'd sleep on orange and green velour without a murmur. Whereas I wouldn't. I wouldn't sleep a wink on orange and green velour. I appreciate the stylistic importance of red vinyl, and they don't. It's elementary."

I must still be looking a bit doubtful, although I do see his point, because he adds, "If it makes you feel better, invite them to the opening. They'll be so grateful."

# 34.

"Interesting," Hugo says when I turn on the light in my apartment. I'm giving him a preview of the club for his article. He seems very curious. Before I can even put my purse down, he is over at the bath, investigating the rubber shower attachment. "How very *European*," he says. "I like to see how other people live. I like to see if they've got more things than I have. I knew you wouldn't have."

"Oh, have you got lots of things?" I ask as I throw my pocketbook in the bath. "What's your apartment like?"

"Very *moderne*," he says. "Very chic."

I wander into the bedroom. It appears to have been invaded by Freddie. Alice, my pale blue organza gown, is spread out on the bed, her skirt puffing out in the breeze from the window. While I pick her up, I can hear Hugo rummaging in the kitchen. "Is this what the club is going to look like?" he calls out to me. "I trust I'm the first to see it."

"Almost," I shout back.

Hugo strolls into the boudoir. "Almost what the club is going to look like or almost the first to see it?"

"Both."

"I want to make this clear, Reality. I'm not going to run the story if there's a chance of being scooped. I warn you, I'm used to having my own way. I'm not going to stick my neck out for you and get it trodden on."

"Do you like the decor?" I change the subject. "It's not nearly finished yet, but you can get an idea—"

"It's all right," Hugo says critically, running his fingers over a panel of wallpaper. "But I don't think I've got a jacket to go with these cabbage roses."

"We could do a wall for you, if you like. Maybe a tartan wall, to go with your Commes des Garçons suit."

"There's no need to bother," he says. "I would never be here long enough for it to be worth your while."

He disappears into the kitchen again. I hear him going through the gray filing cabinet I keep my pots and pans in. He must be looking at my photocopied mural of Veruschka because he calls out, "Have you seen her book? I have a personally signed copy." He wanders back into the bedroom and examines the painted plaster cherub on top of the water fountain where I stash brushes and pins and hair combs. "This reminds me of Rome," he says.

"When were you there?" I ask.

"Oh, I'm too busy to actually *go* there. But I've been invited. And naturally I've seen *La Dolce Vita*. Federico hasn't done anything I like since. I've told him."

"Do you *know* Fellini?"

"Of course. I know him very well. I went to his last press conference."

Hugo sits on the edge of the bed. He picks up Ralph, tosses him in the air, but doesn't try to catch him. "A poodle pajama case! Well, well. It's a bit *fifties* for a girl like you. You strike me as a very 1962 sort of person."

"Gosh"—I blush—"I suppose I am."

"You're very Antonioni."

"You think so?"

"Most definitely. You're almost fascinating."

"Oh," is all I can think of as a response to his compliment.

"Well, Reality," he says, tapping his fingers together impatiently, "I like your room. It's full of character. If I didn't like your room, I'd leave right away. As it is, even though I like your room, I've got to leave right away anyway."

"Why?" I ask, a bit hurt. "I thought we were going to go to a club."

"I don't like to spend *too* much time with one person. People might get the wrong idea."

"I make great coffee."

"All right, if you insist. You're lucky I'm drinking coffee this week."

"I'll just take off my shoes first," I tell him.

"You're short," he comments when I've put my stilettos in their sleeping bag.

"I'm almost five-five," I say defensively. "There's nothing short about five-five."

"Oh, yes, there is," he says, and slides off the bed. "Look." He stands so close to me I can smell the cigarette smoke on his jacket. And he's coming closer. My nose is now buried in the ruffle of his green dinner shirt. He is stooped over me as if he were sheltering me from the rain. Just hanging there like a big bit of mistletoe drooping off a tree.

"Do you like my shirt? It cost three hundred and ninety-five dollars."

"It's fab," I say, maneuvering myself around him. "How do you have your coffee?"

"Very black, very strong, very sweet in a small espresso cup with a twist of lemon on the side, thank you."

My idea of making coffee is to fill an old peeled tomato can with warm water and Maxwell House and let it stew away on the gas for hours. The can is a bit rusty around the edges, but no one has died yet from a cup of my coffee. In fact, I think the rust makes it taste richer. Hugo follows me into the kitchen.

"I can't drink that," he says, glaring at the can.

"I think I've got a Sleepy-Time tea bag somewhere. Or would you like a swig of brandy?"

"I'll take the brandy," he says. "I've got to stay awake. I've got several more appointments tonight. Tina. Jerry. Then Faye. She's one of my best friends."

"You've told me," I say.

"I have?" he asks nonchalantly. "Do you realize you've only got a can of Heinz strained vegetables and a mousetrap in this cupboard?"

"I like baby food," I say. "What's wrong with that?" Do I have to justify everything?

"You don't really catch mice, do you?"

"No. It's left over from the last tenant."

"Just as well. I wouldn't want to be best friends with a mouse killer."

"Are we best friends?" I ask.

"I'm considering it," he says. "What's that noise?" He turns around in surprise. There's a *commotion* coming from my closet.

"You can *hear* it?"

"Of course I can. It sounds like a troupe of flamenco dancers. It sounds like a troupe of flamenco dancers, and it's coming from over there." He strides into the boudoir and points to the curtain draped across the closet.

"Oh, it's nothing," I say.

It isn't nothing. It's my frocks.

I'm shocked that Hugo can hear them. No one else has ever heard my frocks before. Not even Freddie. They can be making a racket and Freddie will keep on chatting over the noise as if nothing were happening.

I'm trying to ignore them, but the rustling gets louder, as if a thousand caged birds were fluttering their wings against the curtain. I can hear silk swishing and taffeta squeaking and layers of net petticoats making loud pouf-pouf noises. I'm hearing the distinct scrapings of metal coat hangers rubbing against each other and the tiny sounds of shoes tapping their heels on the hardwood floor.

There's a particularly loud, rustling sound.

"It's a rat!" Hugo exclaims.

"No, it's not," I say carefully, watching for any reaction. "It's my frocks."

"Your *clothes* are making that noise?"

"Uh-huh." I'm embarrassed.

"How interesting!" he says, patting his pockets. "Do they make that noise on their own?"

"Sometimes."

"You don't have to wear them for them to make that noise?"

"Oh, no. They can rustle all by themselves."

"Without the wind?"

"Without the wind."

"This is amusing. I think I'll make a note of it. Do you have a pen?"

"There's one in your top pocket."

"I know that." He pulls a slim black titanium pen out of his pocket and sits on the bed.

"Do you want any paper?" I offer.

"Of course not. I lose bits of paper. My sleeve will do."

"But you'll ruin your shirt!"

"Oh, that doesn't matter. I've got hundreds of them."

I try to sneak a look at what he's writing.

"Don't!" he snaps, cupping his right hand over his wrist. "This is private. Now tell me. Why are your frocks rustling?"

"They like you." I don't know if this is true or not, but it's a good line.

"They *do*? What in particular do they like about me? Do they like my suit, for instance? What do they think of my shirt? I've never had a dress rustle for me before. They don't bite, do they?"

"Only if you yank the zipper."

"Oh, I wouldn't do that."

"Some boys do."

"Do they? It must be horrible being a girl."

"I like it."

"Why?"

"You get to wear frocks. Boys only get to wear boring things."

"Not necessarily."

I look at Hugo's butter yellow suit and green satin shirt. "Not necessarily," I agree.

"Can I meet these dresses?"

"I'll have to get undressed and put them on. They're shy."

"Fine." Hugo shrugs, as if he couldn't care less. One minute he's excited; the next minute he's bored. I don't get it.

"Do you want to go into Freddie's room? He's out."

"Oh, no," he says. "I can't be bothered."

I go over to the window and pull down the blind. I don't want the man across the way to see. One man at a time is enough. Even if Hugo doesn't really count as a man, strictly speaking.

Hugo stands there writing away while I peel Rita down over my knees and step out of her. It's a real effort getting out of plastic, and when I finally look up, I notice Hugo is staring at my body, somewhere between waist and neck.

"Don't you stick to that thing?" he asks.

"She gets a bit gooey."

"It must feel like walking around in a used condom," he comments.

I screw Rita into a tight bundle and put an elastic band—gently—around her.

"Don't they hurt?" he asks, bending over and putting one finger between my thigh and the garter on my diamond-front thirties step-in, as if my leg were a laboratory specimen.

"Sometimes," I say, and don't move away.

"Then why do you wear them?"

"Because they feel"—I blush to say it—"sexy."

"They hurt and they feel sexy?"

"Well—"

"How interesting. I knew you girls were strange."

Hugo twangs my garter like a guitar string. "I've never been up close to one of these before. Except on a drag queen."

I untangle his finger. He sighs and slides back onto the bed, with his legs crossed neatly. "I'm ready whenever you are," he says.

I go behind the curtain and start slipping into a pale yellow sundress. As I reach for the zipper, I hear Hugo making a phone call.

"Have you read my column?" is what I hear him ask as I smooth out the skirt and slip my feet into a pair of sling-back flatties. "Why not?"

"Da-da!" I announce as I step out of the closet.

Hugo says, "Don't go away," into the phone and squints at me.

"This is *Lolita.*" I do a sort of shimmy around the bed, like a rock and roll step without a partner. I flop down next to him on my stomach, with my chin in my hands and my legs crossed in the air. "Isn't she sweet?"

"Hmmm," he mumbles, and puts his hand on the side of my waist. "Nice fabric."

"Of course, she has to be worn with little white wrist gloves and heart-shaped sunglasses and that straw hat with rosebuds behind you on the bedpost. Where *did* I put those gloves?"

"Never mind," Hugo says. "I can imagine."

I go back behind the curtains and squeeze into a cute little

Lacroix-inspired number with cap sleeves and a short hoop skirt. She is my most headstrong frock and has been fairly bursting to get out of the closet. The hoop in the skirt propels me into the bedroom, and I have to hold on to the curtain to stop from stumbling. Hugo is whispering into the phone.

"This," I say as I catch my breath, "is Marie."

"Oh, yes?" says Hugo, burying the receiver in a pillow.

"She likes dancing," I explain. "When we go to—"

"I don't want to know about that. What I want to know, Really, is this. Does she actually say anything?"

"Of course!" I tell him. "Heaps!"

"Can she recite poetry? Could she talk into this phone?" He holds the receiver out to me.

"Oh, Hugo, that's not what I mean at all. She doesn't actually have a *voice*."

"What does she have? An intercom?"

"No, silly." I giggle, sitting down beside him. "She communicates without words. It's kind of spooky. She puts thoughts into my head. It's like having a little angel on my shoulder."

"Will she talk to me? Could I interview her?"

"Oh, no, that wouldn't be possible."

"What if I got into her?"

"All you boys ever want to do is wear my frocks!" I eye him suspiciously. "You don't, do you?"

"Don't what?"

"Don't want to get into my frocks?"

"Not if I can avoid it. I just thought she might talk to me if we were a bit—*closer*."

"Oh, that isn't necessary. I can interpret."

"Oh." He sounds disappointed. "Do you think my shirts talk to me?" he asks after a while.

"I don't know. Do they?"

"I don't know either. I have a lot of bespoke tailoring done. Do you think bespoke tailoring means that the shirts actually speak?"

"Why don't you ask them?"

"How would I do that?"

"I don't know. Just communicate."

"Oh, I can't *communicate*. That's why I became a writer. It's like a lunatic becoming a psychiatrist. At least that's what my psychiatrist says. Have you any other things that speak?"

"Oh, yes. Barbra's quite a blabbermouth."

"Introduce me then."

"Only if you're going to give her a mention. She's a prima donna. She'll be horrible to live with if you don't."

It's a complicated maneuver trying to wriggle out of Marie, who is reluctant to be taken off, and to zip up Barbra's sailor collar.

"Now what does Babs—"

"Barbra."

"What does Barbra think about the world? Does she have a point of view? Does she actually *think* anything about anything? This, incidentally, is one of my favorite questions to ask celebrities."

"Well, I'm not sure she has a point of view about the *whole* world. But she might have a point of view about *some* of it. I mean, she might have a point of view about shop assistants and coat hangers and people who are careless with their cigarettes. If you look at the world from a frock's point of view, you see an awful lot of dirty laundry."

"What dirty laundry?" Hugo asks, raising one eyebrow, pen and wrist poised.

# 35.

Freddie has done a wonderful job on the decor of The Closet. He has spent days scrambling through trash cans and Dumpsters to find exactly the right elements. The effect is startling. My bedroom looks almost exactly the same as it did before. Which is a relief. He's made it look authentic. He's made it look like an authentic girl's boudoir at the end of the end of the twentieth century. Which it is.

His room has undergone a total transformation, though. There's the red vinyl sofa square in one corner and a lot of black bikini chairs scattered around the place. There are red and brown boomerang-shaped ashtrays on his old boomerang coffee table. There's a curved black Naugahyde bar near his front door, quilted all over, with stools with high metal legs that are losing all their gold paint. There's a big rug tossed over the autumn-leaf carpet. It's got three camels on it and a view of the pyramids. There are some plaster Nubian slave lamps with shades the color and texture of taco chips. There's an Al Moore painting of a girl in a leopard-print bikini—called "Camouflage"—over the bath. Cristobal's *maison*, next door to the toilet, is now a miniature-scale model of Frank Lloyd Wright's Falling Water.

"Oh, Freddie, I love it!" I tell him after a quick inspection. "I feel totally at home."

"The best thing of all"—Freddie beams, digging a little red box out of his pocket—"is that we have our own matches."

# 36.

I've wanted a Chanel tattoo for *months*. And now that I'm going to be in Hugo Falk's column, now that I've having my own club, now that the decor's finished, I'm going to celebrate by getting one. A Chanel tattoo will make me chic and daring at the same time.

"I don't like this," says Freddie, who has taken a crisp white linen handkerchief out of his top pocket and is rubbing a layer of grime off the small window in the iron door. "It's illegal."

"It's not really illegal," I tell him. "It's just a bit unsafe."

"But they don't clean the needles," he says. "Anything might happen."

"Nothing's going to happen! Bad things don't happen to people who are on top of the world."

We're standing on Centre Street, scrutinizing a doorway.

"Well, I don't see a thing," says Freddie, peering through the circle he has made in the dust. "This can't be the place. Let's go home." Freddie isn't very comfortable down in the boondocks. You wouldn't be either if you were wearing a pink and apple green floral frock with a big straw hat on your head and little sling-back pumps on your size 12B feet and you are a boy. Cristobal is so frightened he's baring his expensive dental work.

At this point there's a scraping of metal on metal and the door is opened inward. A man's head appears in the gap and frowns at us.

"Goodness," says Freddie. Freddie says this because the man is completely bald except that his head is covered in a tattoo of hair, with a center part and all. The illustrated hair is dark blue, not quite black.

The man looks at Freddie and me and closes the door again. I knock on it. "He thinks we're the police," I tell Freddie.

"Since when did the police wear six-inch stilettos?" Freddie asks, looking at my feet.

"Don't be silly," I say. "They wear them all the time. When they're *undercover.*"

"A bobby would never do that," is what Freddie replies. Freddie is still annoyed about the time a plainclothes cop pushed him against a wall on Tenth Street and emptied the contents of his purse all over the sidewalk. "I had a dirty hairbrush in there, too," he told me afterward. "It was extremely humiliating."

I bang on the door harder, with two fists. The metal scrapes again, and the door opens. "What?" says the man ungraciously.

"Goodness," Freddie repeats, noticing in the same split second as I do that the man doesn't have a right ear, just a tattoo of one.

Before he can close the door again, I wave a piece of paper under his nose, which might also be drawn on. I can't tell from here. "Can you do this?"

He snatches the paper off me and turns it upside down.

"*This* way," I say, reaching in and turning it back up again. "It's two little *C*'s linked together," I tell him.

"Looks like horseshoes to me," the man says. He looks me up and down slowly. "It will cost you."

"How much?" I ask nervously. "I've only got twenty dollars." Freddie nudges me. He thinks I'm stupid to tell the truth.

"Regular tatts cost eighty. This is more."

"You mean it costs more for two teeny-weeny little *C*'s than it does for a whole Komodo dragon, or whatever you've got down your arm?" Freddie pipes in.

"Dragons are standard." The illustrated man goes to shut the door again.

"Wait!" I push my purse between the door and the doorjamb. I can hear my makeup mirror crack. "You've got to help!" I must sound desperate because the man opens the door wider, and we can hear that he's talking to someone behind him in the shop, but we can't hear what he's saying. We can see a whole bunch of yellowing newspapers stacked up on the floor and tied with twine, but that's all. Freddie and I exchange glances.

"Aw right," the man says grudgingly, turning back to us. "But for twenty she won't do no circle." He's pointing to the circle I've drawn around the two linked *C*'s.

Freddie grabs my arm, "You've got to have the circle!" he cries. "It's not the same without it."

"Shut up," I tell him. "I can always draw it in in ink." I smile at the man. "It's a deal."

He opens the door to reveal an old woman in a brown smock standing by a vinyl dentist's chair with a torn seat. The woman is almost a dwarf. She's got huge bifocal glasses on her nose, the lenses as square and thick as slices of toast and almost the same color. Freddie shrivels up a bit at the sight of the rusty electric needle she is holding in her hand but nevertheless says to her, to break the ice, "*Fab* glasses. Where did you get them?"

"You have to suffer for fashion," I tell Freddie as we are walking uptown afterward.

"Well, in that case, why did you beg her to stop after the first *C*?"

"She hit a nerve," I explain.

"You don't have nerves in your upper arm."

"Want to bet?" I pinch him hard. There's no fat on his arm, just flaps of skin.

"Ouch!"

"I'll draw the other *C* in pen. When the bleeding stops."

"It will wash off."

"Don't be such a wet blanket," I tell him. "Just because you fainted. Besides, as far as I'm concerned, half a Chanel is better than none."

Freddie looks at me with new respect. "You know, you're absolutely right." He squeezes my arm affectionately.

"Ouch!"

"*Sorry.*"


On our way up the Bowery, Freddie stops and looks in the window of a lighting store. He thinks we need more light in his room if it's going to be a nightclub. People won't be able to see the fabric in each other's frocks clearly enough, he says.

"Freddie?" I ask, after a minute.

"What? Do you think that nursery lamp would throw out enough light? I do love Dopey."

"Someone is following us," I whisper.

"What do you mean?" he asks, turning around sharply.

"I've just got a feeling. It's spooky."

"You're imagining things. Everyone's eyes are on you. That's all it is. They know who you are. They're all talking about the club. You're going to have to get used to it when you're a somebody."

"You think that's it?"

"I'm sure."

Out of the corner of my eye I catch a shape like a tent on feet disappearing into a doorway.

"I saw that, too," Freddie tells me casually. "It was only an artist carrying a canvas."

"Oh," I say. I'm almost disappointed.

# 37.

Hugo is three hours late for our next date. When I point this out to him on the sidewalk outside my apartment, where I've been standing since nine, he brushes some lint off his chartreuse shoulders and says, "You're lucky I bothered to come at all."

Hugo has with him a white-haired black-skinned boy called Ronald, who talks a lot and jiggles his shoulders but keeps his hands deep in his pockets. I tag along several paces behind them in Dolores, who is so tight tonight she's making me take two-inch steps while all the time in front of me Hugo and Ronald are deep in conspiracy about something.

By the time we get to the Boa Bar and Hugo has made a big fuss of Lilly, who is the drag queen on the door, and has sent over a bottle of Moët White Star (donated by the barman) to one of the cabaret performers—a boy with a Liza Minnelli haircut who is performing "Maybe This Time" on an Hawaiian guitar—and is generally kissing a lot of people on the cheek as he maneuvers his way to a barstool with the three boys trailing and me crushed between two twelve-inch-high hairdos in the rear, I am feeling a bit, well, *left out*.

I find myself a barstool. Several people stop to chat. To tell me how excited they are about my club. Something fizzy is passed down the bar from a blur in a tuxedo at the far end, and I drink it. Much later I am trying to warm a double brandy in a balloon—compliments of the house, of course—with a borrowed cigarette lighter when Hugo appears back at my side.

"Where's Ronald?" I ask although I'm not even the teeniest bit interested.

"Oh, somewhere. Maybe he's gone."

"Well, don't let me stop you—" I offer heroically.

"Look," he says, "if I had wanted to leave without you, I would have. Without a thought. Do you understand?"

"Well, there's no need to snap," I say.

He sits down splat on a stool that has been vacated by a boy in a cowboy shirt.

"You are supposed to be interviewing me anyway," I say. "Can we begin?"

"Oh, I'm not going to ask you any questions. I'm just going to *observe* you."

"Doing what?"

"I don't know. The sort of things you do every night. All of them. I want to observe you being yourself."

"Does that mean following me to the bathroom?"

"Oh, I don't think so. Unless you want me to go with you. Would you like that?"

"No, I wouldn't," I say, sliding off the stool. "I'll be back in a minute."

"I'll be here," says Hugo.

When I come back from the bathroom, Hugo is gone. Ronald is there, though.

"Have you seen Hugo?" he asks me, looking worried. "I need some cab fare home. You don't have any, uh, cash on you, do you?"

"Sorry, I never carry cash," I say, and Ronald shrugs and ambles off toward the men's room with his hands deep in his pockets.

"Thank heavens he's gone," says a voice behind me, just as I'm thinking of leaving myself.

"You said you'd be here, Hugo," I scold him. "And you were gone."

"I was just trying to get away from Ronald," he says, sitting down at the bar. I stand because there aren't any other stools. We're now about the same height. "It's always the trickiest part," he explains. "Getting rid of them."

"Why do you go out with them then?"

"I don't go out with *them,* if you don't mind. They go out with *me.*"

"All right, then, why do you let *him* go out with *you*?"

"Ronald's a reasonable person to be seen with. He's adequate in his place. He's a reasonably talented writer. But he's not talented enough for me. I couldn't have a really serious relationship with someone who isn't *extremely* talented. The trouble is, they all cling to me. They think I can help their careers. Which, of course, I can."

"Well, I'm not a clinging sort of person at all," I reassure him. "I'm very independent. I have dozens of boys chasing me, but I don't go out with any of them. Just like you. You don't think I'm clinging, do you?"

Hugo brushes my question away with his hand. "Oh, no. You're a girl. That's different."

"Why?" I feel a bit hurt, although I have no idea why.

"Because I don't have to think about a relationship with you. But I have to very carefully sum up every boy that comes my way before I'm even introduced to him. I have to estimate his fabulous rating straight away before I get into deep water. Now, take Ronald. He *looks* fabulous. He passes the first test. He doesn't say anything fabulous, but we can skip that as unimportant. The question is, Does he do anything fabulous? In order to establish that, I've got to have at least one date with him. He'll invite me up to his cockroach-infested tenement, and I'll look at his work. Now, if his writing is *passable,* I might see him a few times, but I'd hate all my critics to think that Ronald was my *boyfriend.* They watch my every step. If I were to date a writer, it would have to be no one less than Tom Wolfe."

"But he's not gay."

"I know that. Although you'd be surprised who is. Everyone, deep down, is gay. No, as relationships go, Ronald and his rather touchingly naive writings about pineapples are definitely second-rate. So I'd never take him to a really fabulous party, for instance."

"But you'd take him out on a date with me."

"Well, naturally. As far as anyone knows, he could be *your* date, not mine."

"But what if I don't want people to think Ronald's my date?"

"That's precisely my point."

I don't get it. "It's very involved, Hugo. When I go out with a boy, I never have to think of anything except how I look and how he looks with me."

"That's because your life is so uncomplicated. I'm sure it must all be very simple from down there."

"It's not simple at all! I've got so much to juggle! You have no idea! I've got to make sure I don't neglect Tallulah too much or she throws a tantrum, and there's the question of boring Françoise by wearing her to some tedious event, and even Doris sulks a bit if she isn't admired more than once in an evening. I have to keep tabs on all that. And then I've got to make sure I don't wear the same thing twice to the same club—imagine what it would do for my reputation!—and I've got to remember which frock I lent to Freddie last and make sure she's cleaned before . . ."

I drift off in mid-sentence because Hugo isn't listening. In fact, he isn't there. Between "Freddie" and "cleaned" he's plain disappeared, like a jelly stain in bleach.

# 38.

"Hugo Falk has been getting around." Phoebe drops into the conversation as we're liberating some hair accessories from a cramped little boutique on West Broadway. "He's been seen out with a few other girls lately. I happen to have it on good authority."

"What other girls?" I try to be nonchalant about this, as nonchalant as I am about slipping a crocheted snood into my pocket.

"Oh, Ricci and Bambi and Margie from Cummerbund. There are *lots* of them." Phoebe is almost smiling.

"Oh, *them*." I shrug. "Hugo is just observing them. He's observing everyone who has come into contact with me in the last few years. I suppose it's what he calls background."

"I saw Hugo with Biba last night when I was walking Cristobal," Freddie tells me over takeout scones and preserves in his room. "In the salon. *Very* late. *Alone.*"

"Oh," I say calmly, "he's only talking to Biba because she does my hair. He's not the type to be interested in a hairdresser. A girl hairdresser. A girl hairdresser with a big nose."

"Hugo was around here yesterday," says Faille as she takes my order for Swedish pancakes at midnight.

"What did he want?" I inquire.

"Among other things," she says, "he wanted to know what you eat."

"You see," I tell Freddie later, "he's researching me."

He's following me, too. I feel it in my bones. I think I keep on catching his reflection in shopwindows. I know I keep spotting him slipping into doorways. Out of the corner of my eye I'm sure I keep seeing him scuttle across the street like a dried-up leaf in the wind. Every time I walk past a phone booth, I'm certain he's in it.

I don't mind. I could get used to being followed. It's almost erotic.

The only thing is, the last time I caught a glimpse of Hugo out of the corner of my eye, I could have sworn he was wearing a frock. A big frock, like a tent. I didn't think he'd go *that* far.

# 39.

Freddie has just finished tacking grosgrain ribbon along the baseboard, and Phoebe is running her finger along the windowsill to make sure there's no dust. I'm looking in dismay at all my frocks, which are scattered in big puffballs of net and creamy lace from one end of the room to the other.

"That's enough, you two," I say in exasperation. "The club is *off*."

Freddie looks startled. He's still on his knees on the floor. "What do you mean, it's *off*? This is rather sudden. Don't you like the room?" he asks. "You've been saying you *loved* it all week."

"That's not it! It's worse than that! It's worse than *anything*! Nothing worse than this could happen. It's the worst thing I could possibly think of. And now it's *happened*!"

"Shut up, will you?" says Phoebe sharply, wiping her finger on the new drapes. "What's happened? What are you hollering about?"

"I've got nothing to wear!" I wail.

"Don't be ridiculous," says Phoebe. "You've got a closetful of things."

"That hasn't got anything to do with it," I tell her. "You should know that."

Phoebe should know that you can have a closetful of frocks and still have nothing to wear. They do not cancel each other out. I don't know why I need to explain this. It's as clear as day.

When I say I have nothing to wear, I mean that I have nothing to wear that is *exactly* the thing to wear in those *exact* circumstances. I have nothing to wear—*nothing*—because I am seeking the thing to wear that belongs absolutely to that one moment when fashion and occasion and mood come together in space and time. Anything else than that one thing would be, well, failure as a woman. I am a woman, and to wear the wrong thing at the right moment or the right thing at the wrong moment is like taking the wrong door on West Fourth Street and ending up in a leather bar. What could be easier to understand than that?

"Calm down," says Freddie, who is still on his hands and knees attending to the grosgrain. "Why don't you try that pink thing? Pink is your lucky color after all."

"She's such a show-off," I protest.

"Well?" asks Phoebe, who is trying on one of my bracelets. "What are you waiting for? She sounds perfect."

This is not the first time I suspect Phoebe of being jealous of me. I slip into Blanche anyway, but I can't find her ruffled stole.

"Too much," says Freddie right away. "What's that apricot thing over there?"

That apricot thing is Myrna, and she's a long satin slip, cut on the bias, with little shoestring straps. I pull Blanche off—it's quite a struggle, she likes to be the center of attention—and slide into Myrna.

"Your stomach is sticking out," is all Phoebe has to say, and I'm out of Myrna in a *second*.

"What about this?" I ask, and show them Sonja, a little red velvet flared skating dress with white fur trim.

"Hmmm," says Freddie, his arms crossed. "Perhaps with a crinoline." I put on a triple-layer white petticoat. "Hmmm," says Freddie.

"Do you have another one?" I step into a crinoline made of stiffened net with little rosebuds around the hem. "Hmmm, not bad," says Freddie. "But you need a hat." I take out a black velvet hat in the shape of a snail's shell. "Hmmm, that might do," he says.

"She can't wear *that*," says Phoebe, who has on a copy of the black wet-look pantsuit Audrey Hepburn wore in *Two for the Road*. "It looks like she's trying too hard."

"But I'm supposed to be trying hard, aren't I?" I ask as I unwind. "It's my club. I've got a reputation to live up to."

"That may be true," says Freddie, who is going through my hat basket and trying on different styles. "But if you look like you care, your career is finished. Phoebe's right. Take it off."

"They're expecting you to look sensational," explains Phoebe. "But they're not expecting you to do it *intentionally*."

"So you think I should just toss on something casual?" I ask. "This mohair sweater? Maybe over my dirndl petticoat with—let's see—that foxtail boa around my neck?"

"Goodness, *no*," says Freddie. "You can't afford to be *random*. From now on everything you wear has got to be planned—"

"To the split second," says Phoebe.

"To an inch of your life," says Freddie. "If they see you Monday night in anything short of *stunning*, you'll be ruined."

"I know." I groan. "What have I got myself into?"

# 40.

I go to Saint Martha's to light a candle to the Holy Virgin to pray for her to help me find a frock. I need a miracle. The club is opening in two nights, and I still have nothing to wear.

Eunice is kneeling in the front row. She gives me a tense nod. She looks as if she thinks I'm going to bite her. I bend over and whisper in her ear, "Where did you get those *fab* rosary beads?" just to show there's no hard feelings. I trot down to the altar, chose the prettiest candle, and light it with a match from a box of The Closet matches, just for good luck. I'm wearing my Cinderella charm bracelet and one of Hugo Falk's black hairs, which I picked up off the bedspread and have been carrying around ever since. I'm hedging my bets.

I'm glad the Madonna is a girl. I'd have less confidence praying to a male saint.

Freddie is waiting for me outside with a stack of posters he has put together to advertise the club and has photocopied at FIT.

"What about this lamppost?" he asks me, fighting his way through a pile of plastic trash bags outside the church. "Is it prominent enough?"

I remind him that everyone walks past Saint Martha's on Sunday to the weekly jumble sale at Saint Teresa's next door.

"Help me, will you?" Freddie hoists himself up onto the lid of a metal trash can and grabs the lamppost for support. I slip the posters out from under his arm and position one of them on the post. Freddie balances himself and gets the masking tape out of his pocket. When he's finished, he asks me how it looks.

"It's a bit crooked, but that doesn't matter. It's very arty." I step back a pace. "It's *fabulous*," I say sincerely.

It is. It's a blowup of one of Freddie's old snapshots of me, all contrasty from being photocopied. I'm moving my head, so my face is blurred and my hair is jagged and wispy like a pineapple top. You can't see much detail in my face, except for the stripes of Glamour Lash and a smudge that is my mouth. Freddie has cut out newspaper type and composed the letters to read:

THE GIRL OF THE MOMENT
THE CLUB OF THE CENTURY
THE NIGHT OF YOUR LIFE

It doesn't say anything else. Not a date. Not an address. Freddie has taken the front table at Café Orlon each afternoon for the past week and is spreading the word to everyone who drops by. This is the way we can exert some quality control on our guests. We don't want a whole lot of suits cluttering up the hallway with their Burberrys and smelling up the staircase with Obsession.

"It's very professional," I say approvingly.

"You think so?" Freddie steps back to have a better look. He forgets that he is standing on a trash can. "Oh, dear!" he says, and wobbles madly, trying to catch his balance. He tumbles off but makes a soft landing on a garbage bag. The trash can rattles to the ground, and the lid rolls into the gutter with a clatter.

"Are you all right?" I rush to pick him up.

"Just embarrassed," he says, rolling off the trash and getting back on his feet. He bends down to pick up the masking tape. His body freezes. "Look at this!" he exclaims, and starts rummaging around in the open trash can. He's got a piece of black fabric in his hand. A piece of black fabric and some pink organza. He keeps pulling at it, like a magician plucking silk handkerchiefs from a hat. Finally he stands up and shakes the fabric out.

It's a frock. Not only is it a frock, but it's almost the exact frock Anita Ekberg wore in *La Dolce Vita*. It's strapless and shapely with six panels of pink organza—shocking pink and petal pink combined—floating from the hips.

"It's a miracle!" I laugh, picking up the panels and tossing them in the air with delight.

"It certainly is." Freddie sighs, pressing the frock against his body. "It's a bit big in the bosoom, but it looks like it was made for me!"

"What do you mean?" I say crossly, dropping the panel I have in my hand. "It was made for *me*!"

"Oh, no," says Freddie, moving away. "I found it."

"That's irrelevant. I was *supposed* to find it. It was waiting for me. It is the answer to my prayer. The Madonna has sent me a frock. If I hadn't asked you to meet me here, I would have found it all by myself. You weren't supposed to at all! It's my miracle! Give it to me!" I try to snatch it off him.

Freddie holds on to the waist and refuses to let go. My blood is boiling. "You're lucky you aren't a Catholic," I tell him. "You'd go blind or something."

"Prove it's a miracle!" he yells at me. He has the waist and I have the hem. I'm not pulling too hard because I don't want to hurt her. "It's *mine*."

"All right, then, I will! Does she have any coffee stains on her?" I ask, looking at the fabric. "Any egg yolk? Any *wine*?"

Freddie yanks the hem out of my hands. He turns away slightly and examines the frock. "No," he says suspiciously, turning back to me, the frock partly hidden behind his back. "It's spotless."

"Then it *is* a miracle," I say confidently. "That proves it!"

# 41.

I'm fifty minutes away from opening the most fabulous club in the neighborhood. Which means, the most fabulous club in the world. It's going to be so drop-dead everyone will *die*.

I'm putting the final touches to my outfit—sewing new fastenings into the back of my "miracle" frock, Anita—when Freddie bursts into the apartment with Phoebe wafting behind him. He's been downstairs buying some ice. He drops the bag of cubes onto the kitchen floor with a crack and runs into my boudoir, his ermine-lined Liberace cape flapping behind him.

"There are *dozens* of people out there!" he pants. "And it's only eleven o'clock."

"Put on some music, will you?" Phoebe says impatiently from inside a flamboyant taffeta cape, which she flings on the bed to reveal a pink and silver fitted party frock with a skirt like spun candy. A marcasite tiara is snuggling amid a cone of twisted brown hair. "A club without music is ridiculous."

"Tom's not letting them into the building until you give the word," Freddie interrupts. "He's says they're getting difficult. I said I'd ask you if you wanted him to open the downstairs door yet."

"What do they all look like?" I ask, stepping into my frock. I always try to step *into* my frocks rather than pull them over my head—that's what professional models do. "Are there any suits?"

"A few Italian ones."

"With the sleeves pushed up?"

"No."

"Thank goodness. Are there any *somebodies*? Is Jackie O here? Did you get that invitation to her?"

"Hand-delivered to the Carlyle," Freddie says efficiently.

"I expect she'll come later. She's probably still dining at L'Acajou. Tell Tom he can start sending the others up the stairs. They can stay in the hallway for a while. No one's coming in here for at least half an hour. I've still got to do my hair."

"Righto," says Freddie, and dashes out again.

"Now," I say to Phoebe when he's gone, "tell me how fabulous I look."

The club has been designed so that it has not just one door but three. I think it increases the frustration. Which increases the relief and therefore the good time people have when they finally get in. There's the door on the street that has a glass porthole covered in wire mesh and leads to another door that's plain battleship gray painted metal. It's very neoindustrial.

The club doesn't look like a club at all. It looks like an apartment building. Freddie has scratched a tiny THE CLOSET into the metal door, nevertheless, as a hidden clue.

The idea is that Tom lets them in downstairs and they then come up to the second floor and huddle around the door to the apartment. This is the real club door. It's the hardest one to get through. Just because you get up the stairs doesn't necessarily mean you get through the last door. It's the final frontier.

Unfortunately, during the day, the neighbors have gotten wind of what is happening. They don't seem very pleased. I don't understand why. They should be ecstatic that our building has finally made a leap into the big time. Freddie says that when I'm famous, someone will put a plaque on the outside of the building, the way they did on that old painter W. H. Auden's place on Saint Mark's. I'd like to see the neighbors complain then. If they're lucky, walking tours of the East Village will stop by here and they all can hang out their windows and be photographed.

Freddie has calculated that we can fit only about one hundred people into the hallway at a time. Why, one hundred people clopping up and down the stairs is hardly a disturbance at all. Even if some of them are wearing tap shoes. We will know it's time to close the door when the club gets so crowded the guests are standing in the bathtub. Freddie thinks the bathtub may well be the best seat in the house. You can see everything from there, if you push the plastic gliding swan shower curtain aside.

One of the best things about Freddie's design for the club is that I can lie on my bed and be on the door at the same time. I've practiced. The plan is this: Every now and then Freddie will open the door to the hall and I will survey the crowd. If three people leave at this point, three people can come in. It will be a breeze. I don't think a proprietor of a club should be seen on the door; she should be found lounging inside as if she doesn't have a care in the world apart from looking glamorous. The truth is, I don't trust anyone else to be on the door. Even Freddie. I wouldn't say this to his face, but he gets some very weird ideas about brocade sometimes.

Phoebe goes over to the record collection. "What's all this?" She screws up her nose and picks up the corner of an album as if it were a dead mouse. "Where's the Henry Mancini?"

"We don't have any," I say, sitting in front of the vanity table. "Come and help me put this wig on, will you?"

Phoebe mumbles something and spins "These Boots Are Made for Walking" on the turntable. "Why don't you have a tape deck, for heaven's sake?" she asks.

"Tape decks are OUT," I say. "So are compact disks. The only things that are IN are twelve-inch records."

"And twelve-inch hair," says Phoebe, going over to my vanity and picking up one of my wigs.

"I'm not wearing that," I explain. "I'm wearing a long blond wig tonight."

"Hurry up and put it on, then, and let's get this place *jumping*," says Phoebe impatiently. "I'm bored already."


I know The Closet is going to be a hit the minute Biba walks into the room, tosses her Dynel ponytail, and says to me, "This is *groovy*." Hairdressers always know these things.

I'm lying on the bed surveying the fifty people I've let in so far. It's a fabulous crowd, beautifully turned out.

There's a black Stephen Sprouse T-shirt with safety pins holding the sleeves together and a short black zippered David Cameron jacket with a flared zippered skirt. There's a black strapless denim frock with snaps down the front and an ebony-colored taffeta evening stole over an old black lace Calvin Klein. There are three black leather biker's jackets from the Antique Boutique. There's a black Norma Kamali jersey evening frock with ruching down the side and an inky sort of cape with ostrich-feather trim. There are at least four frocks, circa 1962, with tiny shoestring straps and an elastic Azzedine skirt with suspenders crossing a black bodysuit. Someone is wearing a divine pair of long black leather gloves that come up right under the armpits. There's a twenties shift, shimmering with jet

bugle beads and several black turtlenecks worn with corduroy jackets and stovepipe trousers. There's a pair of spurs which scrape
Freddie's grosgrain off the baseboard in places and an enormous
black picture hat that never makes it out of the kitchen.

It's a low-keyed sort of night. Which is exactly how it should be.
It's intimate. It's exclusive. Everyone is content to move around the
room and look at everyone else. Except me. I lie on the bed without
once getting up, in a swirling sea of pink chiffon. People come to me
and tell me how fabulous everything is. I'm the center of the room.
I'm the center of a room that's in the center of the universe. Which
means I'm the center of the universe and all these people are black
satellites revolving around me. A girl could get dizzy.

"Reality!" someone calls from the kitchen. It's Faille, in a Pucci print
that looks like it once was the uniform of some foreign airline.
"There's a person here who wants to see you!"

"Who is it?" I call back. "Is it Jackie O?"

It turns out the person is Consuela, who is one of my neighbors.
She's standing in the hallway in an old brown print frock with the
ties trailing on the ground. She has pink furry slippers with bells on
the front. She's holding her baby tight against her chest and patting
him on the back. He's hiccuping.

"What is it, Consuela?" I ask, annoyed at having to push my way
through the crowd smoking Ritz cigarettes in the hallway. "I'm having a party."

"My baby," she says, and pulls him away from her body to show
me. He's got egg yolk all over his mouth.

"Ooh," I cringe. "Put him away." I never did like those floppy
baby dolls. I only liked Barbies and ones that had plastic bodies you
could hold firmly while you did up the buttons.

"My baby," she repeats. "He no sleep."

"He no sleep? What's that to do with me?"

"He no sleep all night. You party."

"Oh, I see," I say. "Don't worry, Consuela. He'll get used to it. Cristobal has already."

"No more sound?" Consuela asks hopefully.

"That's silly. Of course, there'll be sound. We're running a night-club here, you know. Now, I've got to go. My *public* is waiting for me."

Consuela's baby gives an ear-piercing shriek. She's worried about the noise *I'm* making?

"Please," Consuela says. "No noise."

"All right," I say grudgingly. "I'll turn the stereo down."


It's 5:00 A.M. and several people are still frugging at the end of the bed, to Zira and Cornelius's love theme from *Planet of the Apes*. Freddie goes over to the stereo and puts on the sixth Burt Bacharach selection for the night. The tempo of the party is slowing down. Tom's friends Barney and Burt are having a great time, flat out in the middle of the floor with their arms around each other. People have given up stepping over them a long time ago. They are now stepping *on* them.

Freddie comes over to me and collapses on the edge of the bed. "Do you want me to start getting rid of some of these guests? I could put on Richard Harris's *Love Album*. That will send them screaming into the night!"

"I can't understand it," I say to Freddie as I slide over to sit beside him. "Hugo hasn't come. I wonder where he is. I hope nothing's wrong."

"Don't be silly, Reality. You know Hugo, he's probably forgotten the address. He's probably in some bar right now taking notes. He's probably at Faye Dunaway's for dinner. Hugo could be anywhere, doing anything. He's that sort of person."

"But he should be *here.* This is the highlight of the social year. I want him to see me in my element, surrounded by adoring fans. Do you realize there are twenty-three hairdressers here? It's a very important party. And I wanted so much for him to see me tête-à-tête with Tina, talking about her costume collection. That was a great moment. A great moment that should be captured in print. And now she's gone. Oh, I wish he'd just get here!"

"Don't worry about that, dear one." Freddie consoles me. "I'm your press agent. We can always do it again. Stage it. Get Tina back tomorrow. She won't mind. I've always preferred artificial setups to anything *natural* anyway. I hate natural."

"Me, too." I shudder, a flash of my mother's unmade-up face zipping through my mind. I sigh. "Why does that Hugo Falk always make me feel like a sweater that's been put on inside out? You know? Whenever he's around, I always feel like I'm showing the wrong side of me to the world. But when I feel I'm all in place, like tonight, with all the labels neatly tucked away, he's never here to notice. Why is that? He's like scratchy wool against skin. It's *spooky.* I can't explain it. Do you get psychic later in life like you get diabetes? I wonder."

"Stella's just this minute walked in. Why don't you ask her?" is what Freddie suggests, nodding in the direction of the door.

# 42.

I didn't think it would be *this* much work running a club. I've got so much to do. When I get up in the afternoons, I have to make the bed and tidy up the apartment and make sure my frocks are tucked away behind their curtain so no one will see them. I have to sweep the floor and brush all the debris into the hall. Of course, when we're more successful, I'll have someone to do that for me. In fact, I'm going to hire someone to do that tomorrow. I don't think it's right for me to sweep up. It doesn't give me time to be creative.

The major part of my day is spent deciding what to wear. There's a lot of pressure on me about this. To look fabulous. It can take hours to find exactly the right thing. I love lying in bed and thinking about my frocks. It's the best part of the afternoon. But it can be *traumatic.* If the very thing you want to wear needs a dry-clean, for instance. It's shocking you can't get one-hour dry-cleaning around here. It would make my life so much more simple. But I have to live with it.

Today I went and had a pedicure. I recommend Macy highly. I've put a whole stack of her cards in the ashtray. I had to be back here in the afternoon, though, to answer all the calls that are coming in. People *begging* me to be invited tonight. The club has become a *phenomenal* success. Third Street is simply *buzzing*.

Once I am dressed, I have to attend to the flower arrangement and help Freddie move the furniture around and make sure there's someone to supervise the door downstairs. Tom sometimes goes down to the Bowery and he loses all sense of time. Some drunk stole his watch last week. And then, all of a sudden, it's midnight and there's a *flood* of people at the door and I have to lie here and tell them to come in or go away. I don't usually get to bed until at least seven.

I think it's going to be *exhausting* having a club.

# 43.

There are twelve people in the club, trampling all over the new old rugs. Phoebe. Freddie. The photographer's assistant. The photographer's assistant's assistant. The stylist. The stylist's assistant. The makeup artist. The hairdresser. The manicurist. A senior editor from *Frenzee* magazine. A messenger who has arrived with an armful of frocks. I'm about to be photographed for Hugo's story on me. I'm very nervous. I took three sleeping pills last night and tossed everyone out of the club at six so that I won't have bags under my eyes today.

The senior editor has called ahead to arrange the sitting. It's been a week since we opened the club, and I haven't heard from Hugo. He must be busy. It's a relief to know he's actually writing something. I mean, they wouldn't go to all the trouble of photographing me if he wasn't.

The stylist, whose name is Amy ("The *first* Amy on the masthead," she points out when we're introduced. "The six other Amys are all below me. Do you think I should change my name?"), signs the messenger's delivery book and takes the frocks from him. "Peace," the messenger says to Freddie, who has been standing in the kitchen to make room for the delivery.

Freddie comes back into the boudoir. This is not as easy as it sounds. There are so many people, props, lights, makeup kits, wigs, clothes racks in the room that Freddie's return has been like a corset being laced up: You breathe in and pull on the laces in the middle and hope that nothing is going to pop out the top. The pressure is relieved a bit by Barry, the makeup artist, who says he must go to the bathroom for a pee. So he sidesteps the camera cases, pushes his way behind the clothes rack, and edges along the wall until he gets to the doorway at the same time as Freddie is edging around him, behind the clothes rack, over the camera cases, and into the unoccupied plastic chair. I wince when Barry tramples on my favorite pair of cork wedgies.

Several people in the room think they are in charge of the shoot. For a start, there is the senior editor, a woman called Hattie, who is standing in the corner by the blacked-out window with her arms crossed, chain-smoking long, thin cigarillos, which she keeps in a silver case in her top pocket. She holds the cigarillo exactly the same way Phoebe holds hers, with her palm upturned and flat and the cigarette laced through her fingers. It must be the way they do it at fashion magazines. It must be *the* way to hold a cigarette. I always take note of details like this. They're part of the fabric of life.

The hand that is holding the cigarette is trembling wildly. Hattie is making all sorts of comments from her corner. "I don't think so." She shakes her head when Amy holds up a hat. "Too dreary." "Can't you get rid of that shadow?" she asks when the photographer's assistant finishes fiddling with a big light, the sort you see in movies about old movies. "She needs more blush," she calls out as Barry comes at me with a big powder puff. The funny thing is, Hattie is calling out all these directions from her corner and no one is paying the slightest bit of attention to her. The other funny thing is, she doesn't seem to care or notice, just keeps on standing there lighting up cigarillos, only occasionally moving in closer to peer over some-one's head at a Polaroid or the amount of shine on my nose.

Barry, the makeup artist, also seems to think he's in charge of the shoot. He's completely monopolizing me, taking *hours* just to smudge a bit of kohl under my eyes and brush my eyebrows. The lipline takes *forever.* He applies a curler to my eyelashes and then some mascara and repeats the whole thing *six* times. And then he decides to start all over again. As he's wiping off the foundation with big globs of cold cream, everyone else in the room is screaming at him to hurry up. This just makes him go slower. He's muttering to me all the time, clicking his tongue and saying things like "They're so impatient" and "Don't they recognize an artist at work when they see one?" When he is close to the finish—blotting my nose with a tissue and reapplying some white powder—he turns to Hattie and says, "Don't blame *me* if she looks hideous in the picture."

Then there is the hairdresser. He's an ugly guy with a mop of black, curly hair, and his name is Rusty Hanes. Rusty has swarthy skin, all pockmarked and oily, and black eyes like the shiny pieces of jet on the necklace Phoebe gave me for Christmas and then took back again at Easter. He is not very tall, but I notice he is wearing high-heeled snakeskin cowboy boots under his black leather trousers, which have a *lace-up* fly. He has a *very* hairy chest, and the hairs are so long they are tangling up in wet ringlets. I can tell this because he is wearing a white ruffled cotton shirt—like one of those Tom Jones nightshirts—unbuttoned right down to his waist and because he is sitting on my lap with his chest almost in my face.

Rusty has come up to where I am sitting under the light and just plopped down on me and made himself comfortable without even saying a word. I should say here that I am just in my peach satin slip—the one with the old coffee-colored lace edges—and my cone-shape bra because I am waiting for Amy to iron the frock it ap-pears I am going to wear in the photograph and Rusty's hot black leather is grinding into my thighs. I look around to see if anyone will protest and catch Phoebe's eyebrow. She's blowing little smoke rings on her cigarette and looking at the ceiling thoughtfully as if seeking the right word for her IN and OUT page.

I'm finding it a bit difficult to know what to do with this maniac who has me pinned to the chair and has started to run his hands wildly through my hair, fluffing it up and pulling at my scalp and turning my head to the side to see the way that it falls. This goes on for ages, possibly longer than Barry's eyelash curling and certainly longer than it takes for me to get dressed most mornings. Is this hairdressing or pornography?

"Excuse me," I say eventually, "my leg's gone to sleep."

"Fantastic," he whispers huskily in some sort of accent that makes the "fantastic" sound like "funtasteek." "Your hair is fantastic."

"Thank you," I say. He's looking me directly in the eyes now, pressing down on my thighs even harder, wedging his hips into the bend where my top half meets my bottom half.

"And you are so beautiful. So—fantastic, really fantastic."

"Thank you. Would you mind shifting your—"

"I think we could make *fantastic* music together."

What is strange about what Rusty is doing to me is the fact that nobody else seems to notice. He's grunting and he's groaning and his leather pants are creaking as he continues to rock up and down on me and run his fat fingers through my hair. No one else is paying the slightest bit of attention. I know, because I look around in embarrassment to see if anyone can tell I'm blushing. I'm blushing so hard I'm sure my face has gone the color of my hair. Freddie is helping Amy iron the frock while Amy's assistant, also called Amy, is experimenting with some of Barry's eye shadow in a handheld mirror. The photographer's assistant is doing something to an outlet that looks dangerous. The assistant's assistant is taking orders for coffee and sandwiches. Phoebe is still looking at the ceiling. Hattie is lighting up a cigarillo. Barry is on the phone—to Cuba, I think. I try not to think about that. The manicurist is doing my toenails. Cristobal is sound asleep on the bed.

It seems like hours later that Rusty's pants stop creaking and I'm handed an oval mirror. I scrutinize every inch of my visible skin. I notice that my fingernails are now pearly pink. I hate pearly pink. This kind of pearly pink anyway. The kind that separates out into swirls. I hold the mirror up to my face and examine my hair at the front. It doesn't look as if he's done *anything*. I turn my head to the side. Not a *thing*. I don't know if I'm relieved or disappointed.

"It's . . . *nice*," I say to Rusty timidly.

Hattie comes over. "More *height,* Rusty," she says urgently. He gets out a tail comb and starts teasing. Everyone watches with bated breath. It's like watching one of those Japanese chefs chop sushi. When he finishes, I have a little mound on top of my head. He pins a tiny black bow to the center of the bouffant bit. I look like the prizewinning Shih Tzu in a dog show.

"It's *very* Cilla Black," says Freddie. "I think it's fab."

"But is it *me*?" I ask. I think it's a little preppy for my taste.

"Well, it's mod enough," says stylist-Amy critically, one finger on her chin. "It might work. But you can't wear that dress with it." She tilts her head toward the black-and-white polka dot frock assistant-Amy has over her arm. "You'll have to wear that aqua wool suit."

"But I hate aqua!"

"So?"

"I thought I was going to wear my own frocks. I thought this was a story about *me*."

"Don't be silly," pipes in Phoebe. "You're so naive. It's a story about what the advertisers are doing for winter."

"Actually," says Freddie, clearing his throat, "I'm Miss Tuttle's press agent. I want her in her own things. She won't do the picture unless she wears them."

I give Freddie a startled look.

"But what about the advertisers?" protests Hattie. "You can't credit that old thing." She is pointing to the suede fringed vest on the bed I was wearing when they all arrived this afternoon, which seems like a *decade* ago.

"Turn it into a beauty picture then," says Freddie cleverly. "Estée Lauder will be *so* pleased with the mention."

That seems to cheer up Hattie. She goes back to her corner. Barry goes back to the phone, and I hear him ask the operator to connect him to Bahrain. I hope that is a town in the Midwest. I try not to think about it. Rusty is wrapping the cord around his big blow dryer and putting it away. I look at his pockmarked face and matted chest—and at his fly. The top few laces of his leather pants are undone.

The assistant gets his assistant to check my makeup. "Everything OK?" he asks no one in particular. "Will I call Marty?"

"You *may*." Hattie nods very grandly from her corner.

Marty is the photographer. He's almost very famous. He's been published in *Perfect Woman* but not as yet in Italian *Vogue*. So you can see where he is in the scheme of things. Sort of suspended between great and fabulous. Phoebe showed me a picture of his. It was used to illustrate a feature on skin care over forty.

"She's got great skin," was my comment to Phoebe about the model's face. "Marty must be a very good photographer."

"Give me that," said Phoebe, snatching the magazine back. "She's got great *age*," is what Phoebe replied. "That's Garance. She's twelve."

Barry talks on the phone the whole time we wait for Marty, which must be at least an hour. When he arrives, he strides straight up to the camera and looks through the lens.

"I've got to be at dinner in half an hour, so no more fucking around!" he tells Hattie firmly.

"No, Marty," says Hattie meekly.

"You over there," he says to Freddie, "get out of the way."

"Sorry," says Freddie meekly.

"I want that light meter. Now!" he snaps at the assistant.

"Right away," says the assistant meekly, and races to pick it up off the bed.

"Your feet are in the frame," he says to assistant-Amy when he bends down and looks through the lens. "Move!"

"Sorry," says Amy meekly.

"What's wrong with that vest?" Marty says to stylist-Amy after she finishes hurriedly dressing me. "It looks like shit."

"I'll fix it," she says meekly, and quickly comes back over to me.

"Fast!" he screams at her.

"Is that all right?" she asks him after she's almost yanked my shoulders off my torso.

"It'll do," he says. "Get out of the picture!"

"More lipstick!" he yells at Barry. "She looks like death warmed over."

"OK, OK," says Barry as he puts down the receiver but doesn't hang it up. He clicks his tongue in that funny way of his but nevertheless fills in my lips as quick as lightning.

"Get rid of that stupid little bow," he tells Rusty. "She's not a pussycat."

"And you!" he growls at me. "Get on the floor!"

"Sorry," I say meekly. What have I done wrong?

I have to admit Marty is a surprise. He's balding and paunchy around the middle with little wiry hairs at the base of every finger and—worse than anything—dressed in horrible dark blue jeans with white topstitching. Not like David Hemmings in *Blow-Up* at all.

When the photo session begins, I'm on the floor in a corner of the room in my fringed vest and a striped microminifrock with my red platform sandals. Marty snaps at me to put my arms around my knees and look up at him. He's standing way above me on two phone books, peering down through the lens. It's one of those funny old bellows cameras, and I think, This isn't an almost famous photographer; why, the poor guy can't even afford to get a new camera. Topstitched jeans and an old camera. My confidence is flooding out of me and lying in puddles on the floor.

Actually the experience is quite—*interesting*. I try very hard to concentrate on what Marty is doing because I've read somewhere that having a relationship with the camera is the most important thing if you want to come out the other end looking beautiful. "You've got to make love to the camera," Freddie has told me. "That's what Zsa Zsa Gabor did."

"Can't you give me something else?" Marty asks impatiently after looking crossly through the camera at me for about five minutes.

"What something else?" I ask timidly.

"Something more than *cute*!" he snarls.

"Oh," I tell him, "I don't think I can do *that*."

"Fucking amateurs!" I hear him mumble to himself. "Don't just stand there!" he yells out to the assistant. "Change the fucking lights!" To me: "Stop pouting. Don't you know how to smile?"

"Sorry. Is this better?" I make an effort to twist my mouth up at the corners.

"Oh, Christ!" he exclaims, clenching his fists and banging his knuckles together. "Can't you smile straight? It's not too much to ask, is it?"

I try to pull the corners of my mouth down again while keeping the teeth clenched together.

He groans and steps down off the phone books. I try to hold the grin while the assistant's assistant lowers the tripod and the assistant rolls one of the lights closer to the wall.

"Is this all right?" I ask through rigid teeth as Marty looks at me again through the lens.

"It's going to have to fucking well do, isn't it?" is all he says as he straightens himself up again. And then he walks out. Just like that. Out of the room, into the corridor, gone.

"Is it over?" I ask no one in particular.

"No," says the assistant, who is writing something down in a book.

"Did I do something wrong?"

"You were divine!" says Barry, who is approaching me with a huge brush covered in lilac powder. "A real star."

"Well, where has Marty gone?"

"Oh, Marty," says Hattie from the other side of the room. "He's finished for the day."

"Give me a big smile," says the assistant from behind the camera.

"Sixteen at a thirtieth of a second," says the assistant's assistant, who is holding a light meter right in front of my lilac-powdered nose.

"But isn't he taking any more pictures?" I ask.

"Why should he?" says Betty, who is doing Phoebe's nails now.

"Well, he is the photographer, isn't he?"

"Don't be silly," says Phoebe knowledgeably. "Photographers don't really take the pictures. Everyone knows *that*."

# 44.

It's six in the morning, and I run down to the Magazine Rack with Freddie. We've been drinking scotch on the rocks all night to calm ourselves down. Only I'm all jittery. This is my big day. Hugo Falk's article on me is hitting the newsstands this morning. I'm wearing my seventy-five-dollar mink coat and dark glasses in case someone recognizes me. Freddie has a bottle of champagne under his arm. Phoebe, who has insisted on taking a taxi, is there ahead of us, pacing up and down in front of a pile of newspapers.

"Are you nervous?" Freddie asks me.

"Kind of," I say, and shiver despite my coat.

"It's going to be *fabulous*," Freddie says.

"It's going to be more than fabulous," I say. "If there is anything more than fabulous."

"There's fabu-lous." Freddie giggles, dragging out the last part of the word. "And fabulously fabulous."

"But after fabulously fabulous?" I ask. "What's after that?"

"I don't know," he says. "Does it matter?"

"I've got a feeling it does. But I don't know why."

"Oh, shut up, you two!" Phoebe says. She looks drawn. She's dragging heavily on her cigarette as she paces.

"Maybe we should open the champagne now," Freddie suggests. "I'm rather thirsty." He starts tearing off the foil, in a neat little coil.

"Not yet, Freddie!" I try to stop him. "I'm superstitious. I don't think we should celebrate *yet*. Maybe we should wait for the party tonight." Freddie has sent out invitations for a party to celebrate my article. The guests are supposed to come dressed as me. Which is a cute idea. Except that I can't think of anything to wear. I've never had to dress like me before.

"Have confidence in me," Freddie says as the champagne cork flies in the air and pink liquid gushes all over a stack of the morning's *New York Times*.

The wife of the owner, Ahmed, opens the little Lucite window where she sells lottery tickets during the day. She waves her finger at Freddie. "You fashion people!" she complains.

"Sorry," he says, and tries to drain the top copy of *The New York Times* onto the sidewalk.

"You'll have to buy it." I laugh. "Whatever will you do with it? You hate newspapers. The print gets all over your frocks."

"Papier-mâché," he says. "Crazy paving for Cristobal's house." He then goes into uncontrollable fits of laughter.

I grab the champagne bottle from him. "Where are the glasses?"

"Don't be so bourgeois," he scolds, taking the bottle back and putting his mouth around the neck. "This is how we do it in London."

He hands it to me. I shake my head. "I don't think it's right. I think we should wait."

"Oh, come on," snarls Phoebe. "Stop squabbling."

"I'm feeling quite sloshed already." Freddie giggles. "Do you think it was Tom's nightcap that did it? I've never had Thunderbird on top of scotch before."

"Shut up, Freddie! There's a truck coming," I cry out, pointing to the street. A van pulls into the gutter and scatters a group of Jamaicans rolling cigarettes. "Do you think this might be it?"

"Those parcels do look magazine-sized," Freddie observes, putting the champagne bottle between his knees while he unpeels his white gloves. "As your press agent, I think I'll go and inquire."

"Well, hurry up then," I tell him. "The suspense is killing me."

Freddie hands me the bottle and skips over to the van. The truck driver is a beefy Indian wearing a balaclava. I like balaclavas. They're very Courrèges. This is a good omen. I watch Freddie follow the driver, who is carrying a heavy bundle tied with twine on his shoulder, into the newsstand. Freddie shrugs as he pushes past me and whispers, "Maybe. I can't understand a thing he's saying. I knew I should have seen *A Passage to India.*" I can see Freddie under the fluorescent light, digging into his pocket. He takes forever to come back outside.

"*Well?*" Phoebe asks him, tapping her toes impatiently.

He gives me a sad look and then he holds up a magazine in front of me. "Da-da!" He smiles mischievously. It's *Frenzee.*

"Gosh," is all I can say, examining the cover. "What's that?" It's a smudgy photograph of a whole crowd of people. The only thing I can make out is a Polynesian-print shirt on a man in the foreground and the huge earrings on a girl at the top of a flight of stairs. Slashed across the bottom of the page are the words "FABULOUS NOBODIES." "That's funny," I say. "*Frenzee* is running a story on the girls of Third Street in the same issue as a story on me. What a terrible photograph! I like her earrings, though. I have a pair like that myself."

"It's printed out of register and duo-toned," says Freddie. "Maybe they did that deliberately. It's arty."

"Let me see," says Phoebe, snatching it off Freddie. "That's not arty. That's *you.*" She looks directly at me.

"What!" I exclaim, grabbing the magazine out of her hands and scrutinizing the cover. I feel numb. This is the very same photograph I've pasted between the pages in my scrapbook. The one where I'm standing outside Less Is More looking like a junkie. "Oh, no!" is all I can manage to say.

"What's wrong?" asks Freddie. "You're on the cover of *Frenzee*. You're a *cover girl*. What could be better than that?"

"I look funny," I say weakly. "It's not my image."

"It might not be your image," says Phoebe, lifting the magazine out of my limp hands. "But it's certainly you. What page are we on?"

"We?" I ask.

"Look up the contents," Freddie tells her. "That will be quickest."

"I'm *trying!*"

Phoebe flips to the front of the magazine and runs down the contents list with a satin-tipped finger. She goes back to the top of the list and starts again.

"I can't see it." Freddie looks distressed.

"Look up 'Hugo-a-go-go,' " I say, getting more and more agitated.

"Page sixty-six," says Phoebe, flipping over a few pages. We speed-read Hugo's column. "He doesn't mention you." Phoebe closes the magazine. "Not in boldface anyway."

It's Freddie's turn to snatch the magazine and start flipping. "Ooh, look at this outfit. I wonder—"

"Who cares?" My voice comes out in a thin screech. "Go back to the list."

"There is this FABULOUS NOBODIES article. Do you want to try that?"

"Why?" I ask. "That has nothing to do with *me*."

"Of course it does!" says Phoebe. "She's a doorwhore, isn't she?"

"I am not!" I scream at her.

Freddie goes back and forth through the magazine. "The pages are all sticking together," he complains.

"It's because you're drunk." Phoebe is cross.

"Stop! There's a platform shoe!" I point to a photograph. Freddie keeps flipping past it. "Go back!"

It's me. It's me in my club. "What's wrong with me?" I say after we're all silent for a minute. "I don't have eyes that color."

"You're *airbrushed,*" says Phoebe authoritatively.

"It looks good, doesn't it?" Freddie says.

"I don't know," I say. "Do you think so?"

Freddie flips over to the next page.

"That's you!" I point out a black-and-white photograph of our apartment to him. "In the background."

"So it is," he says. "You can only see Cristobal's right ear, however. He's going to be very upset."

"Well, don't worry, Freddie, at least it's an ear. I can see one of your nostrils, Phoebe!"

"Where? Let's see!" Phoebe elbows her way closer. "Are there any other pictures of me?"

"I don't think so," I tell her.

"But Hugo asked specifically for a picture of *me.*"

"I don't see why." I'm surprised. "The story is about *me.*"

"What makes you think that?" Phoebe empties out her cigarette holder onto the sidewalk and refills it.

"Let's go home and read it," Freddie suggests.

"Let's go home and wait for all the phone calls," I remind him. "Do you think I'm famous enough for Revlon now?"

"Indubitably," Freddie says, kissing me on the cheek. "At least six million subway riders must be reading about you right now."

# 45.

Phoebe kicks off her Joan and Davids. Freddie puts our shoes in their sleeping bags. We all flop down on Freddie's rug. Each of us has a copy of *Frenzee*. We lie in a line, leaning on our elbows, in the midst of a volcano of club debris—cigarette butts and crumpled plastic cups scattered on the floor—with the magazines smoothed out in front of us.

Pages eighty-three to ninety are the crucial ones. The headline reads DOWNTOWN'S FABULOUS NOBODIES: DOORWHORES, DEBUTANTES, AND DILETTANTES. The title is so long it cuts the photograph of me on the opening page clean in half.

I study this photograph closely, trying not to get hysterical. In the picture my mouth is open in a big O. A really big O. As if I'd been drawing on lip liner and was trying to get into the corners. That's always the tricky bit.

I still don't recognize myself. Not only have I got bright blue eyes instead of smudgy green ones, but all the freckles on my nose are gone. My teeth aren't crooked anymore. They're white, too, not cream, which they are at street level. I've got two extra cheekbones. I've got extra strands of hair. That stupid poodle bow is back in the middle of my head. I've got a suntan!

"Congratulations," says Freddie. "You look like a *model*."

The thing is, I don't. If I looked like a model, I wouldn't mind. What I look like is the Poor Little Match Girl, or something. I'm sitting in the corner of my club, on the floor, all scrunched up with my arms around my knees. The whole focus of the picture is my feet. I didn't know it at the time, but Marty's assistant has used some sort of lens which makes my feet look as if they're twice as big as my head. I'm wearing my green platform sandals, the ones that I've covered with little stick-on vegetable transfers, and you can see that the sole is coming off the bottom of one shoe, which makes the shoe look like it's smiling at the camera.

Underneath it there is a black-and-white photograph of me at the club reclining on my bed with Cristobal's ear and Phoebe's nostril in the background. But it's not especially flattering. In it, I'm leaning on one elbow as I turn around to answer the phone. My neck looks all wrinkled on account of the way I'm twisting.

"I wish they hadn't used *that* picture of me," Freddie complains, studying a photograph of himself in a snakeskin halter neck, holding Cristobal up to the camera. "I would have shaved under my arms if I knew."

"Hmmph, you needn't worry," says Phoebe. "They've got hold of an *ancient* picture of me!"

"Let's see," I say.

Phoebe flings her copy at me. "There!" In the photograph she's sitting with me in a corner at Velcro. Both of us have our hands over our mouths.

"Why, that's your Jean Seberg phase! You don't wear your hair like that anymore."

"Exactly. I want to *die*."

"Don't do that, Phoebe. Look on the bright side. You're at least twelve months younger in this photograph. Not one of your wrinkles is showing."

"What wrinkles?" she asks, looking distressed.

"What's this little girl doing here?" Freddie waves a page under my nose. "She couldn't be more than twelve. Does anyone know her?"

"Not me," I shrug.

"Well, what's she doing superimposed on a photograph of you sitting at your vanity table? I didn't know you had a child," he insists.

"Beats me," I say.

"But it's you!" Freddie cries. "The caption reads: 'At eleven, in Phoenicia.'"

"Oh, *no.*" I close my eyes and shudder, and my heart sinks to my go-go boots with a thud.

I open one eye, and I look at the photograph again. I'm standing on the veranda with a straggly bunch of daisies in my hand. I'm wearing pink overalls and a striped hand-knit sweater and sheepskin boots on my feet. I remember this picture now. Constance used it as a reference for a clay pot plant holder she was making for my room. A pot plant holder of a little girl in overalls with a hole in her hand where you're supposed to plant a flower. When I was sixteen, I took that pot plant holder down to the bottom of the garden and threw it against the fence and smashed it. It was so ugly. It was ruining my image. This picture represents one of the low points in my life.

"Well, look at this!" says Phoebe, suddenly pouncing on her copy. "Here's a picture of those dear little policemen who dropped in the other night to find out if we had a liquor license."

"What?" I say, and roll over to look at the next page. "Oh, no, who took *that* picture? Freddie, you're my press agent. You should have stopped them!"

"Why? You look smashing in those capri pants."

"But I look tough. I look like I'm about to poke that cop in the eye. *Tough* is not my look. I'll never live it down!"

"Well, maybe no one will notice it," Freddie says cheerfully. "It's only postage stamp size."

He and Phoebe wait for my reaction.

"It might as well be plastered over every billboard in town, fifty feet high," I say. "Millions of people are probably looking at it right now and laughing at me."

"Millions of people don't read *Frenzee*, you dope," says Phoebe. "The last audited circulation was one hundred and eighty thousand."

"I don't care! If even one person sees me looking tough, that's bad enough!" I moan. "I look like a hooker."

"Funny thing," says Freddie, tracing the first paragraph with his finger. "That's exactly what Hugo Falk says."


We lie there quietly for at least an hour—I've lost all sense of time—taking in every word. I notice Phoebe moves her sugar-pink lips as she reads. No sound comes out, though. No one says a thing.

Reading Hugo's article, if I didn't know him better, I'd swear he was making fun of me. It must be some obscure joke. Hugo wouldn't drink all my liquor and go to bars with me and watch me get undressed and then write about me as if he didn't like me. But reading his article, if I weren't me, I'd swear he didn't like me one bit.

For instance, he describes me as looking like a six-year-old playing dress-up. He says I look like a whore. He says my mother should spank me. My mother must have put him up to this. He says I'm a girl who spends more time doing my mascara than thinking about the troubles of the world; at least that's what I think he says. What does he mean by this? What troubles? The world looks just fine to me. There wouldn't be so many people going out and enjoying themselves if there were something seriously wrong with it. Being on the door of a club, you know these things. You're at the pulse.

What's worse, I'm not the only one he has written about. I mean, if he's going to be critical of me, that's one thing. But being critical of me in the company of people I can't stand is another. Like Ricci. There's a whole five paragraphs on Ricci and a photograph of her in a pink Lycra unitard where you can clearly see her saddlebag thighs. She says a whole lot of stupid things about being a doorwhore and how many somebodies come to Less Is More now that she's in charge. It makes me violently ill to be on the same *page*—let alone in the same magazine—as someone so tasteless. It's almost as bad as turning up to a party in exactly the same frock as your best friend.

Hugo has interviewed everybody I know and some people I've never heard of before. Phoebe and Freddie and Faille and Biba and Aurora and even Ahmed's wife at the Magazine Rack. Everyone has been quoted. Everyone has been quoted saying things about everyone else. Most of these things are not nice. Phoebe says I get all my ideas from her. Freddie says I'm messy and I sometimes lapse into bad taste. My old schoolteacher says I always was a show-off. Ricci says I still am.

When I finish this part, I glare at Freddie and Phoebe lying beside me. They look up and then look back down again quickly, ashamed. A few minutes later they look up and glare at me. I feel them boring holes through my Pucci. I don't look up. I'm the one who is ashamed now.

Hugo has betrayed my confidence. He's taken a whole lot of drunken conversations in a whole lot of fashion bars and turned them into seven pages of magazine. I mean, it's one thing to tell Hugo in the privacy of your own home that you're worried about Freddie's attachment to his dog, but to see it in black print on glossy white paper with quotation marks around it, that's another thing altogether. Freddie has just got up and stomped out of the room in his stockinged feet with Cristobal under his arm. I can sort of understand why.

And it's one thing to tell Hugo over a margarita that you think Phoebe is just a pale imitation of Audrey Hepburn, but it's another thing altogether to be lying on the floor with her, watching her lip-read those very words for the first time. It's another thing altogether to have to suffer multiple cigarette burns to your forearm because of it.

It's one thing to have a mother who is a hippie and to mistake Jackie O for a nobody in a cardigan and to pad your bra with cotton sometimes and to draw in the second *C* on your tattoo, but to know that three million people—OK, 180,000—are chomping their way through cornflakes and all your intimate secrets this very second, that's another thing altogether. It's one thing to have a warm and meaningful relationship with the contents of your closet, but it's another thing to have your frocks misquoted in public. Lolita never did say, "The true artist today is the person who knows how to shop well." I said it. Lolita isn't that smart. She's cunning and petulant rather than intelligent. The way Hugo mostly writes about my frocks, you'd think they were just flimsy lengths of fabric. I don't think they'll ever speak to me again. Especially Tallulah, whom he called a "frivolous bit of net." As if there were something wrong with being frivolous.

"How *could* he?" I say to Phoebe, flinching as she waves her burning cigarette dangerously close to my arm again.

"How could you?" She sits up on her knees. "A pale imitation of Audrey Hepburn! Really!"

"How could *you*?" I snap back at her.

"I don't know what you mean. When Hugo came to me and told me what you'd said about my father—"

"Wait a minute, Phoebe. What do you mean, what I said about your father? What did he say I said about your father?"

"You told him about daddy's shoe factory. About those dreadful Reebok rip-offs! That was my darkest secret! And now it's out!"

"I don't think I did that."

"Yes, you did. No one else knew."

"About your father's shoe factory?" I say. "I'm not the only one who knows."

"Well, not *now*, idiot," she says. "The whole world knows!"

"No, only a hundred and eighty thousand of them."

"Very funny."

"Anyway, Freddie knew, too. I told him."

"You told Freddie? Oh, really! That was a secret."

"Freddie must have told Hugo. I'm sure I didn't. I don't think. Did I?"

"Let's find out," says Phoebe. "Freddie!"

"Yes? What?" he says ferociously, coming into the room in his panty hose, followed by Cristobal, who is growling. "I'm not speaking to you ever again." He says this to me.

"Freddie, did you tell Hugo about Phoebe's father's shoe factory?" I ask, ignoring what he has just said.

"Well, yes, I did. So what?"

"I always knew you were a blabbermouth," says Phoebe.

"Actually," says Freddie to Phoebe, clearing his throat, "you got what you deserved. Hugo was very upset with you. He told me that you were telling everyone who would listen that he recycles his columns."

"Which is something Reality told *me*," Phoebe points out.

"I told you that in confidence," I say.

"The same way I told you about my father?" Phoebe asks with narrow eyes.

"I might as well get it off my chest," Freddie interrupts miserably. "What I did tell Hugo was the bit about your real name being Vespa Faske, Phoebe. He told me that you said I was just a boy in girl's clothing. I was very upset."

"You mean, you were seeing Hugo behind my back?" I ask.

"Behind *my* back?" Phoebe corrects me.

"Well, I am your press agent, Reality."

"You didn't show him my scrapbook by any chance?"

Freddie shuffles his feet.

"Anyway," Phoebe says, "I didn't tell Hugo you were just a boy in women's clothing. I said pleasant things about you, too. He just chose not to publish them. I don't know why. You should be grateful to me. Especially after I found out you said I was frigid."

"But I didn't say that." Freddie looks distressed.

"That was me." I own up.

"Thanks a million," Phoebe says.

"Hugo told me you told him about my tattoo. About how it's really only *half* a tattoo."

"That was me!" pipes in Freddie. "I told him that. But you told him my father was a cop."

"Which is *true*," I say.

"But you're my friend," he moans. "You're not supposed to say things like that to strangers. They'll get the wrong idea. They'll think I'm *middle-class*."

"He wasn't a stranger," I say.

"To *any* of us," says Phoebe cynically.

"You told him things about *me*," I tell Freddie.

"Because I thought you told him things about *me*."

"And *me*," insists Phoebe. "He kept on asking all these silly questions about you, Reality. So to shut him up, I told him about your mother being a hippie. But only after he told me what you said about my father."

We all look at each other.

"We've been conned," we say at once.

# 46.

I close the magazine and sigh and roll over on my back. I lie there for ages. I'm confused. I don't know whether this is the best day of my life or the worst one.

It's all very well being the cover of *Frenzee*. But when everyone down here gets a load of Hugo's story, I'll be *over*. Luckily no one ever gets up until after lunch, so maybe I've got awhile before my reputation is in tatters.

At first I feel like a frock that has been put through a wringer. I feel as if all the bubbles have been squeezed out of me and I'm just lying in the sink like a limp, wet, old rag waiting to be hung out to dry. I feel ripped right down the middle, like that Halston I found at *Perfect Woman*. One half of me could cut my own throat. The other half of me could cut Hugo's throat. And then somewhere around stomach level, where the waist of my panty hose always digs in, I feel violently ill.

Phoebe has reluctantly gone to work. Freddie has to run out and have his hair set. I just lie around on the floor like this until the jagged bleat of the phone cuts through the silence like Freddie's pinking shears.

I crawl quickly over to it on my hands and knees. If it's Constance, I'm going to let her have it. To teach her to stop interfering with my life as if she has anything to do with it. I'm surprised to find it's Hugo on the other end of the line. He's angry. Which he has no right to be. "I've been sitting in this bar all morning," he complains. "Waiting for you to call and thank me for the story. Luckily dozens of other people have more manners than you and have been phoning to tell me how fabulous it is. What have you got to say for yourself?"

I'm speechless. But I don't hang up. My hand is stuck around the receiver like rigor mortis.

"Well?" he demands. "I'm waiting."

This makes me furious. "How could you!" is what I finally blurt out.

"How could I what?" he asks. "You sound mad."

"I am!"

"I don't know why. I've just given your career a *tremendous* boost. It's not every day a nobody gets the cover of *Frenzee*. You should be grateful. I had to fight to get you on it. I'm really a kind soul."

"The only soul you've got is on the bottom of your shoe!" I blurt out. This is very clever of me, considering how shaken up I feel.

"I've certainly never had this reaction to an article before," he says lightly. "How curious."

"I don't know who you think you are writing those things about me. I'm not a nobody!"

"Well, not now, of course. Now that I've made you famous."

"And I'm not a doorwhore!"

"Oh? I thought you were."

"I'm not! You're the doorwhore, Hugo, if anyone is. You're the one who says Oh, Yes, You're Fabulous, So I'll Write About You Next Week or I'll Never Write About You in a Million Years You're Not Pretty Enough for Me. You dangle your column in front of everyone like a—"

"Carrot?" Hugo suggests, sounding enthralled. "Go on."

"Not a carrot, an open door to some fabulous club. A fabulous club where you're the only member. Except that when your poor victims get inside, it's *empty.*"

"But that's the nature of fame, Reality. A great door but an empty room. Faye told me—"

"I don't want to know about Faye! You're the one I'm interested in. You're the one who lurks around doorways trying to latch on to some fool who'll let you humiliate them in print. You hypocrite!"

Hugo doesn't sound at all disturbed by what I've just said. "Lurking around is my job, Reality. I happen to be very talented at it. I had to lurk. *Frenzee* magazine wasn't the slightest bit interested in you until I told them there was a *controversial* angle. They wanted an exposé. I told you that. I thought I did it rather well. Complimented you and exposed you at the same time. I've kept a foot on both sides of the fence."

"What about that stuff about my frocks?" I interrupt him. "You made them sound . . . trivial. And I'm never going to forgive you for mentioning my mother. Never! You were just exploiting me! I should never have trusted you!"

"On this matter of exploiting," he says stiffly, "if I recall, you didn't seem to mind exploiting *me.*"

"Exploiting you!"

"I seem to remember an occasion when you almost fell over yourself to be photographed with me. You were wearing a pink dress. It went with my jacket."

"You've suddenly got a good memory. You've never remembered that before."

"I'm vague only when I deliberately want to be vague," is his answer. "In any case, all publicity is good publicity," he adds smugly. "You'll see."

"Don't hide behind that old excuse! I've got an image to protect, and you've just ruined it! Those sheepskin boots! Ricci must be doubled up with laughter!"

"Oh, I don't think so. I've spoken to her this morning. She's mad at you for saying she looks like a hippie. Come to think of it, that's funny, isn't it?" When I make a choking sound, he keeps chattering on. "But, Reality, look at it this way. If I said nice things about you, people wouldn't talk about you at all. They'd flip over the story and think it was just another heterosexual journalist's wet kiss. They'd forget about you as soon as they moved on to the fashion pages. You'd be wrapping up tomorrow's trash. This way people will talk about what a silly, vain, self-absorbed thing you are and be scandalized that the youth of today is so obsessed with fashion, and your moment might extend to *weeks.* You might even last until spring if no one else comes along. You didn't murder anyone or wear a boa constrictor around your neck, so I *had* to think of something. I did you a favor. You should think of it as my love letter to you."

"Love letter!" I stand up in outrage. I knock the bedside table. The plaster blackamoor wobbles on his stand and then crashes to the floor. I stare blankly at the tangle of beads and bits of colored plaster. I don't know what else to say. I'm confused. Hugo makes it sound as if he's been helping me all along. But I'm not sure. He talks so fast. I stop shaking anyway. "The way you write, it sounds like you *hate* me."

"I wouldn't pay any attention to that," he says brightly. "It's just a persona I adopt in print."

"It is?" This stuns me.

"Certainly. It's not me at all."

"Then you're even more despicable than I thought!"

"Now look," he says crossly, "if you continue like this, I might never write about you again."

"Huh!" I laugh. "Go ahead. Don't write about me. I don't care! It would be a *relief.*"

"You don't care?" he asks, sounding hurt.

"No, I don't! Not about you anyway."

"I didn't think you were so mean," he says.

"You're the one who's mean! You write any old thing about anyone just because it sounds good in print. Just because it makes you sound good in print. That's what you said. Admit it."

"Of course, I admit it. That's called being professional."

"And it doesn't matter to you if what you write is downright *cruel*. It's cruel telling everyone that I'm the sort of girl who cares more about putting on her lipstick than anything else in the world. That really hurt. And I happen to care about my frocks. They're important to me. They're not just things. They're people. They need as much love and attention as pets or babies or starving children in Africa. And don't you *dare* laugh! I'm not stupid. I know all you people are sniggering away, thinking how dumb that sounds. Well, if you had ever heard a frock cry, you might change your mind. All these poor frocks madly trying to tell all these women that they're too fat for stretch jersey or their slip's showing or that maroon leather doesn't go with their red hair and the women are just *ignoring* them. If you walked down the street and listened, you'd hear all the incredible shrieking coming from the frocks on passersby. All those frocks desperately trying to get their women to pay attention to them. 'I *hate* those shoes,' they say, 'they're not my color,' or 'You've put on weight, you're *stretching* me.' It's just heartbreaking. All the right frocks on the wrong women and the wrong frocks on the right women. I can't bear to think what it must be like in the morning, millions of frocks screaming and wailing as they're plucked out of their closets, just like that plant—you know—the one that cries when it's picked—"

"The mandrake," offers Hugo.

"The mandrake. Is that what it's called? Anyway, the whole thing's too *horrible*. Some days I can't keep on walking. I have to go home and cry and cry for the pity of it!"

"I didn't think of it that way." Hugo's voice sounds curious. "Do you mind if I take notes?"

"You're impossible!" I spit out.

"There's no need to get upset."

"Yes, there is. There is a need to get upset. Someone has to. All those poor frocks!" I let out a sob. I can't help it.

"Look, don't get hysterical," he says, sounding panicky.

"At least I care about something, Hugo," I go on, ignoring him. "Which is more than I can say for you. It's more than I can say for those Burberrys, too, and those women with platinum credit cards in Bergdorf's and—"

"Calm down," he consoles me. "You're not making sense."

"I am!" I shout. "No wonder I like frocks more than people."

"Well, that's understandable in most cases. Sometimes I think I like my Ken Scott suit more than I like the waiters at Houndstooth for instance. But you couldn't possibly mean that you like your clothes more than me now, could you? Be sensible. You couldn't possibly feel more respect for that rubber dress than you do for me."

"At least that rubber dress has a heart."

"So do I." He sounds indignant.

"Oh, sure," I sneer. "Where is it then?"

"On my sleeve," he says quietly.

# 47.

My frocks are very quiet in their closet. I know they are depressed. I
feel sorry for them. Frocks are so *vulnerable.* There's all this talk
about the poor homeless people and the starving farmers, as if they
were the world's downtrodden. They're not the only ones. It's all out
of proportion. Did anyone ever think of the frocks? There are more
frocks on this planet than there are human beings. Yet you never
hear a single word about the way the frocks suffer. All this stuff
about Biafra and Tasmania, or whatever, and you never hear a peep
out of anybody about frocks. The poor frocks have to hang there and
take it. Take Hugo Falk insulting them in print. It was a waste of
time introducing Tallulah to him. He didn't listen. He just heard. I
close my copy of *Frenzee*—noting with satisfaction that Hugo has
misspelled Lacroix—and wearily get to my feet. I've got to get down
to Aurora's and pick up that silver and blue Lurex Cilla Black-
inspired mini I've been saving for the party tonight. The theme of
the party is going to be me. I think Cilla Black is very me today. At
least Cilla Black appears to be me on the surface, even if I'm crying
deep down inside.

I decide to change into Gina. She's got the right attitude for a day
like today. She's *spirited.* She'll show them. Besides, she's a million

light-years away from sheepskin boots. Everyone will think that photo of me is a *fake*. Facing everybody out on the street is something I couldn't do on my own. Gina will help me.

I dress carefully. Once I've wriggled into Gina—who's raring to go—I comb out one of my hairpieces and pin it so that it gives height to my head. I have a feeling I'm going to need height today. Then I spray myself all over with Opium, the most powerful perfume I know, even behind the knees. Before I'm at the bottom of the staircase, Gina has started to hum the first few bars of "Volare."

Out on Fourth Street a few people say "Hi!" or "Fab frock" as I trot past. This makes me feel marginally better. But no one stops to ask me for my autograph, although I do linger awhile longer than I should outside the Magazine Rack in case someone recognizes me. I guess none of the fashion crowd is awake yet. Gina and I have almost finished "Arivederci Roma" as we turn into Sixth Street.

By the time the basket of old scarves outside Aurora's White Trash comes into view, we've just started humming "Quando Quando Quando." I'm looking up at the decorative brickwork on the roofs of the tenements as I hum, thinking how wonderful oxblood red looks against the blue sky. I'm just starting to think there is life after magazines when something makes me look down and I find myself on a collision course with who else but Hugo Falk.

I stop dead in my tracks five inches short of him. I wobble a bit on my heels. "Stop following me!" I shout at him in shock.

"May I point out," he says, moving an inch closer, "I am coming toward you. Not following you."

"No further!" I warn him, pushing my straw shopping bag between us.

"You're still touchy, aren't you? I don't know why. I thought we solved our little *contretemps*. You agreed I was right."

"I did not!"

"Look, let's not talk in the street. I'll buy you a drink."

"No thanks. Now, would you please step aside?" I say with great dignity and control.

"Didn't you hear me? I said I'd *buy* you a drink." He sounds insulted.

"You'll just have to learn that you can't buy people, Hugo. As far as you're concerned, this door is *closed*."

I give him a little push. Hugo takes hold of my arm sharply. I try to shake it off, but he's too strong.

"I don't understand you," he says. "I was sure you'd be grateful. Grateful enough to—"

"To what?" I demand, giving my elbow another twist.

"Never mind," he says crossly.

"Why should I be grateful to you? You wrote all those nasty things about my friends!"

"Only because you told me. You opened the door. I'm a writer, you know, Reality. I can't resist things like that."

"And you betrayed my frocks. Which is *worse*. Betraying my frocks is like skewering my heart with a . . . knitting needle!"

"I don't see how I did that. Anyway, your frocks aren't you."

"They are me!" I'm getting angrier, if that's possible.

"You're a funny little mixed-up thing, aren't you?"

Gina is itching to hit him. I can feel her squirming around. "I'm not mixed up. You're the one who's confused. Inviting me out to bars all the time as if I'm your best friend in the world and then ignoring me all night while you chase some scoop—or some white-haired boy you fancy!"

"So that's what this is all about," he says with a smirk on his face. "Well, well." He tugs at my arm. "Come on, I'm taking you home!"

"You are not! I've got other things to do."

He doesn't say anything else but pulls me around in the opposite direction and starts dragging me along the street. I cry out and try to hit him with my handbag, but he's faster than I am and snatches it out of my hand. He's pulling me along like this and I'm stumbling and screaming and a whole lot of people are standing out of our way, just smiling at me.

"All right!" I yell out. "I've had enough. If you'll stop pinching my darn arm, I won't run away."

"I thought you'd see it my way," Hugo says infuriatingly. "Let's link arms." He strokes my elbow, gently slips my forearm over his sleeve, and pats it. "There."

We walk along like this for blocks, he in his ice blue linen suit with pale green button-up shirt and lollipop pink tie, looking for all the world like a big melting gelato, with one of my arms linked through his left arm and my straw handbag in his right, me stumbling along beside him in a pair of red high-heeled sandals with one of the ankle straps twisted and digging into my heel.

Hugo squeezes my arm and says he's been dying to touch me like this ever since we met.

This is what he tells me on the corner of First, and this is what he tells me when he pushes his way past Tom and into my building when we get back to Fourth Street.

"Hugo!" is all I can think to say on the landing as he jams himself between the banister and the wall and refuses to budge until I kiss him. "You're not supposed to like girls! . . . Hugo!" I say as I push past him and try to stop him from following me up the stairs. "You're all confused! . . . Hugo!" I cry as he grabs me by the leg and pulls me to the ground on the landing. "You're out of your mind! . . . Hugo!" I scream as he throws himself on top of me and starts pulling at my skirt. "You're hurting me!"

"What do you expect?" Hugo says as he forces his hand up under my bra. "I've never done this before."

I manage to kick him, in the shin, I think, with the sharp heel of my stiletto.

Suddenly he is overcome with shame and sits on the stairs and puts his head in his hands.

"Oh, *dear*," he groans. "I didn't think it would go like this. You shouldn't have resisted."

"I *what*?" I push my skirt down over my panties as I try to catch my breath. "You've made me chip a nail! Look!"

Hugo uncovers one of his eyes. "Oh, *no*." He winces. "I thought of doing this a long time ago. I just didn't realize I thought it until today."

"How can I believe *that*, Hugo?" I tell him as I wobble to my feet. "You like boys."

"Not exclusively."

"Don't be silly, Hugo, of course you do! You don't need to pretend with me. Why, some of my best friends—"

"Reality. I tell you I don't!" He looks up at me with big, innocent eyes. "Not since I've met you anyway."

"Oh," I say, and pull my bra straps back up. "I don't get it."

"I never do anything to them. You don't have to worry about that."

"Never?"

"Almost never."

"Gosh," I say, and sit up on the step beside him, suddenly interested.

After this sinks in, I ask, "What does '*almost* never' mean?"

"Well, I thought I should at least try it," says Hugo, who seems eager to explain himself. He puts both hands on the cold marble steps and takes a deep breath. "It seemed to be the thing to do."

"The thing to do!"

"Well. Yes. I like having boys around me. It makes me feel more masculine. It's fashionable to be gay, in case you haven't noticed. At least it was until people started catching this . . . *thing*." He shifts uncomfortably on the steps. "It was a *tremendous* help to my career.

Don't you realize that most magazine people are gay? Even the girls."

"But all those young boys? Some of them were quite cute. You *never* did it with any of them?"

"I'm not a fool, Reality! I had to keep up appearances, you know. I had to sometimes . . . *fondle* . . . them. And kiss them. That was reasonably pleasant. In fact, I don't deny it was all reasonably pleasant. But it's quite all right not to actually . . . *do it,* as you say, anymore. Anyway, most of those boys are gay for the same reason. They were actually quite *relieved,* I think. That's why I got on so well."

"Have you ever done it with a girl?"

"Of course not! What do you think I am?"

"I don't know."

"Don't be like that! Girls are a different thing. They're soft and smell nice, and they're interesting, like curvy little creatures from outer space. Doing it with boys is like hanging out with your best buddy and doing subversive things that you can't tell your parents about. It's like being in a secret society. It's like being in one big Boys' Own Adventure."

"I can't ever imagine *you* having a best buddy!"

"I certainly did! Travis West. He used to spit on the ground all the time."

We sit side by side for a long time without saying anything. I'm confused. In fact, I'm so confused I don't even know if I'm confused or not. I feel as if I'm a hat that's just been blown off a head and caught up a swirling drift of wind. It's like I'm floating out in space with no ground below me and no sky above. I don't know which way is up.

After a while Hugo says mournfully, "Reality?"

"Yes?"

"You're not *really* mad at me, are you? I've never attacked anyone before. I usually wait until they seduce me. I never have to wait long," he adds quickly.

"I don't know." I am giving him the benefit of the doubt. Of the confusion. "Am I mad at you?"

"Look at you, you funny little thing," he says. "Can I stroke your foot?"

"No!"

He smiles at me. "You're so camp! Only a homosexual could really fall for you. From the first time I saw you . . . wherever it was—"

"I don't want to know!" I leap to my feet, my mind suddenly made up. "Don't tell me!"

"But, Really, I—"

"Look, Hugo, let's get something straight. A lot has happened in one day. You've lied to me. About *Frenzee* magazine. You've led me on. You've called me a nobody! You've pretended to be my *girlfriend*, like Freddie is. And now you're telling me you want to be my *boyfriend*! You've double-crossed me!" I grab him by the collar of his suit and shake him I'm so mad. "Get up! Don't you dare come up here telling me you want to go to bed with me! Don't you *dare* tell me you're not a fag! You're spoiling *everything*!"

"But, Reality, you're not supposed to act this way. You're supposed to be pleased. You're supposed to fall into my arms. Isn't that what girls are supposed to do? Girls who look all girly like you do?"

"Not this one! Get out before I *kill* you!" I'm screaming now, I admit it, and I hear a door open and then close on the landing above, but I'm too upset to care. Hugo struggles to his feet. He just stands there, crumpled and unsure of himself. He fumbles around in his coat pocket for something.

"Do you have a pen?" he asks.

"Why?" I ask.

"I've got an idea for another article."

"Get ooooouuuttt!" I give him a push. He stumbles down a few steps.

"Reality?"

"What!"

"Maybe if we did it just once—"

I spit at him.

"All right, I'm going. You don't have to act like you hate me. It's unbecoming." He takes a few more steps and turns around. "Really—"

"Find someone else's closet to come out of!"

"You do hate me, don't you?"

I don't say anything.

"You funny little thing!" Hugo actually starts to chuckle. He winds his way down the staircase to the first floor. "You funny little thing!" he calls up from below. I stand there and wait until I hear the street door close.

I get the feeling there's someone else in the stairwell. It's Consuela and her baby standing in a shadow on the floor above. As I push my way past them to get to my door, she complains, "My baby no can sleep!"

# 48.

I can feel Consuela's eyes boring holes through my back as I fling myself up the stairs. I slip on the landing on something white and sticky—probably that darn baby's breakfast cereal—and almost twist my ankle. When I finally propel myself into the apartment, a scene of total chaos greets me.

The first thing I think is that Freddie has been trying on my frocks again and has dumped them all over the floor and left them there. Then I think that the frocks have thrown a tantrum because of Hugo's story. I've felt it coming. In my bones. You couldn't blame them. It's awful being misquoted.

But there are not only frocks on the floor. There are shoes and gloves and Chanel chains and hats all jumbled up among the fabric. Even if my frocks have fallen off their hangers in a fit of pique—and they often do—my shoes can't get out of their sleeping bags on their own. Someone has helped them. I call out to Freddie, but he's still not home, even though his door is wide open. His room is tidy, undisturbed. I start to move around the apartment like a zombie, picking up skirts and dusting off hats and trying to work out if anything is missing or hurt.

My frocks—every single one of them except for Tallulah, who has loops sewn in that you can wind around and around her hanger—have slipped off the rack and are lying in piles on the linoleum. There's an enormous mound of tulle and silk and broderie anglais and tufted acrylic and panne velvet and *faux* monkey near the bed. It's sticking up like a big breast with a pink felt pillbox on top as its furry nipple. I sit down on the bed beside it, my arms full of skirts and my mind full of Hugo.

I'm stroking one of my frocks and staring at the pink felt nipple in a sort of trance when I notice the mound starting to quiver. The bits of tulle and broderie anglais are rolling like the whitecaps on a wave. The pillbox suddenly tumbles down the side, and Loulou's petticoats part.

"Ah-choo!" sneezes this person, who is now sitting up, with skirts fanning out all around it like the pajama case bride doll on my bed, the one I stash my cotton balls in.

"Bless you," I manage to say sympathetically, even though I'm flabbergasted.

"Oh!" says the sneezing person, who appears to be female and is now wiping her sleeve across her nose furiously. She looks flabbergasted to see me, too.

"What are you doing under my frocks?" I demand. My eyes are riveted to her face. She's plump with round eyes that are outlined in wiggly purple liner that extends almost to the tops of her ears. She's got straight black hair like Cleopatra. And blue lipstick.

She just sits there smiling at me. "Do I know you?" I ask, although I'm certain I don't know *anyone* who'd have blue lips.

"I'm Brooke," she says cheerfully. "You know."

"No, I *don't* know. Watch out! You've got your foot on Françoise."

"Sorry," she says. "You know," she insists. *"Maria Callas."*

"What?"

"Have I got it right?"

"Have you got what right?"

"Maria Callas! You said I could look like Maria Callas if I tried. Well, I've tried. What do you think?"

"Maria Callas?" I say, still puzzled. "Maria Callas went out weeks ago. I wouldn't suggest anyone do Maria Callas *now*."

"But it was weeks ago. At Less Is More. I borrowed my mom's snake bracelet. Look!" She waves a fat arm at me. The snake bracelet is digging into her arm and squeezing the flesh into raised ridges.

"Very nice," I tell her.

"You really think so?" she asks eagerly, and smiles. When she smiles, I can see the line inside her mouth where the lipstick ends and her wet fat red lip continues. Suddenly I remember her. Standing at the bottom of the stairs in her rip-and-tear six-years-out-of-date tunic. You don't forget a sight like that for long.

"Anyway," I say firmly, "you haven't explained why you're here. Why you're *under* my frocks. I suppose you were hiding."

"Sort of!" she says, and pulls her knees to her chest. I can now see that's she wearing Anita, my miracle frock. I don't have time to protest, because she goes on cheerily. "You see, I've been reading all about you. About the club and all. In *Frenzee*. I bought it this morning. It's so exciting, isn't it? The club, I mean. I knew you'd do something *great*. From the minute I saw you at that door. You've got real charisma. I haven't met anyone with real charisma before. You don't get charisma often out in Metuchen. You've like got to come to New York for it. This is the place to be, isn't it? Right here. The center of the universe, you said. I've stuck your picture on my lunch box. I carry my magazines in it. Some kids think I'm a bit weird, but you said in the article I read this morning that it's important to stand out. I hung on every word. Like you're so inspirational. So I came to see your club tonight. Except that I knew you wouldn't let me in, me looking like me and all. I mean, I'm trying to do Maria Callas, but I know I'm not very good at it. I've had to wear an old negligee around because I couldn't find a caftan anywhere. I've run away from home to find a caftan. As I said, they don't understand me. Especially since I started doing Maria Callas. I read all about her, you know? What a kook! So I like came here to see you. And because I knew you wouldn't want to see me, I sort of snuck in. Well, it was easy, you know, because that drunk guy down below gave me your keys. He said you dropped them this morning. It's funny, but I think he thought I was you. Isn't that a laugh? Considering everything and all. And the door to your apartment was open. I guess you kind of left it that way. Well, I just wandered around and patted all your dresses. They're *so* great. Like you're *so* lucky. And I sat on the bed. And then I thought I better hide. And then I thought, No, it's early, maybe I could try on one of the dresses. That nice blue one. Except that it didn't fit. So I guess I got this bee in my bonnet and kept on trying on dresses and things until I found one that fitted. I'm a size sixteen, you see. That's why you suggested the caftan, didn't you? I understand. You were being great. I heard you come in before and I didn't know what to do because I'd kind of made such an awful mess, so I sort of jumped under these dresses and hid. Except I got the urge to sneeze. You've got a lot of fuzzy acrylic things, haven't you? They're itchy. Oh, well, it was kind of fun. I better be going. . . ." Her voice trails off. She heaves herself off the floor. She's got a Brussels lace petticoat caught around one ankle and a chain belt snared on that.

"Don't go!" I say, suddenly feeling like I want her around.

"You want me to stay?" she asks, her jaw dropping.

"Well, you could at least help me straighten up," I tell her.

"Sure!" she says. "I'll do anything! Anything for *you*!" She tries to untangle herself from the petticoat.

"Watch out for the hat!" I say.

"Sorry," she apologizes, freezing her foot just in time.

I ask Brooke to stay because I need help with the frocks. But maybe that's not the only reason.

There's something reassuring about her. I mean, there's *nothing* reassuring about that wiggly purple eyeliner and those blue lips. It's something else. She says she's been a fan of mine since I turned her away from Less Is More. She thinks I'm great for doing that. She's stuck my picture on her lunch box, the one she carries magazines in. I've touched her life. I've turned her into Maria Callas. I've spoken to her, and she's listened. She might be the only one who has.

"Tell me something," I say to Brooke as I hand her a bunch of coat hangers. "Have you been following me around? In that caftan? Everywhere I go?"

"Sure!" she says. "It was *so* brave of you to have that tattoo! Can I see it up close?"

# 49.

Brooke sits with me for ages. I've completely lost track of the time. I'm stomach down on the bed, showing her the place in my scrapbook where the photograph of me in the chandelier earrings has been torn out, when I hear Freddie come in. He puts his head around the door.

"Do you like my hair—oh, dear!" He comes into the room, with a headful of ginger curls, and points to the mess on the floor. We haven't gotten around to hanging up all the frocks yet. I've been explaining to Brooke the development of sportswear as a fashion statement in the twentieth century. "You pick the oddest times for spring cleaning!" Freddie scolds. "The party is due to start in less than an hour! There are people lining up in the street already."

"Already! Oh, *no*! I forgot all about the party," I gasp. "Can't we call it off?"

"Are you *mad*?" he asks crossly. "This is our big night! We can't turn hundreds of people away. They'll never speak to us again."

"Look, Freddie, I don't feel like seeing people tonight. I just feel like sitting around and eating pizzas and talking to Brooke."

"Who is Brooke?" Freddie demands.

"Me," says Brooke. "I'm a *fan.*"

"Goodness!" Freddie exclaims, noticing her for the first time.

"Brooke is helping me clean up. We've had an accident," I explain, glancing at Brooke, who looks relieved.

"That's rather inconvenient." Freddie sympathizes. "But we've got a party to hold."

"I don't *want* to hold it," I say. "Can't we tell them all to go home and come back tomorrow?"

"Reality, listen to me!" Freddie steps over some frocks and comes up to me and shakes me. "You might have a fan in here. But you've got *hundreds* of them outside. They're your *public.* The public you've been waiting for. Jackie O might be there right now. You don't want to keep *her* waiting, do you? After all the notes I've written to her begging her to come."

"Well, she can wait, too. I haven't finished telling Brooke about Chanel's simple chemise. We haven't got past 1928."

"Are you all right?" Freddie steps back a pace.

"I'm fine."

"You're a mess."

I look down at poor, crumpled Gina, recently violated by Hugo Falk. I automatically touch my head to rearrange my hair and realize that my hairpiece has fallen off somewhere. I run a finger under one eye, and it comes away with one of my false eyelashes stuck to its tip. There's the problem of my chipped nail. The thought of thousands of people seeing me like this brings me to my senses. "Put that bag down and help us, will you Freddie? I'm not even dressed yet," I say, starting to panic.

"I'm glad to hear it. I thought it was a new look. I didn't think much of it, I can tell you." Freddie bends down and picks up a hat off the floor and groans. "I don't think we're going to be ready in time. Then again, it's not really fashionable to be ready on time. It might be good for business. We are going to have to keep the crowd waiting at least an extra hour. They'll be clamoring to get in by midnight.

I can't help you for long, however. I've got to give Cristobal a mas-
sage. Gracious, was that a knock on the door already?"

"Oh, no!" I cry, and start furiously picking up frocks. Freddie
goes to the door. It's only Phoebe, in a white sheet fastened at one
shoulder with a diamond pin.

"How do I look?" is the first thing she asks when she sweeps into
the boudoir.

"Haven't I seen that sheet before?"

"Oh, really, don't you *know*?" She scowls. "*Quel* damage!" she
adds, homing in on the frocks on the floor. "What on earth are you
wearing?" she snaps at me.

"I'm about to change—" I explain.

"You better. It looks hideous."

"What's got into *you*?" Freddie asks.

"Well, now that you ask me—" Phoebe begins. "Who is that?" She
points to Brooke, who is playing with the organza panels of Anita's
skirt.

"Just a fan," says Brooke, looking at her feet, which are now free
of all petticoats and chains.

Phoebe ignores her and looks at me. "What's this? A rerun of *All
About Eve*?"

"Very funny," I say. "You were about to tell us something."

"Yes, I was. That dreadful Hugo Falk accosted me at Café Orlon
just before. He was babbling on about you. Is he a madman? He interrupted my conversation with Quark. So I made Quark kiss me
just to show Hugo—"

"You *what*?" I interrupt.

"I what *what*?" she asks angrily. I've never seen Phoebe angry.
Ever. Her mouth pulls into a thin little line, and her skin goes tight
across her bones. It's not very attractive. Even in a white sheet with
her hair piled up like a Grecian goddess.

"You *kissed* Quark?"

"That's what I said!"

"But you don't like kissing!"

"For your information, I like kissing when I'm kissing the right sort of person." She adjusts the knot of sheet on her shoulder. "I'm not frigid, despite what you told Hugo Falk!"

"But Quark isn't the right kind of person for you. He's the right kind of person for *me*. How could you?"

"I could and I did," Phoebe says. "He happens to be utterly the right kind of person for me. He's a kept man, you know. Just like George Peppard."

"That's a lie!"

"Oh, no, it's true. When I found out this afternoon, I found him instantly attractive."

"*Who* keeps him? I want to know."

"Just some old artist. She's forty."

"Gosh!" I exclaim. "As old as my mother. I can't believe it."

"I bet she looks like Patricia Neal." Phoebe sighs.

"When Quark kissed you, he asked about me?"

"Of course not. He doesn't even know who you are." Phoebe flings part of the sheet behind her like a train, flounces to the window, takes the cigarette out of her long cigarette holder, and stubs it out on the windowsill. "But he's very interested in me. He's very impressed that I work on a magazine."

"What else did you do with him?" I have to ask.

"None of your goddamn business!" she shouts.

There's a long silence. Brooke is frozen by the clothes rack, holding her breath. Freddie coughs. "Well," he says, "I think I'll go and change. It's almost ten."

This breaks Brooke's trance, and she starts to pick up some clothes. Phoebe is pacing up and down now, kicking frocks out of the way.

"Phoebe?" I ask. "How long has this been going on?"

"That's one of my favorite songs," she answers, wistfully.

"Has it been going on for *weeks*?"

"Yes. If you have to know. He dropped into the magazine to show me his portfolio. I said I might be able to put it on the senior fashion editor's desk. But I only kissed him for the first time tonight. At Café Orlon. Not the longest kiss in the world. He had to go home to do his hair."

"Fabulous," I groan.

"Besides, I didn't think you really cared about him. I thought you cared only about yourself. And any fool could see he didn't care about you. I don't know if I care about him either. But I care about Hugo Falk telling the world I am frigid. By kissing Quark, I've just proved that I'm not!"

"Brilliant. You tell Hugo Falk I copy you and you tell him all about my childhood and now you steal my boyfriend. How could you be so selfish?"

"He's not your boyfriend! You dated him once."

"That's enough these days. Just getting a straight boy to buy you a drink is a date these days. You know that!"

Phoebe turns on Brooke. "Can she *leave*?"

"I'll go," volunteers Brooke. "Can I stand on the door?"

"Sure," I say. "Thanks."

We both watch Brooke close the door behind her. I turn to Phoebe. "I can't believe you kissed Quark. I'm shocked."

"I almost went all the way, too!" Phoebe is starting to shake.

Brooke puts her head back around the door.

"There are a whole lot of people outside!" she says breathlessly. "What am I going to do?"

"Oh, God! I knew we should have canceled the party!"

"For goodness' sake, keep them out of here!" yells Freddie from his bedroom. "We're not dressed! Hang on a minute, and I'll come out."

"Sure." Brooke smiles. "This is fun. You should see what some of them are wearing!"

"What do you mean by *almost*?" I ask Phoebe when Brooke closes the door again. I've got the feeling I've had this conversation recently.

"What it sounds like!" She blushes.

"Me too," I say quietly.

Phoebe raises her eyebrows. "You didn't?"

"Not exactly. No."

"Neither did I. Oh, it's pathetic, isn't it?" Phoebe goes on. "The first time I'm ready to give myself to a man and he doesn't do anything. I expected him to ask me home to help him with his hair, or whatever—" She blushes. "Maybe *I* should have done something myself. But I thought looking gorgeous was enough."

"So did I. I think we were *wrong*. There's something else we should have been doing."

"But *what*?"

"I don't know."

"It's beyond me." Phoebe shakes her head.

"He's probably gay," I say, a bit more bitterly than I intended. "They all are."

"I'm sure he isn't *that*." Phoebe doesn't pick up on my tone of voice. "But I wouldn't know. I wish they'd all make up their minds. That's what I like about Freddie. At least you know with a boy who wears dresses. And that Hugo Falk, too, despite what I think about him. At least you know with a man who surrounds himself with pretty boys."

I feel sick. "Don't you start that!" I blurt out.

She looks at me quizzically.

We're interrupted by a loud, scuffling sound coming from the hall, and then a thump.

"I don't think your little friend is being very effective," Phoebe says. "I think they're going to break that door down."

"Help!" I say to her. "Look at me! I've got to get changed."

"That would be smart," Phoebe says. "You look like a bag lady. I'll go and stand by the door while you put something on."

"But I can't put anything on!" I moan. "I haven't got anything to put on! I didn't get to Aurora's!"

"You're not going to pull that routine again!"

"This is *different*," I tell her.

"Why?"

"It just *is*!"

"What about this mini?" She picks up Françoise.

"She's not me," I protest.

"I don't know what all this fuss is about looking like you," she says.

"But I've got to look like me!" I say. "I've got to look more me than me tonight. Everyone else is going to look like me, so I've got to outme them all."

"In that case you don't need to worry," Phoebe tells me. "Everyone else is going to look like everyone else. Just like you do."

"What do you mean?" I ask, but before she can answer, Brooke comes flying through the room with a flood of people following.

"I'm sorry," she spurts out. "They *pushed*."

"Oh, no," is all I can say, as I stand there looking like a disaster, for all the world to see, with my frocks scattered around me like dead rose petals and one chipped fingernail.

# 50.

It's worse than the Thanksgiving sales at Saks. The partygoers stream into the bathroom and fight over who is going to sit in the bathtub. They pour into the boudoir and squabble over what record to play first on the stereo. They push me out of the way to get to the bed and find the best reclining positions.

The only good thing is that no one recognizes me. If it weren't for Brooke, I'd be the plainest girl at the party. At my own party. I shrink against the wall. Brooke has been pushed back into the corner beside me.

"I'm really, really sorry," she says. "I tried to stop them."

"It's OK." I calm her down. "You couldn't help it if they didn't take you seriously as Anita Ekberg in a Cleopatra wig." She says something else, but I'm not listening. I'm trying to take in what everyone is wearing. The partygoers have outdone themselves. I've never seen so much lip liner and glitter eye gloss in my life. There's every kind of Dynel wig. There are fifty-seven different varieties of sequin. There are press-on nails wrapped around every styrofoam cup in sight. Every heel is at least five inches high.

Someone has come as a Stepford Wife, wearing clear blue contact lenses and pushing a supermarket trolley full of defrosting chickens. Another person—possibly Biba, under that huge black wig—is

Diana Ross in a slithering gold mesh halter frock and eyelashes as spiky as pineapple tops. There's a Julie Christie in a blue shift with white frosted lipstick and torn blond hair. There's an Annette Funicello in a pink and white gingham bathing suit with a pointy padded bra. Paige from *Perfect Woman* is wearing a white slip, and I overhear her telling someone she is Eva Marie Saint from *On the Waterfront*. There's the usual Suzy Parker. A boy is dressed like Carmen Miranda and has trouble getting through the doorway on account of all the plastic fruit on his head. Cameron has come as Jackie O. I look again to make sure it's not the *real* Jackie O. It's hard to tell. Cameron is very good at her. Behind him is a very tall Edith Piaf. There's a Stevie Nicks, wearing a frock like a cobweb and too much patchouli. The Ines de la Fressanges are all here. Faille is a skinny Marilyn Monroe. There are two attempts at Gina Lollobrigida, neither of them very good. There's an excellent Emma Peel and a Cat Woman from *Batman*. And a Barbarella in a cut-out plastic shower curtain. Or is it Modesty Blaise? Phoebe is glowering at another Audrey Hepburn. There's a Jean Harlow, an Anna Magnani in the Peasant Look, more Coco Chanels than you can shake a stick at, and a Katharine Hepburn with painted-on freckles. Freddie has come in in a snakeskin-print pantsuit with wide legs. He squeezes himself against the wall so he won't get stampeded in the rush to grab a seat around the bar. "See," he says with a satisfied grin. "Hugo Falk's story has whipped them up into a frenzy. It's a tribute to you."

"What do you mean?" I ask him as I run my eyes over the crowd. "They all look like Suzy Parker or Gina Lollobrigida or Eva Marie Saint."

"But, Really, that's the Reality Look."

"It doesn't look like the Reality Look to *me*. Don't tell me I look like *that*." I point to a six-foot-four-inch drag queen with an Eva Gabor wig, tossing his long neck back and forth to "Only You Can Do It," which is now playing on the stereo. "I don't, do I?"

"Of course, *you* don't look like that! You're not tall enough for a start. But you've inspired him. You're his muse. You're a *goddess*. I don't know why you're so bad-tempered about it. It's what you've always wanted."

"Oh, Freddie," I say, looking despairingly at the drag queen's big chin, "it's all very well being a goddess. But what if I just want to be *a girl*?"

"Oh, Reality, I love you!" Freddie giggles. "You're so camp!"

I glare at him. "That is exactly what I mean!"

# 51.

What's wrong with being a girl? A real *girl* girl? A girl girl with makeup and cleavage and fluttering eyelashes and six-inch heels? Everyone wants to be a girl, even most of the boys. But the general idea of a real girl is a girl who looks like a drag queen. Or a drag queen who looks like a girl.

Freddie is a boy who wears girls' clothes. He appreciates girls. But not real girls. Just the things girls *wear*. He doesn't even prefer boys, like a real girl would do. He prefers his dog. Phoebe, who looks like a real girl, doesn't prefer boys either. Her preference is for *nobody*. Despite what she says. She didn't really kiss Quark, I'm sure of it. She just brushed against his lips with her lipstick.

And then there's my mother, Constance, who doesn't act like she wants to be a girl, but deep down inside her she really does. I'm not fooled by the fact that she refuses to wear makeup. Those macramé tea cozies are a dead giveaway.

Am I the only real girl around here? I'm the one who has devoted my existence to being one. I *look* like a real girl. But when people show up at my party dressed like me, they look like drag queens. Drag queens who look like *other* girls.

*I'm* a girl who definitely prefers boys. Biting Faille accidentally on the cheek once when I was dancing was as physically close as I have ever been to any girl, and *I did not like it.* She tasted funny. But the only boys who prefer me are boys who should prefer boys, too, like Hugo Falk. The only real boy I've dated in months—Quark—seems to prefer Phoebe, who is just a pale imitation of another girl. What's wrong with me? Or is something wrong with all of *them*?

Hugo Falk says I'm so camp only a homosexual could love me. Freddie says I'm camp, and he loves me, too. Could Hugo be right? It's so confusing. I feel dizzy.

The only thing that's constant in my life is my frocks, and even their hems go up and down.

"Reality." Someone is shaking me. "Reality!"

"What?" I hear myself say. "What's wrong?"

I must have gone blank. I can see two purple lines converging and a blur of color.

"Reality, they're treading on your dresses!"

"Who is?" I ask.

"Everybody!" says the voice.

I try to focus. All I can see are the blurs of shiny wigs and the movement of fabric and cigarette smoke curling to the ceiling. And a yellow and blue plaid shoulder edging its way through the confusion toward me.

"Hugo," I say weakly to the two purple lines, which are now separating and becoming part of Brooke's face. She is looking directly into my eyes, urgently, and chewing her lips, and the first thing I think is: Thank goodness, some of the blue lipstick has worn off.

She shakes me again. "I'm going to have to slap you," she is saying. "But I don't want to."

"It's all right." I hold up my hand. "Just get Hugo out of here." I'm aware that I'm sounding as disconnected as Freddie does when he's trying to conjure up the spirit of Balenciaga in one of his séances.

"But there are people stealing your things!" I hear Brooke cry.

She snaps her head away from me. "Get off there!" she screams at someone. "Don't you *dare* touch that!" I turn and watch her snatch Lolita from the hands of a twelve-year-old girl with braids on her head. I think this girl lives in the building.

"I wanna hear a fashion statement!" The girl sulks. I watch unemotionally as Brooke bundles Lolita under her arm and puts her palm right in the middle of the little girl's face.

There are other arms and legs and bodies gyrating about on the heap of frocks on the floor. I can make out a figure—an Eartha Kitt—in the middle of the pile, on her knees, holding Rita up to the chandelier light and inspecting her seams. There's a Virna Lisi standing next to her, wrapping her body in Myrna. There's an Anouk Aimée with three frocks over her arm; one of them is Françoise. A Doris Day is throwing coat hangers out of the way. A Sophia Loren is waltzing around with Tallulah. The Carmen Miranda is tangled up in Jean. Several people are bending over, trying to snatch a hem or a waist. Several more people are trampling all over the frocks, oblivious to what's underfoot. I wince as a lump of cigarette ash topples onto Carmen's bodice. Brooke is there in a flash, trying to stamp it out. Someone is going through my drawers. There's a girl on the bed unzipping Ralph. The noise—a mixture of laughing and screeching and "I'm In with the In Crowd" playing on the stereo—seems to be coming from inside my head, not outside it.

"Go away, all of you!" Brooke is telling them. She's down on her knees, scrambling among the frocks, trying to bundle them all up protectively.

A girl I've seen somewhere before tries on my shoe-shaped hat and looks around for a mirror. Another person—is it Consuela?—is bundling Alice and Anna under her arm. She looks like one of the Italian women who pick fennel in the grass along Route 28. Brooke is flailing around, hitting people and grabbing at their hems and calling to me to help. I don't move. Instead, I watch Freddie trip over the beanbag on his way to assist. I watch as a boy who is pulling on one of my thigh-high wet-look boots kicks a snapping Cristobal across the other side of the room. Cristobal lands on a hot pink sock which may or may not belong to Hugo Falk. Something stirs inside me at the sight of the sock, but still I don't—can't—move.

"Stop that person!" Brooke is calling out. A girl is bolting toward the kitchen with Dolores over her shoulder. I can see Dolores's rubber trembling. Someone puts out a Maud Frizon to trip up the thief. She stumbles and disappears into the crowd in the doorway, dropping Dolores, who is immediately scooped up by a hand dripping in charm bracelets. More people are coming in from the hall, giggling and covering the kitchen like ants. "Call the police!" Brooke cries in despair, throwing all her weight on the remaining frocks, like a football player.

Phoebe is looking out the window, even though the curtains are drawn. She's lighting a cigarette with The Closet matches and then flinging the dead match over her shoulder. I know what she's thinking. This has nothing to do with me. I feel the same way. I watch as a piece of ash from her cigarette floats through the air and lands at Brooke's feet.

"Call the *police*!" I hear Brooke scream again. Freddie has gotten up off the floor and is flinging his arms about, trying to form a barricade. But it's too late. There are dozens of people on the floor, clutching and grabbing and emerging with bits of fabric. A Coco Chanel is pushing past me with a piece of Petula. A Capucine is barreling her way through with the top half of Doris.

And now Brooke is rising out of the middle of it all with Lolita in one hand, held high over her head like the Statue of Liberty's torch. Someone in an orange frock like a flame is pulling at the hem of Anita. Someone else is screaming. And then there's an almighty whooshing sound like calico in a hurricane. Everyone seems to jump back two feet in a split second. Anita is on fire.

Oh, great, I think, Anita is on fire. Oh, great. But I don't feel upset.

It seems as if one of Anita's organza panels has flirted dangerously with Phoebe's cigarette ash and whipped up a flame like bombe alaska. You can see the creamy pink organza wilting under the golden licks of fire. It's almost pretty. Everything slows down like the projector breaking at Theatre 80. I calmly notice several things. The first thing I notice is how quickly the flame reaches Brooke's armpit. The second thing I notice is how the fire spreads up Brooke's arm to Lolita. I look away and notice Freddie trying to stamp out another burning frock with his velvet evening slipper.

There are dozens of wide eyes and round mouths. No one does anything for what seems like a whole fashion era. And then all the frock thieves start flailing around, trying to get away from the stench. They're scrambling and tripping and flinging their bodies in the direction of the door. A Diana Ross is checking her makeup in the vanity mirror before she turns tail and waddles away in her skintight sequined sheath. Phoebe is climbing out the window.

It occurs to me that I should be doing something. Saving my frocks. Saving Brooke. Evicting Hugo. The thought flashes through my mind: Should I save Brooke or my frocks first? I can't decide. I don't know what to do. I'm suspended in time. I can't move. I feel like one of those Frozen Moments, a Coke can pouring polyurethane froth.

I'm standing—*stuck*—in the middle of my room, being pushed around like a pinball, watching strangers stomp all over my frocks and Brooke catch on fire like a bombe alaska and I've got a chipped nail and I look like a mess, and I feel totally uninvolved.

It's like I've been astral traveling and somebody cut my life cord, which is what they warn you might happen if you do it too often. I've always wanted to astral-travel. I've lain in bed on many nights and tried to will my body to fly off into the black sky. To fly over to Bergdorf's and float around the couture department without a soul to ask me if I need any help. Without a soul there except for the other souls who are also doing their shopping on a spiritual plane. It's never worked until now. And now I don't know if I want it to.

And then, as I'm coolly contemplating what to do, Brooke's fire stops, as quickly as it starts. Someone has thrown my chenille bedspread over her. There's a fleeting moment of regret as I visualize brown smoke stains on the pretty pink fabric. I look around me. The room is almost empty. Everyone has moved back into the kitchen, watching. Except for Freddie, who is sitting crying in a corner. And Hugo, who is crouched over Brooke's motionless body, tapping her cheek. There's a terrible stench. Burning wool and organza and Dynel. And fat. "Is she dead?" I ask no one in particular. My voice sounds hollow.

There's silence for a while. And then Brooke starts to respond to Hugo's taps. She groans.

"Thank goodness!" I cry with relief, going down on my knees next to Hugo. "Brooke, are you all right?"

One eye opens slowly. The tips of the eyelash are singed. The other eye opens. She focuses on me, as if she's a baby just coming into the world.

"Sorry," is all she says before she goes limp again. I look at Hugo questioningly.

"I certainly couldn't let her lie there and fry," he explains modestly. For one confused moment I start to think there's a kinder, braver side of Hugo I've never seen before. "Like you did," he adds.

I blush with shame.

"Anyway"—he shrugs—"this girl is *material.*" What kind of material? I don't understand what he's saying. He's being obscure. I look at the charred bits of what is left of Anita poking out from under the chenille. Does he mean organza? "*Magazine* material," he says importantly. "I've had a brilliant idea for another cover story. In the back of my mind I've been looking for a genuine fashion victim, and I think I just found her. Congratulate me."

"Congratulate you?" I repeat. It comes out in a flat monotone. I don't even have the energy to shake my head.

"What's wrong?" Hugo looks surprised. "Aren't you pleased for her? It's not every day a girl gets the chance to be interviewed by me." He pushes himself up onto his feet and bends down briefly to adjust one of his trouser cuffs.

I should feel angry, but what I feel is hurt. Hugo must catch my look of horror as he begins to straighten up because he smiles and says, "Oh, I see. You're jealous." I can't even force out the strangled sound that is stuck in my throat.

"You don't need to be, you know," he goes on. "I wouldn't desert you. In fact, what I like most about this girl, whoever she is, is that she reminds me of you. I could call her the new you, if you'd like. It would mean that people wouldn't forget you that quickly. It would fill in that awkward gap until I'm ready to give you a comeback."

Just then Brooke grunts and tries to roll over.

"I'd get an ambulance if I were you," Hugo says, patting the left breast of his jacket. "She's not going to be much use to me if she expires on the spot." He puts his hand inside his pocket and takes it out again quickly. "You don't happen to have a pen, do you? Mine seems to have melted."

# 52.

The nurse is wearing those white rubber shoes that are going to come back into fashion soon. If I was in a better mood, I'd ask her where she bought them.

Brooke is in the plastic surgery unit because the burn unit is full. The nurse explains to me they've had a rush of homeless people going up in flames in parks. Anyway, she says, the plastic surgery unit is a happy place, with all the patients cheerfully waiting to wake up with the wrinkles sliced out of their eyelids or their nipples cut off and sewn back on again or the skin on their cheeks pulled tight and tied in knots behind their ears. The nurse says the plastic surgery unit is a good place for a girl like Brooke, with minor burns to part of her face, the top of her hands, and the right side of her neck, to recuperate. The plastic surgery unit is *fun,* she stresses.

I'm taken into a room where a woman is sitting up against a pile of pillows with black eyes and tubes coming out of her nose. She's wheezing and making a terrible rattling noise in her throat.

"This is Mrs. Leman," says the nurse, tucking in a stray bed sheet. "She's got a nice new nose."

Mrs. Leman's chest heaves.

The nurse moves across the room to a bed surrounded by curtains. I follow her. She pulls one of the curtains aside. "Brooke looks worse than she is," the nurse says crisply. "But don't you go wearing her out. You've got five minutes. Just a hello and a good-bye." She moves away to tuck in another stray sheet on another bed.

"Hi," I say to Brooke, who is lying on a forty-five-degree angle against a wedge of foam, with her bandaged arms out over the sheets. Her face is wrapped tight like a cocoon with one unbandaged square where her left eye blinks out at me. There are still traces of purple liner at the end of the lid, where lashes used to be. "You look great."

Brooke grunts. There's a slit for her mouth.

"Cheer up," I say. "It's a fact that hair grows back much quicker after it's been singed."

Brooke nods stiffly. She says something. I have to lean closer to hear what it is. "I'm sorry . . . about the dresses," she gurgles without moving her lips. "It was my fault. . . ."

"Don't apologize," I say.

"Are . . . they gone?"

"Yes." I sigh. "Almost all of them. I'm heartbroken. You can't imagine how much I miss them! I even miss their tantrums."

"I'm sorry."

"You couldn't help it. I shouldn't have expected a novice to know how to look after a door. What about your face?"

"It's . . . all right." She gulps.

"For heaven's sake, don't tell them that! Make them give you a new one. Plastic surgery is *wonderful*," I say encouragingly. "You should get some liposuction while they're at it."

Brooke makes an excited choking noise. "I've lost . . . twenty . . . one . . . pounds already . . . the nurse told me!"

"You see," I say. "Everything's for the best. When you get out of here, you won't recognize yourself!"

"Do . . . you . . . like . . . *really* . . . think so?"

"Of course I do! We'll throw a party." I think of the state of the apartment. "Somewhere."

The nurse suddenly materializes next to me. "Come along, now," she says, consulting a stopwatch. "Your time is up. Brooke has to have her dressings changed."

"I've got to go, Brooke," I say apologetically. "I'll come back soon."

Brooke blinks at me. She makes a noise that sounds like good-bye. Then she starts struggling under the sheets, as if she urgently wants to say something.

"What is it?" I ask, putting my ear right near her mouth.

"Next time . . ." she rumbles.

"Come along," says the nurse.

"Could you—"

The nurse frowns.

"Could you bring me . . . some . . . fashion magazines?"

"I'd be happy to!" I smile. "I'll bring the latest *Vogue*. It's seven hundred pages thick." I say this to reassure her that the world outside is going on just as usual. I pat her on the arm. "See, you're getting better already!"

Brooke's one eye looks pleased.

# 53.

Aurora says I can sleep in the back of her shop if I want. She seems to know instinctively that I can't go back to my apartment. I can't live with all those frock ghosts.

Freddie is unhappy about this. He says we're the most-talked-about club in the neighborhood. There's been a paragraph on the fire at The Closet in the *Daily News*. He's cut it out, to put in his project book for FIT. People have been calling all week to ask when the club is reopening. Now that there's been a fire—even such a little one—we're *really* hot.

I'm arranging the frocks on the rack by the wall in graduating colors, starting from ebony black and running through the rainbow to carmine red.

The doorbell tinkles, and I look around.

It's Phoebe, in the beige duffel coat from the Bonjour Paris scene in *Funny Face.*

"Hi," she says sweetly. "I'm sorry."

I go back to the frocks. "It's too late to be sorry. You and those stupid cigarettes."

"I know," she says and then more brightly: "I've changed brands. Courrèges Lights."

"So you should," I say. *"Murderess."*

"They've got the dearest little packages."

"You sound jolly," I say suspiciously, looking up.

She smiles. "I am."

"You're not going to tell me you're still seeing Quark?" I dare ask. "You can leave right now if you're going to tell me that."

"Don't be ridiculous." She scowls, momentarily reverting to her old self, the grouchy self I actually used to like. "I've thought about it seriously, and I'm giving up men. I don't like them. I'm marrying myself to my magazine. Like a nun. Celibacy brings out the cheekbones. That's going to be my first editorial. Now that I'm *junior fashion editor.*"

"Congratulations," I say tonelessly. "So that's why you're crowing."

"I am not!" she says. "And it isn't. I've brought you a present. As a kind of peace offering."

"No, thanks," I say. "I don't want anything from you. I don't want anything from an ex-best friend. An ex-best friend who sets fire to one of my frocks and escapes out the window. And don't tell me where you got that idea from. I *know!*"

She ignores me. "Don't you even want to see your present?" she asks, not put off in the least. "You'll be sorry."

"I'm not corruptible," I tell her, slipping a violet frock between a purple one and a lilac one.

"In that case," she says, "I better take it back."

"Good," I say, turning away from her.

"To Bergdorf's," she adds.

I turn around sharply. She's gloating. Her hands are clasped firmly behind her back, and she's leaning slightly forward with her heels together and her chin up like a schoolgirl being patted on the head by a teacher. "Well?" she asks.

"You *didn't?*"

"*Naturellement.*"

"Give it to me!"

I try to snatch the shopping bag she's holding behind her back. She skips away and giggles like a twelve-year-old. Right now I'd swear she was reverting to Leslie Caron in *Gigi,* which was her look—let's see—early last year.

She suddenly stops behind a circular rack of clothes and asks, "Do you forgive me?"

"You've really pulled it off?"

"Of course I have. Without you hanging around getting nervous, it was a *cinch.*"

"OK. I forgive you."

Phoebe smiles and holds her arm out straight. A mauve Bergdorf's shopping bag dangles on the end of one pearl-tipped finger. I snatch it and pull out the contents hungrily. I scrunch up the tissue paper and unfold the jacket. I shake out the skirt and hold it up to my hips.

"Well, try it on!" she orders. "I didn't risk life and limb to have you stand around gawking."

"Phoebe, you're wonderful!" I say as I wiggle out of my mini and step into the Chanel skirt. "It's a pink one, too!"

"It's got chains sewn into the hem."

"I can feel them!" I cry. "However did you do it?"

"Great courage and determination," she says. "Actually, I borrowed it for *Perfect Woman* and then reported that I got mugged on the way from Bergdorf's to the office. They believe me, of course, because there're so many fashion muggings lately. Not to mention those animal liberationists snatching furs. Faille had her earrings ripped off her ears yesterday. Did you hear about it? By a girl on a scooter."

"It *is* nerve-racking," I agree, sliding my arms into the sleeves and doing up the front. "Aren't these buttons heaven?"

"You know," Phoebe says, following me down to the mirror, "I was thinking maybe we could try a mugging in the garment district. Nothing big to start with. Think of all those racks rolling up and down Seventh Avenue, begging to be pilfered."

"But what about the fashion closet? You've got carte blanche now to steal whatever you want."

"That's no fun," she answers stubbornly.

I swirl around in front of the mirror. The suit is made of some sort of nubby silk. The jacket stops—just so—at my hips. The skirt stops precisely in the middle of my knee. "Maybe the shoes are wrong," I say to Phoebe. "Platforms look a bit ridiculous with Chanel."

She puts her hand to her chin. "No. It's not just the shoes. Something about the neckline."

"It might look better with a few gold chains."

"You know something?" Phoebe comments, staring at my body intently. "It doesn't suit you."

"Oh, I wouldn't go so far as saying that."

"I would," she says. "I'd go further. It's a *disaster*. You look like a librarian."

"I don't know—"

"You *do* look like a librarian! That's exactly it. That suit is so *middle-class*. What do you know! *Quel* horror!"

I scrutinize myself carefully. The suit fits perfectly. It's neat and tidy. It's demure. It's boring.

"You're absolutely right!" I say. "I *hate* it!"

"It's just not you!" Phoebe starts to giggle.

"Yes, Phoebe, but what am I?" I seem to be asking this question a lot lately. Even to strangers in the street.

"Well," says Phoebe, studying me seriously. "We certainly know what you are *not*! That's a start."

She's right. It is.

# 54.

Later in the afternoon I'm down on my knees, rearranging the jewelry on the bottom shelf of Aurora's display cabinet when I hear the bells on the door again. I glance up and see a figure carrying a bundle of frocks in its arms. It's one of the junk merchants who do business with Aurora.

"There's another delivery," I call out to her. Several minutes ago she waddled down to the bathroom and still hasn't come back.

"What's that, sugar?" she calls, and I can see the bathroom door open a crack. There's a long mirror on the outside for trying on frocks.

"There's a delivery," I repeat. "Where do you want it put?"

"What?" she says, and opens the door wider. I can see her terry-cloth scuffs.

"Never mind!" I call out. I turn to the deliveryman whose face is hidden by the green plastic bags of frocks in his arms. "On that chair." I point to Aurora's vacant seat. The man staggers toward the chair and runs straight into the display cabinet. "Be careful!" I say. I go back to rearranging the cabinet. Out of the corner of my eye I see him dump the frocks over the arm of the chair.

"Do I need to sign anything?" I ask as I spread out the fingers of a white kid glove and move a horseshoe-shaped pin along the shelf a bit.

"Yes, ma'am," drawls the deliveryman. "On my sleeve will do." What he says doesn't register. It doesn't register until a lime green sleeve shoots right in front of my line of sight. A lime green sleeve with "YOU ARE FABULOUS" written across the cuff in smudgy blue letters.

"Oh, no." I groan, and keep on moving the jewelry around.

"Don't be like that!" he says. "I'm here to make up."

"Blue doesn't go with green," I tell him, crossly, trying to think of something to say. But it just comes out sounding pathetic.

Hugo comes around behind the counter and crouches down next to me. He puts one hand on my arm. He's got a big grin on his face.

"Well?" I say impatiently, shaking off his hand.

"You *are* fabulous. I'd forgotten how fabulous you really are."

"Just because you saved Brooke's life doesn't mean you can come in here whenever you like and tell me I'm fabulous. I'm *over* that."

"You're even fabulous without makeup," he continues. "And hair."

"I thought you said you were here to patch things up," I say coldly. "Not remind me that my wigs were stolen, too."

"Oh, I've patched things up already," he says smugly. "You'll see."

"As far as I'm concerned, you haven't," I tell him. "You can get out of here! Go interview your new discovery in the hospital."

"You'll change your tune." He smiles.

"You're interrupting my work," I tell him. "Will you please leave?"

"I'll be at Houndstooth if you need me."

"Don't waste your breath."

"Did you know you have pretty nostrils?"

"Get out!"

"What are these, honey?" Aurora asks, pointing to the plastic bags draped over her chair.

"Oh, the deliveryman brought those. I'll move them."

"You were talking to that old deliveryman quite a while," says

Aurora, settling back into her chair. "I didn't know you were friends with the boys."

"I'm not. It was Hugo Falk."

"Oh," she says. She expels a lot of air. I look at her. There's a twinkle in her eye. "Then if it wasn't no deliveryman, sweetie pie, what are in these bags?"


I take out Tallulah and shake her. I pull out Clara and give her a big hug. I unroll Dolores and brush the scuff marks off her. I kiss Petula hello. I welcome Loulou with open arms. I bury my face in Gloria. Her lilac marabou feathers make me sneeze. I rustle Joanna's silver sequins. I dust the ashes off Sonja. I bend Marie's hoop back into shape. I examine Blanche for any scorch marks. I smooth out Carroll's top on the display cabinet. I dance around the room with Carmen, humming selections from Yma Sumac.

# 55.

"How did you get my frocks back?" I demand of Hugo when I eventually find him in the phone booth at Houndstooth.

"Hold on a minute," he says into the phone, and cups his hand over the receiver. "It's *Paloma*," he whispers to me in a conspiratorial way.

"I mean, they were all *stolen*." I persevere.

"Reality, as you know, I'm an investigative journalist—"

"Yes, but how did you get them off the people? When you tracked them down, how did you get them to give them back?"

He hesitates, blushes, and then says quietly, "I *paid* for them."

"Look," says Hugo sharply, placing himself between me and the door to his apartment. "I don't think this is a good idea."

"You thought it was a good idea an hour ago," I point out.

"Well, I didn't expect you to agree." He sounds cross.

"I didn't expect to either," I say grumpily.

"I don't like visitors."

"I'm not going to stay in the corridor, Hugo," I tell him. "It's not the sort of thing a boy asks a girl to do."

"We could go to a bar," he suggests.

"We've just been in a bar. About five of them."

"You'll go through all my things. I can't stand people who snoop."

"Is that what your boys do?"

Hugo looks uncomfortable. "All right. If you insist on coming in, you'll have to close your eyes until I've tidied up."

"Tidied up what?" I ask suspiciously.

"Some confidential documents." He frowns.

"Your next exposé, I suppose?"

"Precisely."

"OK," I agree. "My eyes are shut. You'll have to help me. I don't want to go banging into any terrazzo tables." Hugo sighs impatiently. He grabs my arm so hard he pinches me.

"I'm leading you in. Just take little footsteps, and you won't trip over the books. I suppose you want to sit down. Here's a chair." He guides me into it. It's upright and wooden by the feel of it, without a cushion.

I can hear Hugo start to rattle around. He's rustling paper and opening drawers and flushing the toilet several times. I hear him push a window open. There's a whirring noise, and I feel like I'm the eye of a hurricane. "It's only the fan!" he calls out, and I have to strain to hear him.

"Is it safe to look?" I call out after a while. "I'm going to have to peek soon or I'll die!"

The fan is switched off.

"All right," he says grudgingly. "If you have to."

I open my eyes wide. It takes me awhile to realize why Hugo has been so suddenly reluctant for me to visit. I'm in a room as big as my kitchen. Which is to say, as *small* as my kitchen. That's all. One window. A single bed, hastily made up. Shoes sticking out from underneath it. Stacks of books everywhere. A filing cabinet with a shaky pile of magazines stretching up to the ceiling. A built-in closet without doors. Rows of jackets and shirts, some slipping off their hangers. Sweaters all over the floor. Several full plastic trash bags. Ties looped over the back of the door.

"Hugo!" I exclaim, surprised. "You said your apartment was *moderne!*"

"Don't you like it?" he asks accusingly. "It's home to me."

"Well, I thought it would be more . . . glamorous," I say, not meaning to hurt his feelings.

"Sleaze is *very* glamorous," he says, defensively, slipping a rolled-up ball of something under the mattress. "Anyway, Trotsky used to live in this very room."

"The person who is on those T-shirts they sell on Saint Mark's?"

"The same."

"Gosh, did he leave anything behind?" I go over to the window. "Can you close it?" I ask. "It's breezy. My hair is getting mussed up."

"If I can," he says. He can't. It's stuck.

"Where's your bath?" I ask, looking at the lonely toilet in one corner. "As a matter of interest."

"Down the hall," he says. "This is an SRO. A single room occupancy. The last one left on this street, actually. I'm very proud of that."

"I suppose it is *bohemian,*" I say positively.

"Of course, I'm never here," he goes on. "I have such a busy social life. I'm out all night going to fabulous places. I merely come home to change my clothes. I only need two hours' sleep a night, and even then I don't sleep. I toss and turn. I get up and write notes. I have nightmares. I have brilliant ideas. I'm a very restless person."

"Well," I say, "aren't you going to offer me a drink?"

"I suppose you're going to say you need one after taking a look at all this. I knew I shouldn't have let you talk me into inviting you here. It's not very . . . romantic. Girls like romantic, don't they?

That's what's so easy about boys. They're more matter-of-fact." He catches the dirty look I'm giving him. "We should have gone to a motel."

"There aren't any motels in Manhattan," I say.

"Well, I probably could have got us a room on the house at Morgans. A lot of my celebrities stay there. I'm *known* at that hotel. What are you drinking?"

"Anything."

"I thought so," he says with a note of criticism in his voice. "I've only got vodka anyway."

While Hugo goes over to the toilet tank and picks up the bottle of Absolut on top of it, I look around me again. There's more dirty underwear and socks on the floor than I thought possible from one human being.

Hugo seems to have read my thoughts. He still has his back to me, wiping the rim of a tumbler on his sleeve.

"I could never work out why people bothered to put things away," he explains, "when they were going to wear them again in a few days." This is not the sort of thing I want to hear. The fact that Hugo has been looking more attractive now that he's rescued my frocks may not survive the sight of what is lurking on the floor in his room. The future of Hugo and me is dubious enough without a roomful of dirty boxer shorts coming between us.

Hugo hands me a room-temperature glass of vodka and stands awkwardly in the middle of the room. "I knew you wouldn't like it," he admits gloomily.

"I do," I say encouragingly. "It's just I imagined you'd be . . . neater. Your closet's a disgrace."

"That's because I have less time to think about clothes than you do. I have important work to carry out."

I glare at him.

"Let's change the subject," he suggests. "You always get so bad-tempered when I talk about your clothes."

"I think I'll go home," I say, making up my mind and looking around for somewhere to put down my glass. "This whole thing is silly."

"Are we drunk?" Hugo asks. "Is this why we're here together?"

"I'm sure of it." I get up abruptly.

"I think we should still do it," he says suddenly, crossing his arms in front of him. "It might be interesting."

"*Interesting?*" I repeat. "Is that what you think?"

"Hmmm." He hums thoughtfully. "I think so. I don't think you should go. Now you've seen my room, I suppose it doesn't make any difference if you see the rest of me."

"Hugo, you're embarrassing me." I look away. If I weren't wearing Mary Janes and ankle socks, Hugo would see that even my toes are blushing.

"I am, aren't I?" He ponders. "I'm embarrassing myself. It's a new experience."

"It's just that we've gossiped so much about other people's, well, *sex lives,* that it's a bit awkward having to get around to it ourselves. You know what I mean," I add helplessly, turning back toward him.

"I see the problem," he says, sitting down on the edge of the bed. "I think having to show your own hand should be avoided at all costs."

"But you'd have to if you did it with me."

"So would you. That evens everything out."

"You won't gossip about me behind my back?"

"Oh, Really. How could you think that? I'm very discreet."

"What are those telephone numbers scribbled on the wall? If they're boys' numbers, I'm definitely leaving."

He twists around and faces the wall. "Oh, those?" he asks. "They're the home numbers of several very important magazine editors. For when I get ideas in the middle of the night."

"I don't know whether to believe you or not."

"You're not very trusting. But then neither am I."

"Once burned, twice shy," I recite.

"Literally." He sighs.

There's a silence.

"Well?" Hugo eventually asks.

"I don't know."

"I think *you* should do something," he announces. "You're the one who has done it with the opposite sex before."

"It was your idea. You should go first."

"Go first? I'm not going to do it on my own while you watch. I'm sick of that."

"I mean, make the first move."

I'm standing rigid by the toilet.

"I suppose I should," he says, and doesn't move a muscle.

"Don't sound so enthusiastic!"

"Reality Nirvana, I'm so enthusiastic I don't know what to do!" he cries out, suddenly passionate. He leaps up off the bed and, surprised at himself, puts his hands in his pockets shyly. "I'm just another man to you. But you're the only girl in the world for me!"

My whole body involuntarily sighs. I know what he's saying is true. I am the only girl for him. The first and only. There's something to be said for that. It's nicer than being the 556th, which I usually am.

I stare at Hugo standing there uncomfortably with one mango-colored sock rolled down to his ankle and a glimpse of strong hairy legs where his trousers have bunched up. Everything that was rigid about him now looks all crumpled and vulnerable. His jacket is unbuttoned and welcoming. I never thought of his suits as welcoming before. I just unravel like a sweater. I fall apart at the seams. I'm undone.

I'm on Hugo's bed, lying on my stomach, being stroked like a kitten. We've been lying like this for a while, not saying much. It's unusual to hear Hugo's breathing rather than his voice. It's nice. Ralph, my pajama case, for whom Hugo has paid a princely ransom, is sitting on the pillow watching us.

"Hugo?" I ask, hoisting myself up onto one elbow.

"What?" His eyes look all misty, owing to the fact that he has flung his glasses off minutes ago.

"Do you like girls more than boys now?"

I expect him to say, "Of course!" but he just blinks at me. There's a long silence.

"Reality?" he asks eventually.

"What?" I say sharply, dropping back against the pillows.

"I'll say I like girls—namely, you—more than boys if you say you like people—namely, me—more than frocks."

I don't say anything for a while, and then I answer, truthfully, "I don't know."

"I thought so." He sounds annoyed with me.

"What I mean, Hugo, is that I like *some* people as much as frocks. Almost."

"Oh, well," he says a bit more cheerfully. "That will have to do. It's not a perfect world. Which is very irritating. But it makes more interesting reading. I myself do like some girls almost as much as I like some boys. But I can't be more specific than that."

"Do you think you will be?"

"Will be what?"

"More specific?"

"Oh, I suppose so. Sooner or later."

"Which one?"

"Which one what?"

"Which one is it to be? Sooner or later?"

"You girls always—"

"*Hugo!*"

He looks ashamed. And then he smiles. "How about sooner?" he says as he rolls toward me, nudging the space between my thighs with his knee.

"Fine by me," I say, but I don't need to say it.

# 56.

"Hi Cherry. Hi Sally. Hi Pixie. Hi Christie. Hi Bambi. Hi Millie."

"Hi Hugo. Hi Reality."

"Hi *Ricci*."

"Hi Hugo. Hi Really."

Hugo is striding down Third Street, and I am struggling to catch up with him. He keeps on forgetting that I'm not a blond-haired boy in sneakers but a real-live female in a tight skirt and heels. We're on our way to the Karma Club, which was formerly Less Is More. Ricci is now on the door of Astral Projection, which was formerly Ultra-suede. PVC has turned into Crushed Velvet. Paisley has become Patchwork. Eton Crop has become EST. The Boa Bar is still the Boa Bar. It was the Boa Bar in 1968, too.

"Hey, man," says Brooke, who is on the door at Karma these days. She's wearing the Indian caftan she finally found for Maria Callas, but since she's now doing Mama Cass, she's added an embroidered headband and a crocheted shawl and she's slipped earth shoes onto her chubby feet. Hugo's article on Brooke's being the new me has just come out; that's why she's beaming in triumph. I have to admit I'm quietly pleased that it's more about me than Brooke. These days Hugo can't seem to write a paragraph without putting me in it.

"Peace," Brooke says as we stride up the stairs. The Astroturf has been replaced by sea grass matting. She holds up two fingers.

"Love," says Hugo.

"Oh, no," I groan.

People down here can't exactly put their finger on when it happened, but the general opinion is that the revival of the hippie era began around the time *Frenzee* published that picture of me in sheepskin boots. People followed my example like lambs. Of course, I've always been a fashion leader. It's just that this time I wish I hadn't been so darn ahead of myself. Even Constance is vaguely modish these days.

Club 66 is already changing its sign. It says Club 71 now. Things are moving faster than ever before. The natural order of events is whirling out of control. We're recycling so fast we're gobbling up a decade every few months. Before the year is out, it will be last year again. After we get through punk and Recession Dressing, that is. The way things are going, we'll have to rack our brains for something new to take us into the next century. There are only so many times you can revive the New Look.

My relationship with Hugo is something new. People swear they've never heard of that sort of thing before. Boys leave girls for other boys, but they don't leave boys for girls. I don't know why that should be so. Personally, I'm a great believer in girls. A lot of other people are, too. I think it's the greatest compliment a girl can get for a boy to turn straight for her. Her femininity must be *overwhelming*.

You've got to be adaptable in this life. Goodness knows, if you aren't, you'll go out and spend your whole season's wardrobe allowance on miniskirts when it's actually the eve of the maxi. You'll be ordering margaritas when everyone else wants wheatgrass juice. You'll be dating boys like Quark who never kiss you when there's a whole galaxy of marginal boys on the outskirts who are a lot more—um— *satisfying*. You'll be perpetually out of fashion. You'll always be miserable. And, what's worse, you won't know why. Brooke was like this before I explained to her some of the harsh truths of life. I'm proud to say she was Mama Cass before the idea even occurred to me. She's on the right track.

This is why I depend on my frocks. To help me adapt to the changing face of the world I live in. I don't know how I'd get on without them. Although, since the Chanel suit, I've learned that not every single frock in the universe is meant for me. This is one of the two great tragedies of modern life, which are: Most of the truly desirable men are gay, and most of the frocks don't fit. But when the frocks—and the men—*do* fit, what *bliss!*

A realization is growing in me that no matter how many wigs I've got, there are just some kinds of person I can never be in this life. But I'm not going to get hung up about it. When I die and get recycled, I can always come back as the perfect Chanel person: thin and tanned and brunette with long wrists and neck for all those gold chains. I'll wait until then.

Hugo keeps telling me to stop thinking that I am what I wear. He says he prefers me without clothes as a rule, although he does have a sentimental attachment to Gina. She reminds him of Federico and our first "real" date on the stairs of my apartment. The thing is, I know Hugo's wrong. You are what you wear. I'll never change my mind about *that*. The simple proof is staring us in the face. Brooke. Brooke is wearing a caftan. Brooke likes wearing caftans, even though she lost thirty pounds in the hospital. I, on the other hand, wouldn't be seen dead in one. Not only am I what I wear, but I am what I don't wear. It's fundamental.

You can tell everything about people by what they put on in the morning, even if they are deliberately putting on something that doesn't look like the sort of thing they would normally put on. Even the fact that they would camouflage themselves is a dead giveaway. I've rearranged Hugo's closet, but I still can't talk him into getting rid of those bright colors now that earth shades have made a comeback. That is because Hugo wants to camouflage the fact that he really is a dear, sweet, shy, insecure person underneath. You know, he actually read *The Prophet*—and enjoyed it—before it became the month's hot book again. But most people wouldn't dream that a person who contrasts citrus green with persimmon keeps a copy of Kahlil Gibran under his mattress. The fact that Hugo wears persimmon and citrus green is proof of his complexity. He doesn't just get around in corduroy trousers and llama hair sweaters, which would be too predictable. He is what he wears. What he wears is him. In fact, as far as I'm concerned, Hugo without a touch of a lime green somewhere just isn't Hugo at all.

The truth is, people would be a lot happier if they talked to their clothes more often. Frocks have a lot to say, and what they have to say is not only fashion statements. I know this from experience. If I'm a fabulous person—which I am—it's partly due to the fact that I am in total harmony with the contents of my closet and the contents of my closet are in total harmony with me. My frocks know me inside out. Hugo doesn't know me that well. Not yet anyway, although I have plans. Hugo simply doesn't spend as much time next to my bare skin as Lolita does. But I'm working on it.

I have a whole history with my frocks, and a girl can't turn her back on *that*.

Want More?

Turn the page to enter
Avon's Little Black Book—

the dish, the scoop and the
cherry on top from
**LEE TULLOCH**

*Fabulous Nobodies Revisted*

# A Memoir of the Eighties

> I agree with the gay Englishman [Irishman Oscar Wilde] who said you should either look like a work of art or, if you can't, wear one. Sometimes I do both!
>
> —JULIE NEWMAR

In 1986 I was sitting at my desk—an old wooden thing I'd found on 12th Street and dragged up four flights to my Second Avenue apartment—and attempting to pump some inspiration into a novel I'd begun the year before, about a magazine editor who defenestrates (my favorite word) from the 43rd floor of a swank hotel in despair at the ruthless superficiality of the fashion world that has consumed her life.

Almost twenty years later, this seems like a really *bad* premise for a novel, but at the time no one was writing about fashion in fiction and, besides, for my first novel I imagined myself as a modern day Barbara Cartland, the British romance novelist who had once served me tea at her home and given me a gold-dipped acorn from a tree in her garden that Queen Elizabeth I had planted and who would dictate bestsellers to one of her six secretaries while lying on a chaise lounge under a white mink blanket. In writing this book—I have no idea now what the title was—I had two honorable ambitions: I wanted to make bucket loads of money like Barbara Cartland, and I wanted to wreak a vaudevillian revenge on some of the fashion people who had once employed me.

Before moving to New York City in 1985, I had been the founding editor of *Harper's Bazaar* Australia, but I'd been fired after ten issues for being too "avant-garde." We'd had Boy George (in drag) as a cover girl, the first male to *ever* appear on the cover of a women's fashion magazine. (*Life* magazine did a piece on it at the end of the year.) Our fashion pages had been full of the fashions of the day, which were mostly rip-and-tear fantasies that looked like they'd been pulled out of the ragbag at the local thrift store. (Does anyone remember the Buffalo Girl look?) Worse still, we'd done an issue in China (I'd herded buffalo for one shoot and handed out toy koalas to the peasants who appeared in our pictures) and printed the sayings of Chairman Mao across the published fashion pages. I was a very naughty girl and I had to be replaced by someone who would return the fashion to predictable niceness and make the advertisers feel more comfortable.

The only thing to do was leave Australia. My husband was interested in becoming a photographer so, after a month in Tahiti (where I contracted dengue fever), then a couple of weeks in L.A. staying at an actor friend's North Hollywood house while serial killer Richard Ramirez stalked the neighborhood, we landed in New York. It seemed like a relief. My husband immediately got a job as an assistant on a *Vogue* shoot, we found a ramshackle eight-room floor-through fourth-floor walk-up with marble fireplaces in the East Village (*very* Roman Polanski I thought), and I began my novel.

That night in 1986 was a hot one. The streets outside were jumping. Our apartment was in an old brownstone situated between 12th and 13th streets. In those days—hard to believe now—the area was *very marginal.* The crackheads had taken over 13th Street and only the foolish ventured beyond Avenue A. Later 13th Street would get its own troop of Guardian Angels. I would often have to fight my way through a group of dealers huddled in our doorway. I was once chased down the street by a druggie attracted by my fake leopard-skin coat ("Hey, Leopard Lady!" he shouted.). A family (pimp, prostitute, and baby) took up residence in their ancient Oldsmobile right outside our house. One night, a gang of men tried to pull me into their car. On another, wintry night we'd been to see Jean Cocteau's *Blood of the Poet* at Theatre 80, the revival house on St. Mark's Place, and when we emerged into the street, we almost stepped into a huge puddle of blood in the snow.

But the danger made it fun to be young and alive. The streets below Fourteenth, especially in summer, were throbbing with possibility. There were plays and poetry readings at St. Marks in the Bowery. Motorcycle gangs with elaborately decorated bikes brawled at the bar across the road. Punk icons like John Sex (who reportedly stiffened his white-blond hair with ejaculate) munched on Swedish pancakes at Café Orlin. John Spacely, whose image was once painted on a wall in St. Mark's Place, stalked the streets in a long leather coat and eye patch. People carried ferrets under their coats. Quentin Crisp lived on Fourth Street and Phillip Glass round the corner. You could have an audience with Mr. Crisp if you bought him a meal at Phebes. You bumped into Richard Hell on First Avenue. Down on First Street a young Texan woman called Ellie Covan ran a nightclub/performance space in her lounge room. Battalions of homeless people sold old shoes and magazines at Cooper Square and, if you were lucky, you could nab an original copy of *Flair*. There was a shop on Ninth Street where you could buy old clothes by the pound. Little shopfront art galleries spread like rashes, showing inflatable plastic toys, and their vinyl-clad patrons spilled out on to the street clutching Styrofoam cups of bad wine. Stephen Saban for *Details*,

Michael Musto for the *Village Voice,* and photographer Patrick Mac-Mullan were the chroniclers of the age.

Downtown had a real cachet and the world's eyes were on us. You were proud to proclaim you got a bloody nose if you ventured above Fourteenth Street.

And then there were the clubs. The Saint on Second Avenue, which was once the famous Filmore East. Area (formerly the Mudd Club) in Tribeca. CBGBs. Pyramid. Mars. Save the Robots. Danceteria. The scandalous Limelight, a cathedral of decadence in a deconsecrated church in Chelsea. Later, The Tunnel, where rats ran over your feet. And biggest and hottest of all, the Palladium on Fourteenth Street, only a couple of blocks from where I lived. If you got on the mailing list for these clubs—and you did this in a variety of ways, by an exhausting attention to looking fabulous or knowing someone on the door—you could be at a club "event" every night and get free drinks too. The "Club Kids" were a force of nature and soon this raggle-taggle bunch of drag queens, fag hags, and exhibitionists had become a moveable Factory, no longer restricted to Andy's pad, but desperately seeking attention in doorways and on dance floors (where they'd pose to Cabaret Voltaire and Bronski Beat) all over downtown. The Club Kids became so fabulous they had to rope themselves off in VIP areas to keep themselves apart from the hoi polloi. Soon, a new category of person emerged, the young downtown novelist (Jay, Bret, Tama) and you could find them, joined at the hip, under the glare of klieg lights in the same roped-off VIP lounges.

There was another kind of rope too, and I don't mean bondage (which was a very fashionable style at the time). The velvet rope *outside* the club. Transversing this was sometimes as difficult as pushing a camel (you) through the eye of a needle (the person on the door). The Doorbitch (or Doorwhore) was a totally capricious breed of human being, who paid no heed to logic. There was nothing—*nothing*—you could do to gain entry to the club if she or he didn't like the look of you. You could be dressed to the nines and you wouldn't get in because that night the Doorbitch was *over* people who tried too hard. (The first time I made the cut at Palladium I was just walking by in black T-shirt and shorts, which, I admit, is the last time in history I've ever worn shorts.) That same Doorwhore would reject anyone wearing blue the next night. The following, she'd let in leisure suits. Sometimes you'd wait for hours outside in the cold or rain and when you finally got the nod, you'd enter a vast, cavernous space with three people in it. It was legitimized tyranny because the act of getting into the club was more important than what the club had to offer. Some people got in, had a look around, and made a point of leaving. Many others whiled away the hours in the bathroom. If I recall correctly, Palladium had fabulous bathrooms.

One night, I ventured down to a new club on Fourteenth Street. It was called Nell's. Nell Campbell is a fellow Aussie who had a long inning as an "It Girl" of New York. Her eponymous club opened its doors in the mid eighties and it was an instant hit because of its moody Weimar Republic décor and because, like all New York clubs in their first flush of popularity, it catered to a self-appointed IN crowd. The girl on the door the night I attempted entry was a wistful blonde who nevertheless had the requisite mean streak. I was wearing my gorgeous fake leopard and crocodile shoes and I was accompanied by a friend, a casting director who had discovered Johnny Depp. But I broke the first rule of getting into nightclubs, which is *never* being hesitant. The girl looked us up and down critically and asked me, not quite sure (I have been told I look like a certain movie star when she is having a very, *very* bad day) "Are you somebody?" Fool that I am, I said "No."

Nell Campbell told a magazine at the time that she had a *fabulous* life, lying around in bed all day deciding what to wear to her club at night. But there were other "It" girls and the competition was tough. The glorious Suzanne Bartsch, now an "event producer," was the Queen of the Night, throwing extravagant costume parties where she might, for instance, come as Marie Antoinette with sheep. Chi Chi Valenti ruled the door at the Mudd Club in an S. S. uniform. Another Doorbitch, Sally Randall, set the trend for being famous for being famous. *New York* magazine ran an eight-page story on her, which caused an outbreak of rampant jealousy. Most famous of all was Dianne Brill, bodacious babe-around-town and later, self-help author, now a mother of three and lipstick designer. Dianne palled with Cher and Andy, modelled for Jean-Paul Gaultier, and managed to get her face and cleavage everywhere—a nobody who became a somebody, fleetingly, through sheer willpower and the judicious use of masking tape. She lived on my block and I would often see her teetering by in five-inch heels and a red rubber dress (she'd sprinkle herself with baby powder to get into it), her blond hair piled Bardot–style in a beehive on top of her head.

On that summer night in 1986, Dianne Brill was probably putting on her false eyelashes, Sally Randall was giving an interview to a downtown newspaper, Ellie Covan was moving the furniture in her apartment to better accommodate the crowds, and Nell Campbell was lying on her bed thinking about what she would wear. Is it so strange that I would ditch my fictional magazine editor and her fall from the 43rd floor and start channelling Reality Nirvana Tuttle?

Reality dictated thirty pages to me that night and in the following couple of years it took to finish *Fabulous Nobodies* she wouldn't shut up. In me she found a willing scribe; in her I found a voice for everything I knew about the glorious perversity of fashion ("There are dozens of rules. If you're fabulous, you know them instinctively. If you're not, you don't."), what it's like to be young and clueless ("This is one of the two great tragedies of modern life, which are: Most of the truly desirable men are gay and most of the frocks don't fit.") and the fragile nature of identity ("I've got to look more me than me tonight. Everyone else is going to look like me, so I've got to outme them all.").

She was a girl after my own heart. Ever since I'd discovered that my grandmother had cut the back out of a gorgeous 1940s beaded jacket to use as a dishcloth, I'd been a champion of recycling clothes. Not that I called anything in my closet by name—that's Reality's thing—but I'd seen the messy fashion closets in magazines like the one at *Perfect Woman* that so incensed Reality and I've been devoted to flea markets and thrift shops all my life. I'd furnished our East Village apartment from things I'd found in Dumpsters and on the street. I still routinely go through people's trash, to the horror of my teenage daughter. I still have trinkets I found in New York streets, markets, and junk shops in the eighties, including a handsome pair of ashtrays in the shape of an Arabian man and woman and a beautifully framed print of Leonardo's Madonna, sold to me by a drag queen who insisted it was an "original." And I've kept some of my eighties clothes, including a suit by Azzedine Alaia with shoulders so big they make me look like the Sydney Opera House. Reality can borrow it anytime she likes.

She's a girl after other people's hearts too. When *Fabulous Nobodies* was first published in 1989, a band called Voice of the Beehive dedicated an album to her. This further cemented her fabulousness. Of course, if she were around now (and there are, I assure you, Realitys lurking everywhere) she'd be on cable with her own fashion show. *Reality TV,* she'd call it, naturally. And she would be executive producing another kind of reality TV show—*Fabulous Nobodies,* in which fabulous nobodies show off their talents, rather like *American Idol* meets *Queer Eye*. She always did like TV, even if it were black and white and she could only get one channel (as long as it showed *The Champions.*) Perhaps Hugo, her gossip columnist paramour, would be the Simon Cowell of the fashion world. Both of them would be taking full advantage of the '80s revival, which comes and goes, just like the '70s revival. As Reality says, "we're recycling so fast we're gobbling up a decade every few months." How true, even today.

What Reality didn't know in 1986, and either did I, was how prophetic she was to become about another age. In her need to be a somebody, to be validated in the pages of a magazine, she predates the frenzy of the celebrity culture of today, where the media is a great churning machine that packages nonentities—a certain heiress comes to mind—as somebodies, like a production line plopping eggs into cartons. Warhol recognized it and the Club Kids milked it for all it was worth. But even they didn't realize that one day we'd wake up to a world where we were swamped by it. "The somebodies wouldn't come to the clubs if it weren't for the nobodies standing around wishing they were somebodies," Reality says. "That's why we need nobodies to make the somebodies feel superior. The somebodies wouldn't come if they couldn't be sure they'd have nobodies to trample over. And the nobodies wouldn't come if they didn't have somebodies to stare at . . . they'd sell their mothers for the privilege." But it's a delicate bargain. "The subtlety of all this . . . is that somebodies sometimes don't look like somebodies. They look like nobodies . . . When you're on the door of a nightclub you have to know the difference between a somebody who looks like a nobody and a nobody who looks like a nobody. It's elementary." And, as Hugo points out, morphing from nobody to somebody is a tricky business: "I never write about anybody who *needs* publicity. If you need publicity, you aren't fabulous. And if you aren't fabulous, well, you're just not fabulous enough for me."

I'm not sure that today's army of photoshopped somebodies (remember that Reality and Hugo live in a pre-Adobe, pre-iPod, pre-Nokia, pre-DVD world) would pass Reality's fabulous test. In fact, I'm sure they wouldn't. Like me, she wouldn't be impressed by the current obsession with bland computer-mutilated celebrities. Reality had a higher standard. She might aspire to be best friends with Chloe Sevigny and Andre 3000, but she'd draw the line at Carmen Electra. She'd be snooty about the *Sex and the City* girls, the way SJP appropriated her look. But, then again, she'd be heading towards forty and she may have learned the essential wisdom in Hugo's POV: "That's the nature of fame, Reality. A great door but an empty room."

When I'm not a novelist, I'm a journalist. (I'm both Reality *and* Hugo, to tell the truth.) I've had my brushes with fame. I could care less. Call me perverse, but I have no curiosity for sphinxes without secrets, to use Truman Capote's borrowing of Oscar Wilde. (Two guys I adore, by the way.) Once a person loses his or her individual nobodiness and becomes a somebody, my attention wanes. I don't want to know with whom they were canoodling at Soho House last Friday or whether or not the J. Sisters do their Brazilians. And, while there are certain complicated and talented individuals I wouldn't mind being stuck in a stalled elevator with for an hour or two—Robert Downey, Jr. and Marianne Faithfull come to mind—it's their essential nobodiness that really attracts me. Celebrity is a two-dimensional thing. It's the third dimension I'm looking for.

And, even though she doesn't realize it, Reality is looking for that too. She's looking for authenticity in Reagan's America, where the masters of the universe are faceless men in suits, wound up in their own sense of entitlement. A true little socialist (albeit with a fascist bent) she's on the side of the fashion students, the waiters, the homeless, the shop girls, the aspiring models, the drag queens, the discarded frocks. She might change her hair, her clothes, her shoes, her face several times a day—she boasts of seventy-two different fashion personalities—but who she's really looking for is herself. The much-coveted Chanel suit is, in the end, not *her*. By the conclusion of her story, she's getting closer to self-awareness (although no one could safely assert she's there yet!): "Not only am I what I wear, I am what I *don't* wear. It's fundamental."

A year or so ago I went to an extravagant party at New York's east side Armory, which was presented on the scale of the kind of bashes they threw in the eighties. The vast space was filled with enormous projects of clouds, the champagne flowed, there was a caviar bar, a famous DJ, and a crowd that included Leonardo DiCaprio, Hillary Swank, and a Queer Eye. Standing there, in the middle of this gorgeous room, I looked around and thought, *where are the fabulous people?* The room was populated by suits. Even Leonardo wore a suit. In the eighties, those fabulous nobodies, the Club Kids, would have been top of the A-list. Now the A-list consisted of agency people and media executives. The friend who accompanied me had been responsible for some of the interiors at Studio 54. We both fell glum. Where was the insanity? New York nightlife was now corporate. The suits had won.

I've been reading recently of a company that will escort normal people to popular Manhattan clubs and make sure they're treated like celebrities. By prior arrangement with the club, the velvet ropes will clip open for them, a table in the VIP lounge will be set aside. This is all done for a hefty fee, of course.

Reality would be horrified.

Tony Amos

LEE TULLOCH was born in Australia, began writing about fashion and popular culture for *Vogue Australia,* and has written extensively on the subject for international publications such as *Vogue, Elle, Jalouse, Harper's Bazaar,* and *New York* magazine. She was the founding editor of *Harper's Bazaar* Australia. In 1985 she moved from Sydney to New York, where she wrote her first novel, *Fabulous Nobodies,* and later *Wraith* and *Two Shanes.* With her photographer husband, Tony Amos, she moved between Australia, New York, and Paris for more than a decade. She now lives on a Sydney beach and is completing her fifth novel. Her favorite frock is a black Azzedine Alaia from 1984, which her daughter Lolita now wears.